I0598174

# JONATHAN WILD;

## OR, THE

## THIEFTAKER'S DAUGHTER.

BY

**MBROSE HUDSON.**

LONDON:

W. WINN, 34, HOLYWELL STREET, STRAND,

AND ALL BOOKSELLERS.

# PREFACE.

THE outlines of the following Work, which embrace the fortunes of the hero, are not further from truth than was absolutely necessary in a story of the kind. The incidents, and the characters that help the picture, are, as a consequence, the creation of the author's fancy.

It may not be uninteresting to subjoin a brief sketch of the true career of the notorious thieftaker.

Jonathan Wild was born at Wolverhampton, in Staffordshire. Fielding, who wrote a politico-satirical work, with Wild for the hero, gives London as his birth-place; but the satirist had not true biography in his view, and his sarcasm would have had almost as great an effect, if he had chosen any other rogue for his chief character, and his facts would have applied as well. The parents of Jonathan were

respectable tradespeople, in a small way, and gave their son
a decent education, as times went, apprenticing him to a
buckle-maker, whom he served for some years honestly
enough. As manhood approached, however, he grew idle
and dissipated, and one day borrowed a horse of a friend,
and rode him up to London, where he sold the beast, and
spent the cash in debauchery. After a while, he became a
bailiff's follower; but the occupation did not pay well, and
he returned to Wolverhampton. The first man he met there
was the owner of the horse; but Jonathan talked him over,
and agreed to pay him at the rate of a shilling a month.
He made two or three payments accordingly: then once
more growing disgusted with buckle-making, he started
again for London. On his road, he encountered an itinerant
doctress, with whom he went into partnership; but after
living together some months, they quarrelled, and the lady
threw him into prison for debt. It was in prison that Jonathan first gained the knowledge that, being afterwards
turned to account, made his name notorious. He cultivated
the society of rogues and pickpockets; he learned their tricks
and stratagems, and when the iron hand of justice laid hold
of them, he put such quirks " and evasions in their heads,
said a writer in 1725, " and gave them such advice, as
sometimes proved of great advantage to them, so that he became a kind of oracle amongst the thieves."

When Wild was restored to liberty, he began his trade, that of receiving stolen property from the pilferers, and restoring it to the owners for a consideration. The details relative to the management of his business are correctly given in our story. By degrees he increased in wealth and notoriety, and the thieves who had first set him up as their factor, found him at last their master and their tyrant. It was by occasionally turning upon his dependants, and bringing them to justice, that he conciliated the officers of the law, and he became so terrible at length, that he was said to hang or save at his pleasure. There was not a thief in ondon but was compelled to seek him, and scarcely any property was, therefore, stolen, out of the proceeds of which he did not, in some way or other, derive a very large share.

The wealth that he was supposed to have amassed by this business made many look upon him with envy, and some, tolerably acquainted with the secrets of his trade, set up in practice against him; but none of them kept their ground, and Jonathan, therefore, remained alone in his glory.

As an instance of the manner in which even great people were accustomed to apply to Jonathan for assistance, the story is told, that a couple of thieves, disguised like chairmen, in great coats and harness, stole the young Duchess o Marlborough's chair, as her grace was visiting in Piccadilly while her chairmen and footman were refreshing themselves

at the neighbouring public-house. The Duchess immediately, in person, applied to Wild, who told her grace that
her servants might have the chair the next day if she would
leave with him, there and then, ten guineas. The Duchess
demurred at first; but Jonathan protested that he was a man
of honour, and scorned to wrong her grace: the aristocratic
dame handed the receiver-general the sum demanded, and
was told in return to direct her chairmen to attend morning
prayers at Lincoln's Inn Chapel, and they should there find
the chair, which the fellows did accordingly, and the chair
was found, with the crimson velvet cushions and silk curtains
all safe and unhurt. The Duchess sent an autograph note
to the thieftaker, complimenting him on his punctuality.

In the course of time, Jonathan's acts became so villanously
daring and impudent, notwithstanding an Act of Parliament
had been passed for the suppression of traffic in stolen
goods, that the law could no longer continue blind and deaf
to Wild's conduct, and in the midst of much blustering on
his part, he was seized and committed to Newgate. He was
tried, and afterwards hanged, in May, 1725, according to
some accounts, being only forty-two years of age, though by
others he was supposed to be much older. His career was
altogether one of the most extraordinary which the criminal
annals of our own, or any other country, present.

Having written thus much, it only remains for me to take

my farewell of the reader, thanking him or her (M. or N.) as the case may be, for patience, and pleasant company on the way, hoping ere long to meet again with mutual satisfaction.

AMBROSE HUDSON.

# CHAPTER I.

### THE INTRODUCTION.

THE close of an autumn day in the early portion of the last century is the time chosen for the opening of our scene; the scene itself
the high road to the city of Warwick.

There, upon a meadow-gate, sat a foot traveller, trimming a hedge-
stick.

He was evidently wearied with walking, and his clothes had a thick
layer of dust upon them; he must have journeyed far, for his was not a

No. 1.

frame to be easily fatigued.   Some one or two-and-twenty years of age,
five feet ten in height, of a gaunt large-jointed figure, he gave promise
of a powerful maturity.   His features were strongly marked : the grey
eye was keen, restless, and rat-like ; the nose broad and stubborn ; the
mouth large and sensual, but not wholly without humour ; the under-
chin slightly protruded, the eyebrows were bristly, and the face itself
was pitted with the small-pox.   His dress was a threadbare snuff-
coloured suit, his wig was rusty, and his hat cocked awry.

There was a provoking jaunty sort of desperado air about the
fellow that would have won for him attention in a crowd, but as there
was nobody at that time near him on the Warwick-road, he cut away
at the notches in his stick, free from passing scrutiny.   When duly
fashioned, he put it aside, and threw his hat hollow upwards on the
ground before him, and dived his hands deeply into his breeches-
pockets.

"Two—four—sixpence ha'penny—eight—nine-pence.   Nine-pence
to carry a man to London !   Hem ! I don't think anybody even of the
most economical turn of mind can call that an extravagant amount of
money to take such a journey with.   But stop ! They teach children
that ' Honesty is the best policy,' and as I believe it when there is nobody to rogue but oneself, what is the use of attempting to cheat my
own reason.   I do mean to have in my possession something more
than those paltry coppers betwixt this and great London.  But by what
means ?  Ah ! that is the grand question.   Well, time will tell, so
come along, my trim companion; although I seek it not, who knows but
you and I may have rough work together ?"

Suspending his bundle on this same "trim companion," he shouldered
the latter with renewed vigour, and went on his way cheerily.

He had not proceeded far before the sound of hoofs attracted his
attention; he paused at the top of the hill just gained, and looking
down the road whence he came, perceived a woman on horseback slowly
ascending.

" A fair evening, madam," said he, courteously, when the rider came
within hearing.

The woman eyed the young man suspiciously, but returned him a
civil greeting.

" How far do you call it from this to Warwick ?" asked the foot-
traveller.

. " Three or four miles at most," responded the woman ; " I am a
doctress on my way thither."

" A doctress !" exclaimed the other.

" Aye, a doctress; you did not take me for a member of parliament's wife, did you? A poor doctress," she added, with an emphasis on the adjective, " travelling about the country for the good of the public, and curing the people of all sorts of distempers."

" Say you so? Then, for the love of mercy, dismount and do me what service you can. I am a wretched cripple, and my hip-bone is dislocated," and as he spoke he truly seemed to be what he described.

The woman, who appeared to have some good nature in her composition, immediately did as he desired.

" Poor fellow !" she cried, " why, the bone is out of the socket, and there is a great exuberance. This is indeed dreadful, and, alas! good man, I know not how to help you."

" A doctress, and not know how to help me !"

" Indeed, no! the case is past my skill."

" And that, madam, I suspect is not very great; or else, perhaps, you think that I am poor, and so cannot reward you. Your feeling, then, must be very sordid."

" Hang it !" cried the woman, " I won't be thought such a wretch as that either. I'd sooner tell the truth, and own I know no more of doctoring than you do."

" What! you are no doctress, then? I thought as much "

" Well, then, poor wretch, since the murder's out, I'm not, or I would help you if you had not a tester in the world."

" You would ?"

" I would !"

" Why, then, a fig for your doctoring; you're a good creature, and a comely one too, and I like you, ma'am. And since telling the truth is the order of the day—or rather evening, for the shadows are falling fast—as you are no doctress, why, I am no cripple !"

In a moment the man stood erect and firm again. Profound astonishment, and even fear, showed in the countenance of the assumed doctress, and seemed to chain her tongue.

" Tut! never stare so. Don't you see I tell you the truth? It is a trick for which I am more beholden to nature than to art and it has served me often at a pinch. Why, my unlucky stars have never brought me in sight of a red coat, that I have not passed by in so decrepit and deformed a posture as never failed to move pity in the beholders towards so miserable an object; but the moment I was out of sight of the kidnapping rogues I walked as upright and strong as, madam doctress, you can see me now."

The woman made him no other reply but to ask him to assist her on horseback again. He complied with her request, and they jogged on briskly side by side for some time without speaking.

The woman—she might be about thirty, and she certainly was remarkably well-looking, as well as somewhat handsomely attired—did not appear anxious to quit company with the poorer traveller. She was the first to break silence.

" What was your motive, friend, in practising this imposition upon me ?"

" Partly my humour ; perhaps to excite your sympathy."

" You are very poor, then ?"

" Poor or rich in comparison with those I meet better or worse off than myself. Men are not apt to think ninepence a fortune, and that is all I have to carry me to London; but poor as I am, I would rather do any knavish thing than beg."

" You are desperate."

" I told you ninepence was my fortune."

" I think, my friend, that I could show you how to better it; but we must have no violence, and in everything you must submit to my guidance."

" Submission is not much my creed," replied the fellow, " but so long as you can make it worth my while, to so fair a mistress I will contrive to bow. As to violence, I am no friend to it, though circumstances and my appearance might induce you to think otherwise."

" You are quick-witted, sir, and, doubtless, sufficiently honest for my purpose. I will trust you; and as you lately said you liked me, so I like you."

She put out her hand, and the man shook it warmly, as he asked the nature of the business in which they were about to engage.

She told him it was but to practise the trick, in which he was so great an adept, in Warwick, to lie in bed for a fortnight, and eat and drink of the best—the rest was to be left to her. Was it agreed ? It was.

" And now," said the quack doctress, " I will tell you my name. I am called Madame Dorville, and you ——?"

" Jonathan Wild."

It was a dark night when the two travellers entered the old-fashioned city. One was on horseback, and apparently a dame of modest and reputable demeanour; the other a poor and tottering cripple, who seemed with agony of limb to drag his tortuous way through the ill-lighted streets.

---

## CHAPTER II.

### THE ELOPEMENT.

THERE was a grand ball in the Assembly-rooms at Warwick. It was the first of the season, and all the great county people were expected, Lord and Lady Dumfounder and two Members of Parliament. The announcement was of course sufficient to draw together all the lesser gentry, and the more wealthy of the families of the neighbouring yeomen. The landlord of the hotel where the assemblies were held was giving his last orders as to the decoration of the rooms, and surveying with manifest pride the dispositions of the lights and flowers, the decorations and the rout seats, when his presence was requested, through one of the waiters, by a lady in a room below.

"What is the matter now, John? any of the company arrived, do you say?" inquired Mr. Brown.

"No, sir; it is a lady and a beggarman; missus can't get rid of them without you, sir."

"Can't get rid of them, eh? but I'll get rid of them with a vengeance. We want no such cattle here, I can tell 'em," and the landlord in wrath hurried down stairs.

In one of the rooms on the ground floor stood the hostess and Madame Dorville, earnestly debating, while stretched on the sofa writhed the miserable figure of our hero.

Mr. Brown entered the room to the accompaniment of a deep groan. It startled him from his propriety.

"Good gracious, madam, do you take this for a hospital?"

"No," replied the doctress with great composure; "I take it for an hotel, the Royal George, I think, and you for its worthy landlord—Mr. Brown, I presume?"

"The same, madam."

"I have been telling your good wife here—"

The hostess broke in.

" The lady says, William Brown, that she is a highly respectable lady, that spends her money going about the country doing poor people good, that she picked up this wretched man on the road." Jonathan gave another deep groan at this point. " And she wants to put up here, and have the best advice in the place for him immediately."

" Mrs. Brown puts the case admirably," observed Madame Dorville, quietly seating herself, " but she demurs at our reception to-night, on account of some festivities which are held here. Now, my late respected husband—"

" Begging your pardon, madam, Mrs. Brown did quite right."

" I say," continued the doctress, without noticing the interruption, " that my late respected husband, when he bequeathed me all his property, bade me how to dispose of it, and particularly enjoined me, should I ever pass through Warwick, to stay at the Royal George, where he had himself experienced great attention at the hands of the respectable Mr. Brown."

" Really, ma'am," said the host, looking first at his wife, and then at the doctress, and lastly at Jonathan, who thought it time to groan again, which he did accordingly, " I don't know what to say. You see, ma'am, it so happens that to-night—"

At this moment Madame Dorville, unconsciously, as it were, deposited a purse upon the table, that appeared to be heavily filled with bank notes and gold, and turning to the hostess, addressed her with—

" By the bye, Mrs. Brown, you have some family, have you not ?"

" Five boys and a girl, ma'am." ·

" To be sure, I remember now. My late respected husband, if I recollect aright, called them a remarkably fine family, speaking of them pleasantly as five brothers, and every one of them a sister. I hope, Mrs. Brown, they are all quite well."

" Quite well, I thank you, ma'am, except Betsy ; Betsy's got a bit of a cold, and Tommy suffers a good deal from the growing pains. Don't you think, William," she added, appealing to her husband, whose features had considerably relaxed at the sight of the purse, " don't you think we might find room somewhere ?"

" You will not find me at all particular, I assure you. I can sit with you, ma'am, if you have nowhere else to put me, and I shall be happy to render you any assistance in my power. It was the remark of my late respected husband, when he bequeathed me all his property, ' Adapt yourself, my dear, to circumstances, and don't let your money induce you to look down upon other people.' As to this poor wretch"—Jonathan took up the cue and groaned more acutely than before.

" Has he got the stomach-ache?" inquired Brown. " He'll frighten the guests if he goes on like that. Perhaps a little drop of brandy will do him good."

Wild seemed to think it would, for he managed to leave off groaning and looked up directly, but his mistress immediately replied,

" Brandy, Mr. Brown! on no account at present!"—Jonathan fell back again, and a prolonged sigh escaped him. " His hip is dislocated, and we must have the first doctor in Warwick to examine him. As to the noise," my good man, addressing Jonathan, " you must moderate the expression of your sufferings. As my late respected husband said when he——"

" Ah! Christian lady," murmured Jonathan, " your respected husband never dislocated his thigh. Oh, I feel faint—a little drop of the gentleman's brandy ;" the patient appeared to be unable to say more without the stimulant, which the landlord fetched immediately, and Jonathan swallowed with great relish, smacking his lips afterwards.

" How do you feel now ?" said madame.

" Better, kind mistress, better considerably."

" But your leg ?"

" Ah! my leg—O—O—yes—my leg! my leg is as bad as ever," and he rolled on the sofa.

" A bad case evidently !" said the landlord. " But since it must be so, Mrs. Brown will arrange about the rooms. The poor man had better be got to bed directly. Dr. Humdrum will soon be here to the ball, and he can see him at once. You will excuse me, ma'am." Mr. Brown bowed himself out.

" And I must leave you for a few minutes," added Mrs. Brown. " I will send some of the ostlers to help this poor cripple to a bed, and then, perhaps, you will not object to step into my parlour, as we shall want this for a cloak-room."

Madame bowed and the door was shut. Our adventurers eyed each other intelligently. Jonathan clapped his fore-finger to the side of his nose, but the lady pressed two of her digits on her lips. She was right, for there was a tap at the door, so the patient lay down again with one of his old groans, and the landlord re-entered.

" I beg your pardon, madam, but you said, I think, the gentleman knew me. You did not mention the name of your——"

" Of my late respected husband, you would say. Doctor Theophilus

Dorville, of Tooley-street, in the Borough, and Dorville Hall, in the Isle of Dogs."

Brown expressed profound respect in a bow, and once more retired. It was to himself he muttered as he hastened to the front-door—

" A great man, no doubt, and a very old friend of mine, I dare say; but I never heard the name in my born days before."

This time on being left alone with the doctress, Jonathan put his thigh in the socket, and skipping across the room, threw his arms round the neck of the comely woman, and saluted her with a hearty smack of the lips.

The guests were arriving : among the first who came were Farmer Hodson and his wife and daughter. He was rather an important man from his position in the county, farmed his own land, and was said to have a very considerable sum of money in the funds. He appeared to be ill at ease in the ball-room ; but he was there in deference to the wishes of his wife, who had not often an opportunity of meeting great folks, and parading her brocade and her point and her garnets, and he was somewhat flattered by the evident admiration which his daughter excited. Even the Dumfounders, who were very grand indeed, and kept pretty much to their own end of the room, condescended to notice charming Ellen Hodson. And truly she was worthy of their praise.

Her face was pale as Parian marble. She had a soft hazel eye ; her nose was delicately chiselled, and the expression of her mouth was sweetness' self. Contrary to the fashion of the time she wore her glossy brown ringlets in a silken crop about her neck, and the lilies in her hair were the only ornaments that she had borrowed. Her little hand seemed to be oftener sought than any other for the stately dance then in vogue, and her fairy figure, as she moved to the measure, was watched by more than one pair of eager loving eyes.

" Ellen," said a good-looking young fellow, called Tom Thornton, the son of a neighbouring squire, " Ellen, you promised that to-night you would tell me if you would accept my love."

" I did, Tom," replied Ellen falteringly, " and—and—"

" And what, Ellen ?"

" I will keep my word."

" Your friends and my own are favourable to our marriage, we have known each other from children, our ages agree, I love you, Ellen, fondly—why should we not be happy ?"

" I hope you may, Tom, with all my heart. But we will speak of this by-and-bye. They are going to dance."

" Will you be my partner ?"

" I am already engaged."

" To whom ?"

" Captain Austen.   You see he is coming to claim me."

A tall, dark, handsome man advanced, in full regimentals, to where Miss Hodson, her lover, and parents were positioned.  He muttered some common-place in a low tone to the young lady, bowed graciously to the mother, and led away her daughter without deigning notice to the farmer or poor Tom.  The latter exclaimed bitterly,

" Captain Austen again !  I shall find a rival in that man."

" Dont'ee say so, Tom," replied the farmer, " Ellen can never think of him."

Tom Thornton shook his head gloomily, and slowly moved away.

" And why, Farmer Hodson," asked the dame of her husband, " why shouldn't our Nelly think of such a handsome, pleasant, dashing gentle-man as the Captain, pray ?  I'll be bound thee couldst lay thy finger on as much money as he ?"

" Thee'rt a fool, dame," replied the farmer, " and as readily caught by a red coat as e'er a child of them all."

The old lady bridled and arranged her head-dress, but she said nothing.

" Doctor Humdrum, Doctor Humdrum," said Mr. Brown, the land-lord, as the doctor stood in the doorway.

" Ah ! Mr. Brown, what is it ?"

" A case, Dr. Humdrum, and you're wanted."

Doctor Humdrum was a pursy little man, in a full-bottomed wig, and a suit of black.

" Dear me ! how very inconsiderate of any body to be taken ill on a night like this."

" But it is not far, doctor."

" How far ?"

" Only upstairs."

" Upstairs !  One of the maids got the colic ?   Give her a dose of jalap."

" Worse than that, doctor."

" Worse than that !  Mrs. Brown brought to bed ?"

" No, doctor, but a poor fellow has his hip dislocated, and a cha-ritable lady who has brought him here is willing to pay all charges."

" Dislocation of the hip, eh ? very good—charitable lady, pay all charges—um !  I'll follow you."

" Where are you going, doctor ?" inquired Captain Austen, approaching on the instant.

" Merely to set a limb.  I think you said the patient was a man, landlord."

· " A man, doctor."

" Then come along, Captain, you shall be my assistant."   The Captain and the Doctor followed the landlord upstairs, and in the far corner of one of the galleries in a little garret, they found, stretched on a truckle bed, the hero of our history.   On a rush chair by the side stood a lantern and some cold brandy and water.

Doctor Humdrum speedily ascertained the nature of the lameness, and asked Jonathan how long ago the accident happened to him.

" About eight years," whined our hero.   Madame Dorville and the landlady entered the bed-room at this moment.   Mr. Brown pointed out the former as the kind lady who had brought the sufferer into Warwick, and desired the doctor's assistance.

" Madam," said the doctor, " it would be no less than a robbery to take your money, for there is no possibility of serving this poor fellow; the bone having been so long misplaced, has contracted a new situation, and the head of the bone forms a socket so formidable, it would be unnatural to remove it thence, so that we must let it rest as it is."

This did not at all seem to satisfy our lady.

" I am sure," said she, " the limb may be reduced to its proper place with due care, if you will apply fomentations and other topical medicines to the part, for the relaxation of the ligaments, and so forth, in preparation for the reduction."

The doctor argued and the patient groaned, while madame quoted the opinion of her late respected husband when he bequeathed her all his property.

An adjournment was proposed, and the disputants, with the landlord and his wife, descended to a more convenient apartment, where the affair ended for a time, as is often the case in such matters, with a wager of fifty pounds, the lady to have the sole conduct of the sufferer, whereupon she proposed to have him blooded the following morning, and commence her treatment with embrocations, fomentations, &c., and the result was accordingly looked for with great interest by a number of people who got whisper of the case, and again told it to others.

Captain Austen lingered behind the rest in the garret of Jonathan. When they were gone, he sat down upon the low bed, and looked keenly at our hero. The adventurer fancied for a moment that his trick was discovered, but he returned the other's gaze with imperturbable calmness.

" Can you keep a secret, fellow ?" asked the officer.

" If it is worth anything," replied Jonathan.

" I am engaged in a masquerading frolic to-night," continued Austen ; " will you exchange coats with me ?"

Jonathan looked at the gold lace on the soldier's, and then at his own threadbare garment hanging on the chair beside him, and replied,

" For how long a time?"

" Nay, if I exchange I shall not cry off at any time."

" Well, as I don't think I shall lose anything, I will."

" Let me have your thick shoes, hat, and wig for mine, and I will throw you in five guineas to boot."

" Done," cried Wild eagerly, sitting up in the bed, and forgetting his hip.

" Your leg seems better," said the Captain sarcastically.

Jonathan laid down again, and felt it necessary to twist a wry face as though the motion had given him great pain.

" Now, then, my fine fellow," resumed Austen, " I shall be here again in half an hour to complete our bargain. You will be discreet for your own sake ; a whisper, and the compact is at an end." The Captain was about to leave the garret, when a sudden idea seemed to strike Jonathan.

" Stop ! come back !" he cried.

Austen returned, and Jonathan sat up boldly in the bed, and put his hand upon the shoulder of the other, who had stooped down to listen.

" This is not a plant, is it ? you hav'nt been cracking a crib, and. want to get me lumbered ?"

" What does the fellow mean ?"

" Burglary or highway robbery, change of toggery, and the wrong man taken prisoner, eh?" Jonathan had looked round the room with great caution before he said this, and he spoke it in a whisper. The officer at first seemed inclined to be angry, but turning it off with a laugh, whispered Jonathan in turn, " Nothing of the kind ; it is an affair of gallantry; a lady in the case—mum!" Then they both laughed, and the captain left the room.

" Right again," said Jonathan with a chuckle; " I thought I should go to London with more than ninepence in my pocket."

The ball was at its height : the old people were engaged at cards, the young ones in the dance.   Farmer Hodson was earnestly debating a question of agricultural interest with a considerable landholder. Tom Thornton had been refused by Ellen, and Ellen and the Captain were conversing in the balcony of the great bay-window.

" Do not hesitate, dearest," said Austen, " you have no cause to doubt."

" Oh ! it is not that—no, Heaven knows I do *not* doubt you—but to leave my parents thus—"

" Have I not told you of the present necessity, that it need but be for a short time, and then all shall be publicly owned ?"

" And why not—yes—we will wait till then !"

" Are you playing with me, Ellen ?"

" Playing with you, Edmund ?"

" Aye, playing with me ?   Are you a child ? Is not every arrangement made, even to the disguise you are to assume ? and yet you balk my hopes, and idly talk of waiting."

" Do not be angry with me, Edmund.   Pity my weakness."

" I do, darling ; but you have sworn to be no other's, and you are too fair a prize for me to resign my claim, Ellen, love.   Now listen. Are you calm ?"

" Quite, Edmund, quite calm," and the trembling girl clung nervously to her lover's arm, and her soft eyes and white face were upturned to his.

" Your father and mother are both engaged, and our absence will not be noticed for the next hour at least.   In ten minutes' time proceed to the room underneath this ; you will easily do so without attracting notice ; it is only dimly lighted, but on the first chair to the right as you enter, under a horseman's cloak, you will find your disguise.   It is but to slip it over your own dress, and you will look like a peasant girl equipped for a journey.   The window, which is open to the ground, leads directly to the garden that you now see before you.   Beyond the shrubbery is the gate ; it will be unfastened ; walk to the corner of the lane a dozen yards beyond ; I shall be waiting for you.   My appearance will wear the same character as your's ; in half an hour, dear Ellen, we shall be on the high road to London."

" Hush !" said the farmer's daughter,   " what was that ?   Something touched the curtain."

" Nonsense, love.   You are nervous to-night.   Believe me it was nobody. Come, let us walk through the room once more ; this dance is over. Are you prepared to do as I have bidden you, Nell ?"

" I know the wrong that it will be, dear Edmund, but I pray that ere long all will be happy—and—"

" And what, my trembler?"

" Nelly puts her trust upon her Edmund's love and honour."

The soldier kissed away the tears that started unbidden in the eyes of the country girl, and drawing her arm through his, for the last time returned to join the assembly.

" In half an hour on the high road to London," muttered Thornton, who, in passing the window, had caught the last sentence of Austen's speech, and startled Ellen as we have seen. " I must prevent this. I am refused, it is true; but if I may not be Nell Hodson's husband, I *will* be her brother ! That fellow's a damned scoundrel ; I thought he was a villain from the first. I could stop this at once, if I liked, by informing her father ; but I won't have a bobbery here and expose her. I will stay them on the high road, as he says, and tell her what the villain means, and bring her home again in triumph—then, perhaps, she mayn't think so meanly of me—who knows ? I'll do it—I'll do it, or my name is not Tom Thornton !"

" Well," said Jonathan Wild, in his garret, after the exchange of clothes had been effected, amusing himself with flicking the guineas from his thumb-nail and catching them in the palm of his hand, " this is a rumbo start to a certainty ; but first to examine the pockets," and he turned up the ample sides of the officer's coat. " Why, what the devil's this ? A snuff-box, as I live, and gold, by the Lord ! Five guineas ! why this is worth another ten at least. Bravo, Jonathan ! A fellow would not look bad in a coat like this, though," the rascal thrust his arms into the sleeves as he sat up on the mattrass. The sound of the music below broke upon his ears. " Egad, I don't see why I should not join the dancers ; I have coat, shoes, wig and cocked-hat to match. I can make up the rest. I'll be hanged if I don't," and clapping his thigh into its socket, he hopped out of bed and began to dress himself forthwith. True, his brown breeches and worsted stockings were rather a ludicrous contrast to the rest of his attire ; but confident in his disguise, and satisfied that the poor cripple would never be suspected, if he could only reach the rooms, he resolved to essay the attempt for the fun of the thing ; it really was very dull lying there in a miserable garret, with the sounds of revelry proceeding below.

A few minutes afterwards and general attention was directed to the remarkable figure of a tall young man in a very handsome but ill-fitting military coat, who wore his wig awry, and carried his feathered hat under his arm ; the costume of his lower limbs was peculiar, and his grey hose looked very warm and slightiy dirty, perhaps ; but his shoes and buckles were elegant, and the magnificent snuff box that he tapped with so much grace, gave him a very grand and noble air.

"Dear me ! who can he be?" ran through the company in a buzz.

" Some distinguished foreigner, no doubt," exclaimed Doctor Hum-drum.

" Evidently an eccentric nobleman," vowed Lady Dumfounder, and the master of the ceremonies was commissioned to ask the stranger's name.

" My name," replied Jonathan ; " oh! ah! yes, of course—take a pinch of snuff? You see I am in the army, and I'm a lord as well—Lord Donohoo."

The name of Lord Donohoo was echoed in audible whispers, and some distinguished families were presented to the young nobleman, who, one or two crabbed people thought, had taken the ball for a mas-querade, and come in character. The majority were, however, decidedly in his lordship's favour, particularly those with unmarried daughters, and as many of the girls were remarkably pretty, Jonathan in the guise of Lord Donohoo took a great deal of notice of them. Indeed, he went so far as to offer to kiss one in a recess, and met with lit-tle opposition. As a proof that his manners must have been very engaging, he actually poked Lady Dumfounder in the waist with his extended forefinger, pronouncing an unspellable word, like " ketchee, ketchee," while he winked his eye, and thrust his tongue in his cheek, and danced on one foot.

Lord Donohoo escorted Lady Dumfounder to the card-room. Lord D. was deep in the mysteries of whist.

" When," said the great county lady to her husband, " when will your lordship be ready for home ? It is one o'clock, and the carriage has been waiting some time."

" I must play this rubber out, my lady," replied the peer of a hun-dred and fifty years ago, " and then I'll go. In half an hour's time, there," and he lugged out an immense gold watch nearly as large as an ordinary saucer, set with diamonds round the face of it, with a great chain and greater seals pendant, and deposited it on the table beside him.

" Then I'll return to the dancers," replied her ladyship. " Lord
" Donohoo, I leave you to look after Dumfounder."

"I'll bet a pot on the odd trick," said Jonathan, staring at the
watch that was set down just before him.

" What ?" inquired Lord Dumfounder.

" I say Il'l bet a pound on the odd trick," replied Jonathan, recol-
lecting himself, chinking his guineas, and tapping his gold snuff-box.

" Oh, very well —done! "

" Done it is."

In the next room there was great excitement. Ellen Hodson, the
belle of the evening, was gone; gone none knew whither. Captain
Austen too was missed. They had searched within and without, and
neither of them could be found.

Farmer Hodson was well nigh beside himself. He raved and
stamped, and even cursed, and bitterly upbraided his wife, accusing
her as being cognisant of her daughter's flight.

The ball was at an end.

And Thornton—Tom Thornton, where was he? He had been seen
by the servants half an hour since to hurry to the stables, and himself
saddle his horse, and gallop hastily on the London road.

"London!" cried the farmer, "ay, that be it, and he be after them.
That my child, my daughter Nell, that I ha dandled on my knee,
and thought to give wi a handsome dower to an honest yeoman,
should live to run away to London to be the mistress of a Captain.
Curses on the villain who could rob a father of his only one—curses
on—no, no, I *cannot* curse *her*. I cannot curse my child !" and the
old man burst into tears as the affrighted guests gathered around him.

" That will do," said Dumfounder, "and now the rubber's over,
I will trouble you for that pound."

But the eccentric young nobleman alluded to had vanished, and with
him, terrible to relate, the gold watch set with diamonds and the pendant chain and seals of my Lord Dumfounder.

The valuables were safely deposited in a water-spout that ran outside the window of a certain garret, wherein lay Jonathan Wild, with
his head in a white cotton nightcap, filling the air with deep and
agonising groans. Between the mattrass and the bedstead were the
coat, shoes, and wig of the departed Captain.

And the Captain, where rode he? On the back of a swift horse,
with the slender arms of the armer's daughter about his waist.

It was a fine night, the stars were out, and the moon was keeping watch over her sister earth.    Away they went, and as they rushed through the night-air, it kept the girl from fainting, and the spirits of the soldier mounted.  At the turn of the road a horseman met them.

"Hold!" cried he, imperatively; and as he crossed they were obliged to stop.

"So, Captain Austen, this is your return for an English yeoman's hospitality.    To pour poison into his daughter's ear, to steal her in the night like a thief, and carry her off to infamy."

"By what right"—— begun Austen.

"By what right?   By the right that every honest man possesses to do his best to stop a deed of villany.    By the right of friendship for the parents, and love for the child, I bid you give her back to me, pure and untainted, as she now clings to you."

"Stand back

"Nell Hodson, if you were ever taught to prize virtue, honor, duty, love, heed not that villain.  If you would not have your mother die with grief, your old father sink with shame—if you would not live yourself an object for the poorest clown to scorn—a painted wanton—"

"I'll hear no more," exclaimed Austen, drawing his sword, and spurring on his horse.

"Then look to yourself, for Ellen shall be rescue ."   The young squire's stout cudgel wheeled in the air, and shattering the officer's sword, struck him heavily in the face.   Ellen shrieked piercingly, and Austen was almost blinded with his streaming blood.   Scarcely knowing how he aimed, he drew a pistol from his breast, and fired it at Thornton.   The latter fell almost within a moment to the ground, and and his horse, without its rider, started off again in the direction of Warwick.   Ellen had fainted, but her lover upheld her, and gallopped on his way.

Within a week, to the wonder of Warwickshire, Jonathan's dislocated thigh was set right by the doctress, and the wager of fifty pounds duly paid.  Madame Dorville, in consequence of her great success, and in accordance—she said—with the desire of her late respected husband, who left her all his property, cured distempers for the mere price of the medicines, and our hero was employed all day in powdering brickdust and rhubarb for moneyed sufferers.

When our adventurers left Warwick, they found they had to divide between them a net produce of a hundred pounds.

## CHAPTER III.

LONDON.—JONATHAN AND THE DOCTRESS.—DIAMOND CUT DIAMOND.

SOME months had elapsed since the events of the last chapter.

Jonathan Wild and Madame Dorville had taken up their residence in the metropolis, after their departure from Warwick, and, though they did not entirely reside under the same roof, yet their apparent relationship partook of the character of man and wife. They had seemed either to have formed a joint-stock bank, or else—as was more

No. 2.

probable—the gentleman perhaps had first spent his own money, and then fallen back upon the lady's,—at all events, it was the question of the right of cash which made them opponents on the evening we again introduce them to the notice of the reader.

It was in Westminster, at the lodgings of the doctress, who still pursued her vocation, and with success, that the following dialogue ___ :—

"___ you, Madame Dorville, that I have not a rap."

"___ I tell you, Mr. Wild, that is no business of mine."

"___ devilish cool kind of an answer that, ma'am, in all conscience."

"And what kind of answer, sir, in all conscience, could you expect ___

"You ___ a little feeling, I think," murmured Jonathan

"Feeling ___ the dame.

"Aye, feeling, Madame Doctress! Is there anything very extraordinary in the word ?"

"Not in the word, perhaps, Mr. Vagabond, but certainly in the sentiment, coming from your lips."

"Why, Mr. Vagabond ?" remonstrated the gentleman.

"And why anything else ?" replied the other ; "have you not acted like a vagabond ? were not you a vagabond when I met you ? and did not I feed you, and clothe you, and put money in your purse, and and make you what you are ?"

"And no thanks to you, either, for, if a vagabond still, my condition cannot be very sensibly improved."

"Were not you next to a beggar when I found you on the road to Warwick ?"

"No ; but I was next to a rogue when I walked by your side *into* Warwick."

"Did not I take you by the hand ?"

"And in return for your hand, did not I put out my leg ?"

"In short, wouldn't you have starved but for me ?"

"And, in short, didn't I requite you by making your fortune for you? Stuff, Madame Dorville, we are quits, and shall gain nothing by this bandying of words."

"Then, why did you begin it, pray ?"  This question was so exactly the fashion of a woman's argument that Jonathan laughed when he heard it.

"I won't be laughed at, sir! who are you that you dare to laugh at me ?"

Wild had a point to gain, so he subdued his face and his t___:—

"My dear Jane—" he began coaxingly.

"I am not your dear, sir, and I know it," pouted the lady, tw___ her shoulder.

"Yes, you are, Jane, 'pon my soul; but—"

"Don't but me, Mr. Wild; I've been butted enough, I can tell you."

"You're out of temper, love, or you would'nt talk in that way. I'm sure, for my part, I wouldn't annoy you for the world, and, after all, I merely said I was without money. If that is to be an off___, old woman, why then God help the world, I say; that's all."

Jonathan Wild said this so pleasantly, and slapped Mad___ orville so playfully on her fat white shoulder that she al___ ___ as she looked up into the remarkably plain face of our ___ ___ed him what it really was he wanted after all.

"Now, Jane, begin to talk reasonably, and though I know it is a great deal to require of one of your sex, yet you will, perhaps, do me the favour reasonably to listen."

"There now, Wild, bother! go on."

Mr. Wild went on accordingly to urge that it was exceedingly distressing for a man moving in the world to be without cash; that to one with the tastes and habits of a gentleman it was absolutely unbearable; there was money to be made; he knew the means; but, as in everything else, capital was required.

"And these means, Mr. Wild?"

"The gaming-table, Madame Dorville."

"The gaming table! are you mad, sir? If you had been born a gentleman, instead of a—"

"A what, ma'am?"

"A journeyman buckle-maker, at Wolverhampton, you could not have more airs and graces."

"'Airs and graces,' is an expression, Madame Dorville, which I have very often heard you make use of, and I believe to be common among ladies, though I have not the smallest notion of its meaning; but without any more parleying, Jane, lend me five pounds, there's a duck!"

"To throw away at the faro table, sir?"

"My dear, where there are so many losers, there must be some winners."

"I have never heard of your winnings, Wild. You ought to be ashamed of yourself to be such an idle lounging fellow as you are, after the capital start you had at Warwick, and now to be doing nothing, but

living apo_ a poor fond fool, and always plaguing her for cash to get rid
o__ the gardens, the tavern, or the gaming table: it is horrible!"

"_s to being idle, my dear, I cannot for the life of me understand how
you support that charge. Who looks after the medicine-chest if I don't,
I should like to know? and, let me tell you, with your business, that's
no such light matter. Why, I was all day yesterday making some
thousands of pills out of a quartern loaf; and only the day before I broke
up a whole bag of hearthstones for worm powders, while I'll be bound to
say there is not a drop of the Revivifying Lotion, or a smell of the
Married Woman's Elixir, if you would give a guinea for it."

"Th__ __r goodness sake, dear Jonathan, get in the senna and the
Holland__ _____ _or there's nothing goes off like the Lotion and Elixir."

"Oh, _____ _ dear Jonathan now. Come, then; idler as I am, I
do something __ service, and that's one charge answered. As to the rest,
I *had* a start down at Warwick with a capital of fifty guineas. I ought
to have done great things. But you are a woman of the world, Madame
Dorville, and should know that money is of no service if we have not the
wit to use it wisely. I am not going to acknowledge, however, because,
instead of doubling my bank, I have broken it, that I have lost my start;
no,—my cash is gone, it is true, but it is only out at interest. and Experience will one day repay me more than cent. per cent., my love."

"I know you can talk, Mr. Wild."

"That merit is not peculiar to myself, Jane, eh? Do you remember
how you bamboozled all the people at Warwick with 'my late respected
husband, when he bequeathed me all his property?' 'Ha, ha!' said I,
'that is a woman in a thousand; she knows what life is, and the effect
of gold upon human nature. She would wheedle the devil—she would;
but the devil, and a lawyer, and a nightingale, wouldn't wheedle her.'
From that moment, Jenny, my darling, I, who had never loved before,
loved devotedly; I wrapped you up in my heart, and in my warm affections you were as snug as a bug in a rug!"

"Was I, Johnny, though really?"

"Now, don't ask such d——d nonsense, Jenny, don't. Haven't I
proved it in every way? Haven't I stuck to you ever since?"

"You have, Jonathan, you have."

"And do you think I'd leave you while you had a pound in the
world?—I'd scorn to do it."

"You are not handsome, Jonathan."

"Eh?" said Jonathan, making a wry face,—for our hero had his
weak point, as well as the woman he was fooling.

"No, Jonathan—you are not. The small-pox has a great deal to answer for to your natural beauty, and your complexion is not good. I know you can't help it, but it makes you look sometimes—particularly when you are bilious, dear—like tripe boiled in pea-soup. But what of that? as my late respected husband—"

"Stow that, Jane, until there is somebody to play upon. You forget!"

"I really beg your pardon, Jonathan,—the effect of habit. Where was I?—Oh, I recollect. I was saying you were not handsome; but that made no difference to me. I think you do care something about me; and, if you are not good-looking, you ARE clever. What a pity it is you won't earn a little more, and spend a little less!"

"I will, my dear, to-morrow. I'll begin to-morrow, 'pon my honour! I say—can't you let me have that five pounds to-night?"

"You don't love me," murmured the doctress.

"Yes!" replied our hero.

"No!"

"Yes!"

Jonathan put his arms round the lady's waist; but she turned from him, and whispered remonstratively, "Oh, go away, do!" and so he did —to the other side of her chair; and then he kissed her; and, as she had not the heart to refuse him, he walked away with the five pounds.

Madame Dorville lived by preying on the follies, the weaknesses, and the ignorance of the world, yet possessed neither the wisdom, the power, or the knowledge to resist the cajolery of an undoubted rascal, whose own weak point was so evidently prominent in his shallow vanity. Do we not find such and similar instances at every turn in this great city? But to return to our story;—and the next sentence is but a further illustration of the contradiction of human nature.

Jonathan Wild, the Shrewd, was gone to the gaming-table, and Madame Dorville, the Quack, to consult a fortune-teller!

# CHAPTER IV.

### THE FARMER'S DAUGHTER.—NIGHT AND THE WATCHER.—THE FARO TABLE.—THE GAMBLER'S DEATH.

IT is a handsome apartment in a large house in the neighbourhood of Lincoln's-inn-fields. The curtains are drawn, the fire burns cheerfully, and a beautiful girl in elegant attire rests her elbow on the table, and her little hand supports her marble forehead.

A sigh escapes her,—another: alas! she is unhappy. And what can be the cause of her distress;—the distress of one so young, so free, so beautiful? As the wind is tempered to the shorn lamb, why fan not the breezes more gently the fragile flowers?

See, the tears are trickling through her fingers—those fingers be-gemmed with rings! She removes her hand,—she upraises her pale fair face,—it is Ellen Hodson! Soft!—now she speaks:

"My father!—my dear father!—hast thou forgotten me entirely?—Dost thou love me still?—Am I yet in thought the child of thy heart?—No!—I dare not think it!—I have no right to think it!—I am too guilty for such happiness!—You have blotted me out—erased my image from the tablet of your memory!—I am no more your child! And my mother—my poor, dear mother! I tremble to breathe her name—it is an insult to virtue. I have no parents now. Oh, this is cruel work! Why does not he redeem his word? He pledged it a thousand times, and called on Heaven to register his vows. Why, in the face of the world, does he not make me his wife, and give me back to honour, and the right to bless my father with the knowledge that I am worthy to be called again his daughter? He *shall* do it! He leaves me here to ponder on my wrongs, and they rise up in judgment, and inspire me with unexpected strength: frail, weak girl that I have been, I'll now be so no more; this state of wretchedness must end!"

She rose as she spoke, and paced the room with agitation, the colour mounted to her cheeks, and her brow was flushed. Suddenly she stopped: the watch was crying the hour:—

"Past eleven o'clock, and a starlight night!"

She went to the window, drew back the curtains, and looked into the street.

It was, indeed, a beautiful night in the early time of spring; and there were few people abroad. Our grandfathers kept better hours than we do; and by eleven o'clock good citizens were mostly in bed.

The way was feebly lit with oil, but the moon and the stars and the white pavement, and the clear keen air, made every object of ready discernment. Ellen pressed her pale cheek to the glass, and looked eagerly towards the corner of the street.

"Oh, that he may come now!—now, while the blood courses freely in my veins;—now, when my wrongs set my heart beating, and my brain working;—now, that I may bravely tell him how the timid victim claims to be made his wife!"

Now she heard footsteps, and she thought they were his, and she strained her eyes, peering into the long distance,—but in vain. Some sober citizen sought his way towards Temple Bar, or dapper clerk his roosting-place in Gray's Inn.

Again the watchman went by:—

"Twelve o'clock, and a starlight night!"

Midnight! and the lights had nearly all disappeared from the windows of the opposite row. In one or two houses she had seen by the reflection of the candles against the blinds that the inmates were retiring to rest. A half-tipsy roysterer would now be the only passenger in the cold, narrow streets. Ellen's determination was fast subsiding, and, as her blood chilled, she turned to rake up the dying embers in the grate. The lamp, too, was fast going out, and she would not disturb the people of the house at such an hour. She drew a shawl about her shoulders, and again sought the window.

There was a bustle out of doors, nor could he be the cause of it.

No; it was the voices of Irish chairmen that she heard. They were bringing home an old lady from a card-party. They stopped next door, and Ellen drew a little on one side, as she feared the glare of their lights might reveal her a watcher. The old woman, in powder, and patches, and paint,—a little stricken by the palsy, it is true, but still firm withal, —alighted from her conveyance, and—her mind still fixed upon the pieces of painted pasteboard, and her toothless mouth still mumbling lowly of aces, and diamonds, and trumps,—she passed into her house. The chairmen drank from a jug that was presented to them by the great fat porter; and then, putting out their lights by the aid of the iron extinguishers which, in different parts of London, may even now be discerned sprouting from the iron railings, slipped their leathers over the arms of the sedan, and jogged on their way.

The street-door was shut with a bang, and again all was still.

"Past one o'clock, and a fine bright morning!"

So late!—Ellen drew her little shawl about her shoulders tighter yet, and wondered would he *never* come. The fire was now gone out wholly, and the lamp flickered to its close. The chilliness that comes with the early hours of the morning was creeping in the chamber.

Where could he be? No business could detain him till such an hour. Hark!—those were the chimes: one—two—three!—three-quarters past one! Should she go to bed?

If——no, no!—the thought was too dreadful—it could not be!—and yet——he had grown neglectful of her of late;—there was a coldness in his tones he never used to note. Oh! could it be possible? Pshaw! she was foolish—wicked—to stand conjuring all sorts of phantoms. The neglect was nothing—the coldness in her fancy; and—yes!—that was his step!

Again he sprang to the window, and knew that he was coming now. Nearer and nearer the steps approached, and her heart leaped boundingly, and her resolves and resentment together vanished, and she was ready to receive him—her betrayer—with open arms! He must be close now—he would mount the steps directly—why did he not knock?—Alas! the passenger had passed, and the footsteps were fainter and fainter; 'twas not her Edmund—'twas not the object of her hope.

She threw herself upon the sofa, and exclaiming,

"God help me!—I am lost, indeed!" burst into a passionate flood of tears.

*  *  *  *

Jonathan Wild was disporting in a west-end gaming-house with the five pounds—almost the last—wrung from the doctress, Madame Dorville.

Our hero had staked a guinea and won; he doubled his risk, and won again; a third time he left down his first stake and his winnings; he was once more successful. A grin seemed to be trying to effect a mastery over his features; but his vanity—which desired to show the thing as a mere matter, in which the gentleman was, of course, wholly unconcerned—battled with and conquered it.

"You are fortunate to night, sir," said a player of apparent position at Wild's elbow.

"Tolerably so," replied Jonathan, who, thinking it not unadvisable to borrow a leaf from the book of Madame, added, "It was the remark of my late respected hus—I mean, father, when he bequeathed me all his property—"

"I beg your pardon," interrupted the gentleman who had just addressed him; "but I think I have heard that or a very similar expression some-where before?"

"Possibly," replied Wild, with all *nonchalance*. "Young men will have respected fathers, even in these days; and respectable parents will sometimes bequeathe their sons all their property." As he made this little flourish, he drew a handsome gold snuff-box from his pocket, and tapping it with an air, offered a pinch as a sort of clincher to his new acquaintance.

"I thought we had met before," said the player, "and this box confirms my opinion."

"This box is mine!" exclaimed Jonathan, snapping the lid hastily, and putting it in his breast.

"I don't dispute it," replied the other, "by right of possession; but you will find my name inside it."

"And that is—"

"Edmund Austen."

"Then you are—"

"The officer with whom you exchanged clothes four months ago at the 'Royal George,' at Warwick."

Jonathan looked closely at the speaker; and, though the latter was now plainly attired in the ordinary evening costume of a civilian of the time, he could not doubt the fact; while a little whistle of astonishment broke from his lips.

After regarding Austen for a moment or two, Wild said, "Follow me," and walked towards a recess, where, turning sharply round upon the captain, he asked him, bluntly, what he meant to do?

"Receive back my own again, fellow," replied Austen.

"By what means?"

"By any, if fair ones fail."

"Can you deny that you gave it me?"

"I did so, it is true, but unintentionally, you know. It was no part of the bargain; and for you to appropriate it was felony."

"I shall not resign it."

"How if I compel you?"

"You cannot do so. Attempt to molest me as I quit this house, and I will blow you to the devil!"

He drew a small pistol as he expressed his determination, and pointed the muzzle towards the captain's heart.

"A word from me," said Austen, "will bring every man in the room to my rescue, and your apprehension will follow in a moment."

"But that word spoken," replied Jonathan, "and you die!"

"Your own death would necessarily follow."

"Not 'necessarily:' this is a public gaming-house; the men who keep it, scoundrels of the blackest dye. They would rather dispose of your dead body than, by bringing me to justice, bring also upon them the fangs of the law."

"You are a calculating villain."

"Better a calculating villain than a headstrong fool."

"Come," said the captain, "put up your pistol, my good fellow. You are a thorough-paced rascal; but it is a pity that your career should be cut short. Who knows but you may be destined for greater deeds? You have served me at a pinch before now: you may do so again; meanwhile keep the box."

"Stay—you seem to have work in hand for me?"

"I may have."

"Then, before we proceed further, irrespective of payment for such service hereafter to be rendered, this trifle is mine?"

"Are you the Prime Minister in disguise, or an Old Bailey lawyer?"

"Neither," replied Jonathan, plucking up his shirt collar, "but I may be one or both before the end of the chapter. Is it agreed?"

"It is."

"Enough; I am satisfied. Let us return to the table."

Jonathan spoke with the air of a diplomatist effecting a national nego- ciation; and the captain could not fail to be amused at the rogue's monstrous impudence.

The men about the table were composed of different sets. There was the idle lounger, who risked his few guineas and sipped his punch, and cared not whether he won or lost, but picked his teeth, and whisked his lace handkerchief athwart his nose, as though the loss or gain of such a thing as a few gold pieces could be a matter of no moment to a gentleman. There were one or two of these, no more.

Then came the determined gambler—the man who, in the possession still of means, risked them night after night in the accursed hell,—social ties, wife, children, family, and friends, forgotten all, in the infatuation that led him—hastily, or by degrees, as Fortune favoured him—to ruin, —certain, irrevocable ruin.

Next, the man who had been at one time or other like the last—the beggar with his pieces scraped together—hard-wrung from trusting friends or poor affection—watching now with flushed and miserable intensity each turn upon the table, till his all was swept away, and then half imbecile,—his straining eyes fixed still on where had stood his hopes.

The half-bully, half-gentleman—all rogue,—the man who had been once a pigeon, now turned Greek, or pigeon-plucker, in pay of the house, luring others on to play when play grew scarce,—made up the list that Captain Austen and Jonathan Wild now joined.

There was one young man in particular who attracted their attention: he was young, pale, and his features were cast in a melancholy mould: he had a small heap of gold before him, and his fingers twitched with it nervously, and it almost seemed that he would wear out his eyes with gazing on the chances. One hand clenched his forehead feverishly as he leant forward on the table, and stretched his bloodshot eye-balls across the baize. His lips quivered, and there was a hectic flush in either cheek.

"Lost, lost again!" he murmured wretchedly.

"My God!" said Austen, "do but look on the agony in that young man's face!"

"Doomed!" whispered Wild.

"How say you?"

"I have seen the thing before," replied our hero, in a low tone; "now mark my words."

Again the young man staked and lost. His heap of guineas had dwindled to a few. His losses had been great, and all other play was for the moment suspended.

"Now, now! or—" The rest was unheard. He threw the remainder of his money on a card: the card was turned; the bank had won—the player was without a shilling.

"Water, water!" he cried, clasping his throat, in a state apparently bordering on frenzy; "water, lest I die!"

They gave it him, and he seemed somewhat to recover, as he pressed his hat upon his brow, and staggered from the room.

"I have seen too much to-night," said Austen, "come with me, and I will tell you the business with which I am about to entrust you as we go."

They left the place together, and, it being now night, or, rather, the early hours of the morning, the Captain did not hesitate to take the arm of Jonathan.

"I think I told you," he said, "when you did me the honour to mistake me for a housebreaker, or some other equally-respectable gentleman, in Warwick, that I was engaged in an adventure with a lady, that induced me to take the step I then did?"

"I remember, and I believed you.   Was it not true?"

"Quite true.   That lady now resides under my protection.   You can serve me."

"You don't mean you want a husband for this wench, do you?  Is that what you are driving at?   You will have to come down handsomely if you keep me in your eye."

"Pshaw!—you quite misunderstand me.   The girl is sensitive."

"Is she, by Jove?   I am the very model for a sensitive girl."   And Jonathan laughed.

"I tell you again, you are mistaken.   I am the only husband the young lady requires or will accept.   Now, as I am not disposed at once to enter into all the heavy responsibilities of that position, in a strictly legal sense, it has struck me that the difficulty may be avoided by procuring a parson of my own selection."

"What is to be my reward?"

"Ten guineas and the undisturbed possession of the snuff-box."

"Sink the snuff-box, which is already my own, and make the sum twenty guineas, and I am your man.   Agreed?"

"Agreed."

They had reached the end of the street; and the report of a pistol disturbed the stillness of the night.   They hurried towards the spot.   The young man who so recently left the gaming-house—the ruined player—had blown out his brains, and to-morrow a widowed mother and a wretched maiden might weep the gambler's loss!

Austen and Wild, finding life extinct, hastily quitted the spot as the watch arrived.

When the two men parted at the Captain's door, the latter said—

"To-morrow, at twelve," and Jonathan replied, "I will be here."

It was noon the next day when Wild retraced his way to Lincoln's Inn Fields.   He was arrested on the door-step of Captain Austen, for thirty-seven pounds ten, at the suit of Madame Dorville,—a result consequent on her visit the previous evening to the fortune-teller!

# CHAPTER V.

## THE FORTUNE-TELLER—A MYSTERY AND AN INTRIGUE.

IN a second-floor back in King-street, Long-acre, lived one of the most notorious characters of her day. Like Madame Dorville, she practised the art of healing; but her supposed skill in reading the future was that which had secured for her the patronage of the public; and some of the highest in the land, perhaps, and great ladies, had been known constantly to leave their carriages in Covent-garden, and at nightfall and on foot to hurry to the lodgings of the fortune-teller, who was known as "Mother Stammers."

Mrs. Stammers was not an old woman, but she looked considerably advanced in years, and in her face might be traced the effects of ever-restless cunning, violent passion, and a strong love of ardent liquors. She wore her own gray hair, which was long and thick, loosely hanging, and on this was an old and much-stained red cloak that reached to her waist. She was supposed to have lost the use of her lower limbs, and propped up in bed she received her visitors. Her sole attendant was a little wretched and deformed old man, believed to be her husband. The man was humble as a child to her, and took without complaining the bitterness of her invectives and the weight of her passion—the latter often exhibited by the discharge of any handy missile at the head of the miserable attendant.

On the evening of which we write—that which preceded the night of the last chapter, the temper of Mother Stammers seemed to have attained almost an ungovernable pitch. She rocked and swayed her body about, and railed at her companion, and told him she should live to do him a mischief yet.

"I have done nothing at all that you should abuse me so," muttered the old man, warming his thin hands over the embers in the grate.

"Done nothing?—no!—and that it is that puts my blood up. You're a villain—an idle villain!"

The poor wretch was used to such epithets, and he seemed to mind them but little.

"Where have you been these four hours?—answer me!"

"I haven't been away four hours, Peggy."

"Dare to call me by that name again, you shrivelled wretch, and I'll beat your life out!"

"I beg your pardon, Mrs. Stammers. I—I didn't wish to offend you. I didn't, upon my honour!"

The trembling creature was seized with a fit of coughing, and could say no more. The black eyes of the fortune-teller gleamed in her head like living coals; she bit her lips with rage, and round about her mouth there came a bad white circle.

"To dare address me by my christian name!—you, by whose side a dog—the meanest cur that lives upon the refuse of the streets—shows a noble creature!—Ugh! how I loathe you!"

The man scarcely moved from his position before the grate—unless, indeed, to turn a little, that, by a furtive glance, he might see there was no article of attack within the fortune teller's reach; but, mumbling and muttering to himself, continued to hold his outstretched palms close to the coals for warmth.

After awhile, the woman became more calm, and asked him if he had been to the place she desired.

He had, he said; but he had not been able to get her the information she wanted. He was sorry for it, and would try again.

"And spend more money, I suppose," exclaimed Mrs. Stammers. "What have you done with that I gave you?"

"It is all gone—all gone, Mrs. Stammers."

"Gone!"

"Yes; but I didn't waste a farthing of it."

"You spent it in drink, you mumbling dotard, you did!"

"I was obliged to treat the servants with it, or they wouldn't have told me anything?"

"Whose servants?—what servants?"

"Mrs. Rushton's servants—the coachman and the groom."

"And what did you ascertain?"

"Nothing—nothing more than you know already. I could not see Charlotte, or I might have learned from her."

"Then you have heard nothing of a will?"

"Nothing: I dropped several hints, and even spoke about the property and wondered what he had done with it; but they could tell me nothing."

"It is of little consequence."

"What could you want to know about the gentleman's will, I wonder?" muttered the old man, more to himself than her

"And what has that to do with you, driveller?" replied Mrs. Stammers savagely; "if you are kept, fed, clothed, warmed, and all by my means, is not it enough, and more than enough, for such as you? What right has a thing like you to have a thought at all?"

"None, my dear; no right, none," replied the poor wretch, meekly.

"'My *dear*!'—I spit at you, reptile!" Mrs. Stammers ground her teeth, and hissed the last word through them, while the old man still warmed his hands, and see-sawed his shrunken frame before the low fire.

"Put more coals on," she continued after awhile, "and then go out for an hour or two; I expect company."

He made up the fire, and poured out the spirit from a basket-bottle into a tea-cup, and placed it by the bedside.

"Draw that curtain close, and trim the lamp." He did so, and the room looked snugger.

It was plainly but not poorly furnished. The bedstead, which was of black oak, stood in a recess facing the window, and the hangings were of a dark-coloured velvet that had once been handsome. There was an oval mirror in a great filagree frame upon the wall, and about it several tawdry-coloured prints of scripture subjects, that, from their poverty of execution and appearance, contrasted badly with the more ambitious furniture. The table and chairs were massive, and had evidently belonged to a person in a better sphere than the fortune-teller. A pack of cards stood side by side with the brandy-cup, and a huge black cat lay coiled at the foot of the bed.

"And now," said the woman, with an imperious wave of the arm, "begone!"

"Whither?"

"It matters little to me,—where you please."

"The night is cold and miserable, and I have no money."

"Is the night colder than your heart—darker than your ways, or more miserable than once you made me?"

"I can't tell—I can't tell."

"But I can, Martin Dormer, and I say—No! Then why should you fear to face it? Go, and shiver in the highways, crawl upon the bridges, look upon the black waters, and—if you will—plunge headlong into them! And yet I doubt if you have weight enough of flesh to sink," she added in a lower tone.

"Don't be so cruel, Peggy!—you—"

"Again!—have not I warned you a thousand times never to call me so? Is not all such compact broken? You were the monster, tyrant, once;—it is my turn now! We are no longer wife and husband. *I* am the tyrant, and you the wretched, crouching slave!"

"I am in your power, I know," faltered the man.

"My power, Martin Dormer—"

"Hush, Peggy, don't speak the name so loud. I gsh!—you can't tell who might hear, and then—"

"Then, they might give information to the officers of justice, and you would be dragged to gaol, and I should live to see you hanged!"

Old Martin (so we will call him) cowered before the flashing glance of his wife, and implored her to be still. She regarded him for a moment with supreme contempt, and then a calmer expression crossing her features, she said:

"You have your saving clauses, too, Martin;—you can ferret out intelligence, and your imbecile foolery allays suspicion; you know how to be discreet."

"I do my best—I do my best."

"Go to the Cock, in Marybone—you know it, near the Gardens,—and pick up all you can respecting the family of the lawyer, Graves, who has lately gone to reside in that part; and be sure to remember all you hear."

"I will, my dear—" began Martin.

"Mrs. Stammers, you mean," suggested the fortune-teller.

"I will, Mrs. Stammers; that is what I was going to say; but my memory now-a-days is not so good as when—"

"You were younger, and I more beautiful!" laughed Mother Stammers derisively. "You had, perhaps, better not allude to that time: it does not tend to make me calmer, or to regard you more pleasantly."

"I wouldn't for the world do anything to annoy your feelings, my dear, or exasperate you, I am sure," whined the old man.

"You're a noble hound," sneered the woman. "Oh, as you return, call upon the laundress in the Oxford-road, and ask her to describe the person of the young officer who is cousin to Lady Nugent. Write it down, lest you forget it;—height, figure, colour of eyes and hair, his complexion, cast of features, gait, temper, disposition, and peculiarities."

"Anything else?"

"Yes; a correct list of the articles stolen from the jewel-case of Mrs. Manvers. Ask her also if she mentioned me, as I paid her for doing, to the maid of Lady Nugent, and when she thinks I may expect to see the dame."

"I will."

"Enough. Here is a shilling for you. Don't drink too deeply, but keep your wits about you; and, above all things your tongue as still as possible. Upon your discretion depends your safety, and—"

"I know, my dear; I know all about it;" and he took the shilling, and put on his hat, and meekly left the chamber.

When he gained the landing-place outside, his whole bearing underwent a complete change: he threw his head erect, compressed his tooth-

No. 3.

less gums, and, while a momentary sparkle stole into his sunken eye, he clenched his withered fist, and shook it at the closed door, and muttered savagely—

"It will come—it will come—the sweeter for delay! Revenge—glorious revenge! Ugh! I could hug the feeling. It is only to save it—only to save it!"

As he descended the stairs, he heard footsteps of somebody coming up. He crouched on one side, and a lady apparently of a tall slight figure, but heavily-veiled, passed him on the landing, where stood a tallow candle, with a long snuff flaring with every gust, and guttering on the floor.

Old Martin waited long enough to hear the lady knock at the door of the room which he had just left, and enter it after a moment's delay. Chuckling to himself, he then continued to descend, and, sneaking on-wards, but ever close to the houses and the railings, pursued his way.

It is our business to return to the room of the fortune-teller.

"Be seated, madam," said Mrs. Stammers, to her visitor, somewhat in a tone of command.

The lady bowed, and in a voice slightly tremulous, but low and musical withal, began—

"Your name, Mrs. Stammers, having been heard by me—"

"And business," interrupted the other.

"And business," conceded the lady, "being anxious to hear what you might say to me."

"You are come, madam, to consult the fortune-teller. Few, lady, visit me now for any other purpose. Do not confuse yourself by seeking to find an excuse for your anxiety, or curiosity, or whatever name you may give the feeling, but compose yourself, and think of the questions you have to ask me. Here are the cards; you will cut them thrice."

The veiled lady did as she was desired, slipping at the same time a guinea on the table, and said while the fortune-teller was laying them out upon the bed—

"I shall be glad to have some proof your knowledge, however slight."

The bed-ridden woman stopped for a moment in her work, and, shaking back her long grey hair, that fell in serpent-like coils, looked up peeringly at her visitor—

"What proof will satisfy you, Mrs. Rushton?" The lady started, as though she had received a shock of electricity!

"Good God!" she cried, "you know me, then!" and she removed her veil, while Mrs. Stammers went on to spread the cards.

Oh, that face! how pale, and yet how beautiful! Her eyes were large and lustrous, and iron-grey, fringed with a long black lash. Dilated now, they looked upon the fortune-teller. Her features were classically regular; her little mouth, half-opened, now revealed a glimpse of the white teeth. She wore powder, after the fashion of the day, and was plainly but most handsomely attired. She drew her glove from her hand, and passed her palm across her brow, as with a sudden emotion. Her exquisitely-tapered fingers were girdled with many rings, and the bright stones glittered in the faint light, while the little white hand itself might have served as a model for the sculptor's art.

"You know me, then?"

"It seems so, lady."

"And where may you have seen me before? I do not remember your face."

"Strange, madam, if you should. I have not left this room these sixteen years."

"Then you are—"

"Bedridden."

"But you have had some intimation of my visit?"

"You best know, lady, that such was impossible."

Mrs. Rushton bethought herself, and looked with astonishment on the gray-haired woman. Still, she believed there was some trick.

"You are the young wife of an old husband—"

"Knowing me, you must know that necessarily."

"Interrupt me, Eleanor Rushton, and I have done!" exclaimed Mrs. Stammers, angrily.

"You assume a strange tone."

"I am acquainted with a strange world, and pursue a strange craft. Your husband is an usurer, and loves his gold better than his young wife: she, in return, loves him not at all."

The lip of Mrs. Rushton quivered slightly.

"But there is one whom she regards with more affection."

"His name?" faltered the lady.

"I cannot tell that yet."

"Describe him."

"Tall, slight, dark, even-tempered—an idler and a rake."

For a moment the lady's eyes flashed with indignation, and she thought to leave the room directly, but her curiosity was too strongly excited, though she still thought she might be the dupe of the woman's cunning and previously-gained information.

"And does he—does he love this young wife, as you say she wickedly regards him?"

"He does not."

"How so?—is he insensible to love?"

"As poets paint the passion—yes."

"'Tis false!"

"I forgive you, lady, for your excitement proves that I can foretel you truth, and I am pleased to know that my art does not desert me as I grow older."

"You will not tell me that in that pack of painted pasteboard you expect me to believe?"

"And did I ask you to credit them?—do they speak, or I?"

"I hear you only."

"And shall believe me—*shall*, Eleanor Rushton—as here I lie, a worn-out, wasted, and decrepid wretch! I have a power you know not of—no matter whence it comes; these"—and she took up the cards, and flung them round the room—"these are but the puppets in my hands. I knew your person when you crossed my threshold. I know your history, and can read your heart, as I can read mankind."

"But not my fate?"

"You contradict yourself, lady, and speak what your judgment dictates, while you believe what your credulity and wishes point at: else, why seek my humble room to-night?"

"Tell me of Edward Maberley."

"Your cousin, madam; you have helped me to his name, but I had known it otherwise before you left."

"Tell me of him, I say, and to the one guinea I have paid you, I will add four more."

"A secret passion is consuming you: *he*, your husband, all the world, are ignorant of it—all save you and I, Eleanor Rushton. Poor as I am, you see the power I possess!"

"The power!" and Eleanor started, and grew paler than before.

"The power by my knowledge to direct your happiness."

"I understand." Mrs. Rushton placed four more guineas on the table.

"Give them to me; they must not be left there; I might be murdered for as much. Pretty shiners!" she exclaimed, taking up the gold pieces and kissing them, "I love *you* now, because in you there is no treachery, no deceit. You are always true; and then—your power! Oh, heaven! how many souls and bodies both have these things bought!" She took one of the coins in her palms, and seemed to weigh it, as she said, "God made man, and look you now what man has made a God!"

Mrs. Rushton looked at the fortune-teller in astonishmen; but the

latter, securing the money, went on to the purpose of the interview—
"Your husband has doubtless willed everything in your favour?"

"Indeed, I know not. I have never thought upon the subject."

"Old men will not live for ever, especially when young wives love handsome cousins."

"Good heaven!—what would you insinuate?"

"Nothing. You are too quick."

"I do not seek my husband's death."

"It would not serve you were he to die to-night. The man you love knows not of your love. You cannot declare it in express terms, because, even were you free, the world—the generous world—denies to woman the privilege it accords the stronger sex. She gives away her heart, but may not claim another in return, and—silent—weeps and pines for ever."

"You have loved yourself, Mrs. Stammers."

"I loved?—I?" replied the fortune-teller, and her whole countenance underwent a striking change. "Don't speak to me of that, and I will do your bidding;—I will open for you where you please the Book of the Future; and, in the language of my trade, tell you of strange things to happen in the time to come. Bury your secrets in the centre of the earth, and I will dig them out, and show them you in their unvarnished nakedness! Ask me how to compass miracles, and I will tell you; but do not speak to me of the loves and hates that have seared this heart and brain of mine, when erect, like you, I walked this teeming earth as fair a thing to look upon of God's own handiwork as you might meet with on a summer's day."

"I am sorry if I recalled that which is painful; but you who can so well counsel others, should derive some solace from the knowledge you enjoy."

"Ah! madam, is the physician never ill? but enough of this. I have received your fee, and must make you re-payment in kind."

"I listen with impatience."

"This cousin of yours is wild, dissipated, and reckless of the future. His mother doats upon him with all the fondness of her nature, and yet he spends his patrimony, and draws largely on her lean income."

"Alas, I know it!"

"The mother wants fortitude to endure, and strength to combat. You must supply in some measure that watchfulness and guiding power which she so much needs."

"I would do anything to save him from the dangers by which he is surrounded."

" Your husband regards him with a friendly eye."

" He looks upon him like his son."

" Oh well he will repay that father's fondness,—but that is not now our consideration. Is your husband fond of travel?"

" Indeed, no, his heart is fixed in London."

" Because London is the market of his usury; we must abandon that idea. Set the lamp upon this chair. Give me yonder packet of paper —the blue one on the shelf—and the large water-vase that rests upon the window-seat."

Mrs. Rushton did as the fortune-teller requested her. The latter sprinkled a portion of the powder in the water which the glass vase contained, and straight a sweet perfume arose, and a blue spiral smoke ascended, and Mother Stammers chanted, in an indistinct tone, the burden of an old song.

The lady under ordinary circumstances was not easily possessed with superstitious fears, although the reputation of the fortune-teller of King-street, had induced the visit of that evening: yet the appearance of the woman, the apartment, and mysticism preserved, all led towards the assistance of an effect desired by the chief actor in the scene.

As the smoke slowly cleared from the orifice of the vase, Mrs. Stammers held the clear vessel between herself and the lamp, as though she could read in the depths of the water the fortune of her visitor.

"What see you there?" inquired Mrs. Rushton.

" Much trouble, sudden woe, and a violent death."

" For whom, woman?—for whom?"

" I see three figures: there are two men; the one is old, the other young; a young and beautiful woman stands between them,—it is the semblance of yourself—a smile crosses her features as she holds a cup in her hand on which is written in legible characters the word— 'POISON!'"

Eleanor Rushton bent forward eagerly and her large eyes grew larger, and her cheek grew paler, as she peered into the withered countenance of the bed-ridden fortune-teller.

It was a strange contrast—that young and lovely face whereon Time had scarcely set his seal, and the shrivelled form, and witch-like features of the counsellor and guide. The fire had burnt out its last in the dull grate, and the small lamp, with its sickly light, seemed only to make more dark the corners of that sombre room.

No word escaped from the lips of the inquirer, but, with her fore-finger extended, she pointed to the vase, and, with the eloquence of action, asked for an explanation of the future.

"I cannot tell," said Mrs. Stammers, "for whom the fatal bowl is meant; it may be typical of sudden close of life, and yet the blow may fall where least expected, and dealt by other hands than those that seem to promise. Put back the vase; we can learn no more to-night!"

"I am confused—bewildered," said the lady; "and I have learn nothing!"

"How! learnt nothing?"

"To guide me to the future."

"Seek to remove Edward Maberly from the pernicious influences about him, indirectly, and in a thousand ways, you can do much. Talk to him, soothe him, counsel him; he will listen to the soothings of so sweet a monitress, and the result may be, that he will quickly learn to appreciate the love that prompts you to encounter the whispering of scandal for his welfare. Away, there are footsteps on the stairs. Our interview is over; let me see you in a week."

Mrs. Rushton drew her veil over her face and about her shoulders, and made her way from the room and the house. As she left the apartment of the fortune-teller, Madame Dorville entered it.

---

## CHAPTER VI.

### THE COMPTER—THE THIEVES, AND THE REVELS OF THE PRIGS.

When Jonathan was arrested, it was, as we stated some chapters back, at the suit of Madame Dorville, and thta lady had been induced to take that step by the supposed revelations of Mrs. Stammers, the fortune-teller, who had stung the doctress to revenge by declaring that Wild was unfaithful in his love. Madame had long held over his head *in terrorem* the acknowledgements which our hero had given her for money lent, and the climax, therefore, was easy of attainment.

Jonathan was taken to the City Compter, as was customary in those days; and here, where a considerable latitude was allowed the prisoners, he became acquainted with some of the greatest rascals of his own or any other time. It must be understood, however, that if Wild had either money or friends to become bail for him, he would have been spared this compulsory association with thieves and pickpockets.

At first, he treated the matter with great contempt, making little doubt but Captain Austen would either advance the money or bail him forthwith; but when he sent to that gentleman's lodgings, in Lincoln's Inn-fields, it was only to ascertain that he had left, in company with the lady, and the people of the house had no further knowledge of them. The next plan to attempt was that of softening the heart of the doctress, but this proved a more difficult task than Jonathan ever could have believed; she replied neither to letters nor messages, and refused to visit our gentleman. She said that the law must take its course. There was nothing left, therefore, but to make the best of a bad business, and this, Jonathan, who was of a philosophic temperament, did to the utmost in his power. The money he had won at the gaming-table, though insufficient to procure him liberty, after purchasing a new suit, wig, and silver sword, to visit the Captain becomingly, was yet enough to procure many luxurious privileges in the Compter. Jonathan soon learned to spend his cash to advantage by treating such of the rogues as he could gather anything from; he was, in consequence, regarded as a good fellow, whilst, to use an expression common among the class, he was, in reality, only "sucking the brains" of more accomplished scoundrels than himself.

"What a noble-hearted bloak you is, Mister Wild!" said a fellow named Blueskin, one day.

"Sir," replied Jonathan, "the man who has no money is bound to share it with the man who has not."

"Exactually my opinion, Mister Wild, it is the principle my mother taught me when I was a kinchin, and first learned to *nim the doll.*"

"What the deuce was that?"

"Why, you see, Mr. Wild, to *nim* is to *prig*, as all the world knows: werry good. Now, priggery ain't to be learned in a day, no more nor any other honest trade; so, you see, anxious parents as wishes to get their babbies on in the world—"

"You mean *up* in the world," suggested Jonathan, indicating by a wry twist of his neck the last effort of the law.

"I mean what I say," responded Blueskin, with some sharpness, "and I never says what I doesn't mean, and what I means I'll stick to."

"No offence; take another pull at the binge, and go on."

"Werry good. To return to the anxious parents as wishes to get their babbies on in the world. They hangs a stuffed figure, which has got coat, and waistcoat, and breeches on the same up to a line as runs across the room, and this 'ere thing sticks all over bells, and puts a turnip in his fob, and a snuff-box in his waistcoat, and no end of wipes in his pockets. If the kinchen gets the warious articles out o' their different recepstickles without ringing of the little bells, they is perfect in their perfession, and fit to practise on their own account. This is what I meant when I talked of nimming the doll. In order to carry the principle into practice—'That the man as has got money is bound to share it with the man as has not,' which beautiful bit of philosophy extends to tickers, and wipes, and snuff-boxes, and-cetera, and-cetera, to the end of the chapter."

"Did you ever take to the road, Mr. Blueskin?"

"Sir, I've taken to everything upon the board, as naturally as heart would desire. I look back, sir, sometimes with pride, and sometimes with regret, when I goes over my career."

"The greatest of us, Blueskin, might do the same."

"Mister Wild, what a pity it is you wasn't brought up a prig!

"Why so, Blueskin?"

"Oh, it's a fine perfession, Mister Wild! You'll say there ain't much difference between them, perhaps, but—dash my wig, sir!—a prig is better off nor a lawyer! You see, what has always kept me in the background is this 'ere: I never had nothing to fall back upon, Mister Wild."

"How do you mean?"

"Well, I mean in this way: when a gentleman has been on a bad lay [an undertaking, adventure], and things is looking queer with him, sometimes it is better for his health to live in a sort of retired kind, which he can't do if he ain't nothing to fall back upon, Mister Wild. Werry good. Then again, everybody knows in this blessed world there's nothing like keeping up appearances, especially among rogues, Mister Wild, and a gentleman in our perfession should visit Hockley-in-the-Hole, Marybone Gardens, and the Pantheon, which ain't convenient, Mister Wild, if there's nothing to fall back upon. Werry good: here's a case in point,—I was always ambitious—fond of the 'High-toby spice' [the path of distinction], and turned up my nose at the 'Sneaking-budge' [shoplifting], or 'Fogle-prigging' [pocket-picking]; but what has been the consequence?—why, when one thing failed I was obliged to take to t'other, and so, sir, while my soul has been on the road or at Hounslow, because I've been hard up for the togs, the snappers, and the nag, these blessed fingers have been forced to wander in the depths of other men's pockets, a-seeking whatsoever they could clutch. Now sir, I put it to you, as a discriminating character, whether a man of my figure would descend to such low pursuits, if he had anything to fall back upon?"

"Perhaps not, Mr. Blueskin, still the men who most distinguish themselves are those who, as you describe it, have nothing to fall back upon. Their poverty is an incentive to exertion, and they oftener rise in the world."

"Rise in the world!—you don't mean—"

"Certainly not, Mr. Blueskin; nothing of the sort!"

It was from such idle conversations, then, that Jonathan acquired a considerable amount of information with reference to the pursuits, habits and characters of the thieves of London. How he turned all such knowledge afterwards to his own benefit is a matter of history which these chronicles will in due time dilate upon.

The room in which our hero slept contained thirty beds and as many prisoners ; the latter were regularly marched to their apartments at a tolerably early hour, both in summer and winter, and the key was turned upon them forthwith, till the following morning, neither fire nor candle being allowed meanwhile. As it was in the winter-time when Jonathan was incarcerated, their long evenings would have been insufferably dull but for the never-failing spirits of the rogues themselves. The stories they told of their past lives, the adventures and anecdotes they related, all assisted to swell that store of information which our hero was steadily acquiring with a view to the future.

It was customary to get up a sort of "sing-song," and Jonathan was sometimes called upon to preside. An outline of the scene of one evening will give an idea of the others, which were all pretty much alike.

The prisoners were in their beds then, and the bright moon that streamed through the great barred window served to lighten the darkness.

"Mr. Wild in the chair," "Mr. Wild in the chair," came from several voices, some of which were evidently under the blankets.

"Mr. Wild, I have the satisfaction of informing you that you have been unanimously called upon to preside on this highly-influential meeting of respectable prigs,—and it's blasted cold, I can tell you."

The speaker was a villainous looking rascal, who had somehow managed to get a cut head, which was now bandaged, but not sufficiently so to prevent the red blood showing through the white rag, and as he sat up in the moonlight, it fell directly upon his pale bad features and his black unshaven beard.

"Send I may live, Jack Hall," said a little man popping up his head

from the opposite bed, " but I wish to the Lord you would lie down again
you looks more like a ghost nor a prig."

The laugh being against Mr. Hall, that gentleman made himself as
snug as his cut head would allow him.

" You must have a bad conscience, you must, Mr. Mosely," said Blueskin, from his mattrass to the last speaker, " or else you would'nt go for
to be afraid of ghostesses. Did you ever slit a gentleman's wizen ?"

" Good gracious ! no. I would'nt do such a thing for the world."

There was a roar of laughter at the excessive squeamishness and affectation of Mr. Moseley in pretending that he had a prejudice against
throat-cutting. Sam Hall said it was as bad as a man saying he did not
eat onions.

" Well, but, gentlemen," remonstrated little Mr. Mosely, " consider I
never was more than a fogle snatcher. I was born a tailor, and I ain't
been so long in the profession as you have; besides I don't mind telling
you though I objects to murder, I've done a bit of bigamy."

" Mosely for ever! we will make a man of you, yet," cried Blueskin,
" but, gentlemen, how's this 'ere? we are forgetting business. What has
become of the worthy chairman?"

" Fast asleep," responded Hall, " don't you hear the beggar snoring?"

" Mr. Wild ain't no beggar, Mr. Hall, and I sticks up for him during
his trumpery abstinence in the world of nod."

" Thanky, Blueskin; but Jonathan Wild can stick up for himself and
fight his own battles any day in the week."

" Why, what a beggar you are, Mr. Wild!"

" Am I, Mr. Hall ! That's an insult, and I never take an insult from
any man. Wait till your head is well, and I will give you a drubbing
to prove that I don't brag when I say I'm your master!"

" My head, you whisking wapstraw [lying greenhorn] ! Damn my
head, I'm all the cooler for it. Come out, and I'll box your liver for
you !"

Jack Hall, who was a big man, was dancing about the floor in a moment,
and his shirt fluttering in the moonlight as he threw himself into defence.
Jonathan leaped after him, crying out—

" It will be a warmer, at all events," and, amidst the applause of the
other gentlemen, who sat up in their beds, and doubled their knees to
their chins, and brought their blankets to their mouths, the combatants
began.

Both were experienced men. Jack Hall, though perhaps the bigger,
appeared the more active, and popping in, planted a facer, and danced

away again, before Jonathan seemed to expect it. Elated with success, and being greeted with great applause, Jack tried the same manœuvre again; but he was expected and prepared for this time. Wild met him, and prevented much mischief; then followed him up—one, two, three—left, right, left—closing with him. Both now fell, Jack Hall under, and together rolled beneath the beds.

The room rang again with cheers and laughter; suddenly there was a noise from where the battling men were sprawling, as of broken crockery, and then there was a gushing sound, and Jack Hall exclaimed, "Damme! I'm deluged!" while Jonathan shouted—

"Confound the thing! to stick it there—and my shirt is wet through!"

There was a loud knocking at the door, and a voice halloing—

"Order there, you prisoners! or the Governor will show you all into separate cells."

There was a cessation of hostilities, and Jack and Jonathan crept to their respective beds.

"Ask the Governor where he'll find the cells to put the very bad boys in?"

"You don't want me to come in and handcuff you all, do you?" continued the gaoler, for it was he.

"If you does," replied Blueskin, "it must be to one another, for we is such capital friends, we cannot afford to part, nohow."

"Then don't kick up such a row any more, but behave yourselves like respectable prisoners in the Compter."

While the sound of the retreating footsteps was heard, all continued tolerably still. Mr. Moseley was the first to break the silence—

"Notwithstanding this 'ere little bit of a breeze, my nose is as cold as the end of a tombstone in the frosty nights of December. Botheration!" added he, punching his nasal organ with playful activity, "I can't bring the life-blood into him nohow."

"You be damned!" said Blueskin; "what warmth do you expect in the tip of a tailor?"

"Mr. Wild is in the chair, hurrah!" cried a voice from the far corner of the room.

"Jack," said Jonathan.

"Jonathan," said Jack.

"How do you find yourself?"

"None the worse, barring the wet."

"Same here. Are we friends?"

"Of course we are."

"Then on we go again."

"Gentlemen," resumed Jonathan, "I am in the chair, and I presume we are met here—"

"Because we can't help it," cried a little man, who was discovered to be Moseley.

"Silence!" exclaimed our hero; "shut your ivories, or indignation will compel me to heave a vessel at your head!"

"Bravo!" cried the company, "drown the tailor!"

"No, gentlemen, we will not drown him, at least in that way. I know what it is, and the tail of me sticks to my back; but we will insist upon his silence."

"I am as quiet as a mouse."

"Then, gentlemen," resumed Jonathan, "as harmony is the word, let us be merry. You will please to imagine that you are charging your glasses. Now, then, are they all charged?"

"All right, Mr. Chairman!" from several quarters.

"Our first toast will be, gentlemen, Success to Priggery!"

The toast was drank with becoming honours, and Mr. Blueskin was called upon for a song.

"Really, my noble Romans, I hopes to be excused to-night, for I has such a cold in my windpipe. You see misfortune makes us strange bed-fellows, and only the wery week afore I was nabbed for prigging a wipe in St. Paul's Churchyard, circumstances compelled me to take to street wocalisation—"

"How damned low!" muttered Jack Hall.

"You be flummuxed!" responded Mr. Blueskin; "I should like to know, did you never—"

"No; I never did!" answered Jack Hall, indignantly.

"Order! order!"

"Gentlemen, I must really require you to maintain decency. Mr. Blueskin is on his legs."

"With all respect for the worthy chairman," replied the gentleman alluded to, "as Mr. Blueskin is in bed, instead of being on his legs, he is on his quite t'other."

Another roar from the company threatened again to bring the gaoler, to enforce quietude.

"Order, order, gentlemen!—for shame!"

It was as much as our hero could do to keep the rogues within bounds.

"Do you sing, Mr. Blueskin, or not?"

"When I was interrupted, I was explaining with all the logic of the Lord Chancellor that street singing had spoiled my voice, and though I never used none but the genteelest of tunes, I cotched one cold o' top o' t'other, till I did'nt know 'Water parted,' from the 'Minivet in Ariadne."

"Then, just by way of starting the thing, I'll sing for you," said the chairman, "conditionally upon Mr. Hall favouring us afterwards."

"Oh, with all my heart!"

"Bravo! bravo!—Long life to Mister Wild!"

"Have the goodness, gentlemen, to be a little more piano in your applause, if you please. We don't want to be sent to the Black Hole, I suppose?"

"Certainly not, Mr. Wild."

"Then shut your peepers, and open your ears, and listen to me."

Every head lay down again, and every blanket was drawn up close, while the moon threw its silver light upon the black floor of the prisoner's resting-place, and our hero chaunted the following—

### JONATHAN WILD'S SONG.

They have torn me from my own true love,
    And boxed me up in the stone crib here,
But what need a man for the whole world care,
        With bacca and beer?

O, we can't indulge in kisses now,
    But memory tells us they were dear,
And is not remembrance made more sweet
        'Mid bacca and beer?

Now this is the point of my chaunt, boys,
    As we can't have our old women here,
Let us hope, at least, they are not without
        Their bacca and beer.

There was great clapping and knocking of hands when it was finished, but Jonathan restrained it as much as possible, and called upon Mr. Moseley for a sentiment.

The little man—who, by-the-bye, wore a red nightcap that added considerably to the effect of his small but grotesque features, immediately replied with—

"A wife to every man, and only two to the devil!"

The bigamist's toast was responded to in imaginary bumpers, after which Mr. Jack Hall duly called upon by the chairman, favoured the company with his ditty:

## JACK HALL'S SONG.

(From which the "Sam Hall" of the present day is a plagiarism.)

My name it is Jack Hall, chimney-sweep!—
My name it is Jack Hall, chimney-sweep!—
My name it is Jack Hall,
And I've robbed both great and small,
And now I pay for all,
When I die.

My master teach'd me Flam—teach'd me Flam—
My master teach'd me Flam—teach'd me Flam—
My master teach'd me Flam;
But I know'd it vos all bam;
And through him I shall hang,—
D——n his blood!

Then I goes up Holborn-hill in a cart—
Then I goes up Holborn-hill in a cart—
Then I goes up Holborn-hill,
At St. Giles's takes my fill,
And at Tyburn-gate,—
There we part!

The Sheriff he will come—he will come—
The Sheriff he will come—he will come—
The Sheriff he will come—
And look so gallows glum,
And talk of kingdom come,
Blarm his eyes!

The hangman will come too—will come too—
The hangman will come too—will come too—
The hangman will come, too
And twist the rope about my wizen,
And then I shall be his'n,
So, adieu!

"Mr. Hall will oblige the gentlemen of the college with a toast."
Mr. Hall had great pleasure—

"When called upon to dance a hornpipe, may it never be in fetters—
under a leafless tree—or do-a-do to a cart."

"Brother prigs, and Romanses in general, I have great happiness in
proposing the health (Loud cries of "What are we to drink it in?")—or
rather, gentlemen, as we are without max or bingo of any kind, it will be
more in harmony with the general aspect of affairs, if I propose the
future success of, and long life to—don't you twig, my nabsmen?—
Jonathan Wild, Esq., the chairman of our conwivial assembly, this
evening, and my late opponent at fisticuffs, when we both rolled under
the bed, and got wet through with—

"Order, order!"

"Order it is, boys. Mr. Jonathan Wild, and long life to him!"

How Jonathan returned thanks, and proposed new toasts, and how there were more rows till the gaoler knocked again, would be to repeat an occurrence of every night. One song, however, without the risk of being tedious, we may here record, as it was the effusion of Mr. Moseley, the tailor—

### MR. MOSELEY'S SONG.

Prigging's the life for a cove to lead,
Steed and deed and I nammus breed ;
   And diddle go daffy, diddle !
Flashy go flipper, new rag and lag,
And fag, and I nammus mag,
And flashy go flipper, new rag !

Nimming a wipe is a charming thing !
King and wing and I nammus string—
   And diddle go daffy daddle !
           CHORUS,—Flashy, &c.

Milkens may boast of cracking a crib—
Ribs and bibs and I nammus dibs,
   And diddle go daffy daddle !
           Flashy, &c.

Bridle culls preach of the moonlight ride—
 Shide and tide, and I nammus bide !
   And diddle go daffy daddle.
           Flashy, &c.

But nix as safe as prigging a wipe—
Tripe and dipe and I nammus wipe
   An d diddle go daffy daddle !
           Flashy, &c.

## CHAPTER VII.

ELLEN HODSON sat alone and in sadness in the new lodging that had been provided for her by Captain Austen.

It was not less handsomely-appointed than the last, but nearer the court-end of the town, whither business now often took the man we must still call her lover. He had hitherto delayed to make her the reparation he had so long and so earnestly promised, and indeed there seemed no great prospect of its fulfilment. The evidence of deep sorrow was written

No. 4.

in the pale cheek of the young girl, and though it cannot be said that her love had decreased, yet bitterly did she already mourn the step she had so rashly taken.    The remembrance of her parents and her village home was ever present to her mind ; she tried hard to suppress every painful feeling, more particularly in his presence, but the thought of the old time would come back, and then the tears started to her eyes, and she was angry.

On the morning of which we write, Austen had been more than usually grave and silent.    He had matters, he said, of importance to transact, and on his return would bring her news.

She heard him, and tried to brush the melancholy from her brow, and conjure up a smile.    Her face was placid as the calm surface of some silver lake, but her smile was faint; the mouth refused to play the hypocrite to the heart.    Alas! what news could she care to hear that he would bring?    The outer world was to the yeoman's daughter but as some frozen unknown region.    It was without knowledge of, or sympathy for, her; what was it to her, or she to it?

If, indeed, from home; but that was impossible: besides, how would she dread—although she longed—to hear!    As to aught else affecting him or her, why the great question of her heart was irrelevant of news.

His manner softened as he was about to leave her.    And she—so keenly sensitive to every tone of that dear voice, from which she first drank knowledge of the mysteries of love—hid her face against his breast, and, while the big drops stood unseen in her earnest eyes, blessed the man who had betrayed her.

"Come, come, Nell, rouse yourself.    You must not give way.    We never know how soon we may need the strength we wantonly expend. God bless you!" and tore himself from her embrace.

Ellen dried her eyes, and took her place in one of those old-fashioned windows that bayed out into the street, and watched his retreating figure as he went on his way.

Thus, when silent and alone, his words came back to her—

"We never know how soon we may need the strength we wantonly expend."

To what did he allude?—could it have relation to her?    Was it necessary that she should reserve her strength for any great or untoward event?    What news could he bring her that would hasten such?

There she sat and pondered, and, as women will do, conjured up a thousand evils far beyond the probability of occurrence.    It was true, her only hold was upon her affections, and for awhile past, at times, he had seemed to chafe beneath the exaction they entailed; but, as it was wrong of her to dwell upon these things now, she would remember only his goodness, and the trembling voice in which he declared his love. He would fulfil the vows he then pledged to her, and called upon his God to witness there was time yet—he would make her his wife—she should return to her childish home, and bless again her parents in their age, and why should she doubt him?

Reader! how is it that a woman clings even to the memory of her first love, before all the world beside?—battling with a positive truth, to embrace the shadow of a dream?

There she sat for a long time, watching his return, and in fancy passing again the happy hours now fled for ever. She wore the day away in reverie, and scarcely moved from her position. Suddenly, she remembered that he liked to see her handsomely dressed, and she went into her bed-room to complete her toilet.

She became the costly things in which she decked herself, but she did not regard them. Once, in opening the wardrobe, to select some article of attire, her eyes met the dress in which she had appeared at the Warwick ball, and an involuntary sigh escaped her.

"When these fingers fashioned thee," she said, " it was in my father's house, and I was innocent and full of hope. If only to live again one hour of that blissful time, I would give a whole ten years of my life to come. The future and the past, to my poor mind, have—one weighed against the other—no comparison in worth. She kissed the hem of the dress she had made herself; then, closing the wardrobe, completed her array and hurried back to the old seat in the great bay-window.

It was long before his usual time before he returned, and when he did so, it was not in his customary mood.

"Something, dearest, has occurred to vex you," said Ellen, leaning her hand upon Austen's arm, and looking up in his face, after hastening to meet him.

"Well, I have been annoyed, it is true, but—"

"Yes, Edmund Austen."

"Scarcely more than I anticipated: let me go in."

He met her eyes with a kind glance, but it was only for a moment; they sought the ground directly, and he did not seem to be at ease. He put his arms round her waist, and led her to the sitting-room. There was an expression of weariness in his face, as he threw himself into the great arm-chair, and sent his feathered hat spinning to the furthest corner. It would have made a graceful picture—that pretty country-girl, dressed in the court fashion of the day, with her huge white-powdered head-gear, low boddice, enormous petticoats, and high red-heeled green satin shoes, as she hung about the chair, and smoothed the brow of her lover, who now, in full regimentals, sat moodily grasping either arm of the chair, and desperately stretching—toes upwards—his great jack-boots.

"Was your annoyance, Edmund, connected with the business of the morning?"

"I can't but say it was. You know I told you I should bring home news."

"But, if you expected it beforehand, it is better than if you had been suddenly informed of it. I dare say it is not so very dreadful, after all."

"I fancy I shall hear you say differently, by-and-bye."

"Me!—Edmund?"

"Yes, you, baby-face!" Ellen turned paler than before.

"You have nothing to tell me of—"

"Nothing. I know, of course, where your suspicions point. I have not heard of them."

"Do not keep me in suspense, Edmund. It is cruel."

"You said, just now, it was better not to be suddenly informed of a disagreeable or painful circumstance."

"Ah! but that was only—"

"Only what?"

"I don't know."

"But I do, Nelly. A further proof that everybody can give anybody very good advice which nobody thinks of following."

Austen laughed, but his laugh did not sound genial.

"Are you playing with me, sir?"

"No, girl, no! Give me some wine, girl."

"Wine, Edmund?"

"Yes, wine, Miss Hodson. Do I not speak plainly."

"Quite, Captain Austen, quite plain. It would have been kinder, perhaps, if you had spoken my name less loud. They call me here by yours—alas! I know I have no right to it!"

"I did't mean to hurt your feelings, Nelly. There—give me the wine!"

Ellen now, for the first time, perceived that he had already been exceeding, though he was very far from tipsy.

"Will you have more wine, to-day, Edmund," timidly suggested Nelly.

"Yes."

Ellen Hodson did as he desired her, and, fetching the wine, filled her a glass.

"A bumper, Nell!—a bumper to the future!—you must drink it!"

"I would rather not; I have not eaten yet."

"Not eaten! Why, my dear girl, have you not dined?"

"Without you?"

"But you might have known, when I did not return at the usual hour, I should dine elsewhere."

"I could not eat alone: I—forgive me, Edmund—but I never did."

The Captain seemed to be struggling with his better nature, as to some communication he had to make; and each little evidence of Ellen's affection, displayed unconsciously, seemed to assist in unmanning him."

"You have not told me yet what it is that has been disturbing you."

"I will. It must be done, sooner or later, Ellen;" he leant forward as he addressed her, and taking her up by the two hands, gently forced her into the seat before him. "Ellen we must part."

"Part!"

"I am compelled to join my regiment. It is ordered abroad."

"And our marriage."

"Is impossible!"

No word, no sound escaped the ashy lips of the betrayed girl; but as she tried to rise, his eye dilated, and a deadly pallor overspread her face, and the next moment, as with a crush, she fell heavily at the feet of her seducer.

A week had elapsed since the occurrences stated subsequently. And all that time poor Nelly Hodson had never left her room. Profound quiet had been prescribed by the physician at first called in to attend upon her. No allusion had therefore been made to the one-absorbing subject of Ellen's dreams, by day and by night. Austen had been unremitting in his attentions to her, and she sometimes hoped that he had not meant all that he said, and that heaven would never suffer him to do her so much wrong.

On the eighth day she returned to the sitting room; and though it was easy to read in her countenance how severely she had been tried, her illness had scarcely detracted from the measure of her beauty.

When Captain Austen left her that morning, as he did now every day, he bade her farewell with the greatest tenderness, and she thought she read in the soft glance of his eye and the subdued tones of his manly voice, increased affection for the future and repentance for the past.

With all the delicacy of her nature, she forbore to address him on the painful theme.

"God bless you, Ellen, be careful of yourself."

"For your sake, Edmund."

"For your own, dear girl."

"For mine if you will have it so.   You will not be long gone."

"No longer than I can help."

"But you will not be long?"

"Again, God bless you."

He took her little head between his palms, and kissed her on her lips, and cheeks, and eyes, and then, apparently at seeing her so pale, so broken and so bruised a flower, with the back of his gloved hand brushed the drop from his lid, and then hurried from the apartment and the house.

To detail how all that day she watched, and thought, and anxiously waited for his coming back, would be but to repeat that which we have told before.   Suffice it to say, that when nine o'clock in the evening came, and no Austen, the flush of fever was in her face, and she paced the room with renewed but unnatural strength.

"A gentleman is below, madam," said the landlady, entering the room, "who is desirous to see you."

Ellen clung to the chiffioneer for support, as the word "father' escaped her parted lips.

"Oh, no, madam, this is not your father, I am sure, he is quite a young gentleman, and he gave me his card, 'The honorable Robert Scamper.' "

"It's a mistake, Mrs. Parsons, I do not know the gentleman, I never heard his name.'

"He says he is a friend of the captain's, madam, and is sure you will see him, because he comes upon urgent business."

"A friend of Edmund's! pray heaven that he be not ill, I will see him, show him in."

The landlady left the room, while Ellen flung a rich Indian shawl about her shoulders, and prepared to receive her visitor, who now entered the apartment.   He was a little spare built man, elegantly attired, and of a rather fair and effeminate complexion.   He bowed politely to the bewildered girl ; but seemed to hesitate before the landlady, who left the room, however, almost immediately.

"I—I need not ask you if I am addressing Miss Hodson. Such beauty is not easily mistaken."

Ellen was not only surprised, but very indignant at the speaker's tone

"Mr. Scamper," she replied, referring to the gentleman's card, "I understood that you were the bearer of a message from Captain Austen."

"I have the honor—but do not distress yourself; may we not be seated." And with an easy air, he resigned himself to a seat. Ellen bit her lips, but forced herself to do the like, murmuring only, as a sad forboding crossed her—

"Your message, sir, your message?"

"I should not like to distress you," said Scamper, "I can't bear distressing women, especially when they are pretty, and I suppose you are prepared to hear what I have been asked to break to you."

"I am prepared, sir, go on."

"I am decidedly glad of that, because it saves so many unnecessary preliminaries. Austen has left England."

"Left England?" She could do no more than echo the words of the speaker.

"I believe, in fact, he told me that circumstances over which he had no control, prevented him making any settlement upon you, but as I promised to do all in my power to repair that matter, poor fellow, he left with his mind tolerably tranquil."

He appeared to wait for an answer, but receiving none, went on. "I believe he said something about a promise of marriage, but of course you never believed him, so we need not talk of that. I told him exactly as I tell you now, what I could do, and what I would; and my word, as they say in the city, is as good as my bond. I have four thousand a-year, and I can't give up my houses; but I have no objection to furnish you a house in good style, provide you with a suitable equipage, and allow you five hundred a-year; but you can't take my name, I won't allow that, Austen did, I know, and I always told him he was wrong; however, you see, my dear girl—" And he rose from his chair, and advancing to Ellen, put his arms round her waist.

Then, and not till then, did she seem fully to understand him.

Her eyes flashing, and the blood glowing in her cheeks, and throat, and bosom, she seized him by the wrists, and hurled him from her.

His head struck heavily as he fell against the corner of the marble mantelpiece, and the blood started from his nose and mouth, and showed him bedabbled on the floor.

With a wild shriek, Ellen rushed into the street, and returned to that house—the tomb of all her hopes—no more.

# CHAPTER VIII.

### THE RELEASE—THE MARRIAGE, THE WIFE, AND THE LOVER.

ONE morning Jonathan was informed by the gaoler that a lady was at the gate who desired to speak with him.

"With me, Mr. Turnkey? what is the lady like?"

"Well, Mr. Wild, she is like a lady, and a lady is like nothing else in natur—leastways, that's the result of my experience, Mr. Wild; I didn't go for to examine her pints."

"Is she young?" inquired Jonathan, arranging his morning attire and plucking out a lace end not scrupulously clean, for to say the truth the prisoners in the Compter were not remarkable for their spruce or dandy airs.

"Middlingish, Mr. Wild."

"Tall?"

"Very good height for you, Mr. Wild."

"Stout or thin, Mr. Turnkey?"

"What I calls a comfortable size, Mr. Wild."

"And her name?"

"Madame Dorville."

"Zounds! you scoundrel," exclaimed Jonathan in a passion, and perhaps a bit of a flurry, "why the devil didn't you tell me that before?"

"Because you didn't ask me, Mr. Wild," replied the turnkey with a grin, making his escape, as Jonathan caught up the first article near him to fling at the delinquent's head.

Wild made his appearance as engaging as possible, which was not, however, saying a very great deal, for, as we have before hinted, our host was anything but an Adonis. It is astonishing what may be done with an air, and Jonathan did what he could. He bent his back, stuck out his right leg, bowed his arm like the handle of a teapot, and resting his right palm upon his right thigh, while his left arm falling straight by his side, compressed his three-cornered hat; winking his eye, elevating his eyebrows, and puckering his mouth, as he regarded himself in three inches of shaving-glass, pinned against the lath and plaster wall, he muttered complacently, " I thought she'd come at last. I knew she'd relent.I should like to know how any damn'd fine woman could resist me !"

Had Jonathan's portrait been sketched at that moment, it would have done for the hero of that old song, the burthen of which runs—

" I'm the boy for bewitching 'em."

He was not in the habit of shaking hands with himself, or his grasp would have been remarkably warm upon that occasion.

He slowly descended the stairs, with his cocked hat still under his arm, rehearsing in his mind the speech with which he should greet the doctress ; but as he had two opinions, he tried two styles, the one grand and lofty—the other soft and conciliating. As usually happens in such cases, when he met the lady, he forgot them both.

Madam Dorville looked remarkably handsome that morning, and Jonathan could'nt help telling her so. She made no allusion to herself as the cause of his incarceration, and he thought it more prudent not to refer to the subject himself, at present.

" Is there no other place but this where we may converse ?" asked the doctress, as they paced the yard together.

" Well, my dear, there's the general reception room, there are the bed rooms, and the cells for the wicked ; the infirmary is on the other side : perhaps we had better adjourn to the visiting room."

They accordingly sought a large apartment, divided off into compartments, somewhat after the fashion, though more rudely, of the coffee shops of the present day. The tables were deal, and not particulary clean, and on them and on the walls were cut the names and initials of more than half the rogues of the metropolis. There were benches to sit upon, and the floor was sanded. It was an atmosphere of stale tobacco smoke and fog. There were damp spitoons of sawdust wet and blackened, that seemed to be festering in the corners, and the whole place gave you the idea of many rabbits being kept therein too close together and no great attention paid to their domestic comfort.

" What will you take, my dear, to drink ?" inquired Jonathan. " Spirits are not allowed, but my friend Grabbs, the turnkey, makes that square for me ; so if you like a drop of bingo, say the word. "

" Oh, Jonathan, so early in the morning! I really could not do such a thing. "

Wild had known her do it, however, before she got out of bed, but as
the lady appeared to forget the circumstance, it was not for him to
remember it; therefore he was willing to suppose that it was early in
the morning.

"Still, my dear, a little drop will do you no harm : which shall it be,
brandy or gin ? "

> "Brandy or gin
> Fly up in the skin
> And make a man feel very queer ;
> But, blarm my eyes,
> If ever I tries
> To rob a poor man of his beer."

The song came from a gentleman with a shade over his eye sitting at
a neighbouring table.

"Be quiet, Blueskin, can't you," said Jonathan in a low tone, "and
let a gentleman alone with his woman ; I shan't forget you when the
bingo comes, I dare say.   Well, my dear," added he turning to the lady,
"what do we drink?"

"I think brandy is the best thing for the colic."

"Then brandy be it ; here, Grabbs, my good fellow," and he whispered in the turnkey's ear.

Mr. Blueskin, the gentleman with the patch, broke out again—

> "For Johnny loves good ale and wine,
> And Johnny loves good brandy ;
> But Johnny loves his blowen more,
> She's sweet as sugar candy."

Wild threw his hat at the thief, and sitting down beside Madam
Dorville, put his arm round her waist !

"And when, my pippin, are we to be as happy as we used to be?"
whispered our hero in his most insinuating tone.

"You cruel man, how can you ask me ?" simpered the doctress, as she
sipped the liquor that the gaoler had brought.   Jonathan handed the
glass to Blueskin, and thought as he did it, it's all right here : I shall
wheedle her charmingly.

"You must know, my good Jonathan," whispered the doctress, when
he returned to her, "it was your own fault that you ever came here."

"Well, poppet, I have always been inclined to see with your eyes,
but, dash my wig, if I can make out that."

" You know, if I hadn't thought you paid more attention to other women than poor me, I should never have been jealous, and you in a nasty place like this."

" Well, it isn't, perhaps, so comfortable as it might be, though I have learnt a vast deal since I have been here; enough to make both our fortunes when I get out again: but who was it that planted the seeds of jealousy in your pretty little bosom ?"

" Well, then, I heard a great deal from Mrs. Stammers."

" Mrs. Stammers, the fortune-teller, in King Street?"

" The same."

Mrs. Stammers was down in Wild's black books for ever. and the probability was, that very bitterly she would have to rue the circumstance.

" If, Jonathan, I might trust you now."

" You may, you may; I have sworn it to you a thousand times, and now ten thousand fold I feel it."

" You love me?"

" From the lowest depths of my heart."

" And will prove your love?"

" Before the assembled world, if you could possibly get it together on any occasion."

" Then marry me, and you are free."

Jonathan drew back a step or two, and looked at her from under his shaggy brows, with monstrous sharpness in his quick grey eye ; then giving a loud whistle, he thrust his hands into his breeches' pockets, and paced the room in deep thought. In less than a minute, he had revolved both the advantages and the disadvantages of such a matrimonial arrangement.

He knew that the doctress was a shrewd woman; he had experienced that out of the produce of her practice: both might live, and he had every reason to believe, that in the execution of the new designs he projected, she would prove not only a useful, but a most valuable auxiliary. He looked at her, as there she sat upon the narrow bench, sipping the brandy without affectation from the black bottle, and in his own mind he said—

" You are a valuable woman, and, no one can deny, a pretty one. It is but one plunge—one great shock, and all is over. I will e'en take the leap."

" Well, I'm sure, sir, it isn't every man would have such a chance, and I'm sure, of all I know, there, not one would refuse such an eligible offer. Heyday, and who are you, sir !"

Jonathan saw it was high time to settle matters, so advancing to his mistress, with the gravest possible cast of countenance, he said—

"My beloved one, think not it is for my own sake I hesitate; that would be impossible. I did but pause, thinking whether I should be justified in linking your fate—the fate of one whom I so dearly prize, with that of so uncertain a rogue as myself."

"The devil he would a wooing go,
    Foll de rol lol, fol de rol day;
But to make up his mind to say yes or no
    Took him very much more than a day—"

"Will you be quiet, sir," exclaimed Jonathan, addressing Blueskin angrily, who only muttered to an old tune,—

"Oh, quietude is never known
    To dwell in matrimony."

"You believe me, dearest," whispered the lover to the lady.

"You men are cruel deceitful creatures; but I'll trust you this once."

"Well, considering its only an affair of marriage, which people are not in the habit of going in for every day, as they do their breakfast or their dinner, that qualification was, perhaps, unnecessary."

"If we tilt before we go to church, Mr. Wild, we shall come to an open rupture afterwards."

"Never believe it, my adored one. When shall the ceremony take place: name the happy day, and night by night until it comes, I'll lie awake, and paint what joys my fortune has preserved in store for me. Oh, name the day, but let it be an early one."

"An early one, my Wild? Will to-morrow, dear, be yielding to you too soon?"

Wild thought it was rather coming to the point; but he expressed himself wonderfully delighted, as he muttered in her ear,—

"To-night, then, to-night, I shall be at liberty."

"Oh there's never a bird upon all the trees
    To be cajoled—to be cajoled,
As a woman, my dear, with salt on her tail,
    As I've heard told—as I've heard told."

Madam Dorville looked very indignantly at Mr. Blueskin; but the gentleman pursued his task of polishing a shoe-buckle, and Wild did his best to withdraw her attention.

" We may consider the matter then settled," said our hero.

" Since you will have it so, love," replied the doctress, as though the proposal had never come from her, and with all a maiden's blushing simpleness, she yielded to her ardent lover's ardent prayer.

The lady and Jonathan held some further conversation, in which the marriage of the morning was arranged. They also entered into some discourse as to their future profession; and our hero contended that the quacking need only be secondary henceforward to the grand adventures in which he proposed to embark. After much persuasion, Madam Dorville consented, to take " another thimble full." " More," she said, " would get into her head before she departed," and Mr. Blueskin, who had prospects of almost immediate release, which, perhaps, in a measure caused his jocose hilarity of the morning, was invited to join Wild and his betrothed.

When the latter parted, it was with all apparent affection, and Blueskin slapping the former on the shoulder, as the doctress was bowed out at the gate, said in a confident tone,

" You're a made man, Mr. Wild, and I shall live to see you the hornament of your age and the delight of your posteriors."

Three months had gone by, and Wild had established himself in a novel business. He was married too, and sooth to say, the doctress made him no bad wife, while we may add, by way of parenthesis, that our hero himself was not the worst among the husbands of his day. At first he drove but a peddling way of trade, helping people to writings which they had lost, letters and papers that had been stolen, and things of no value to any but the owner. Even in traffic like this, when he began his profession, he had so much fear, that he never delivered the property desired into the hands of the parties seeking for it.

The evasion was an ingenious one. Taking the visitor into a particular room, de tapped on the panel, which was immediately withdrawn, and two hands presented themselves to the seeker. One contained the property sought, and the other was open to receive the stipulated reward. The person who performed this office was habited in a black cloak, and wore a mask.

After a time, however, Wild grew more bold, and did business on a more extensive system. He no longer confined himself to papers and writings ; but restored to the owners, on payment of little more than the absolute value, the articles of which they had been robbed. He organised a regular band of thieves, whom he kept under his command, and in hourly fear of him ; for, by the recent act of parliament, the man who turned evidence against his companions was allowed to escape, and it became Wild's policy, when one of his gang offended him, to play off the practice, and hang an obnoxious knave whenever he found him.

It was about this time that he encountered Mr. Blueskin, one evening, in the neighbourhood of Smithfield.

" Whither away so fast, my rory-tory cove?" inquired Wild.

" On a crib-cracking lay, Mr. Wild," replied Blueskin. " I have'nt a moment to spare."

" Indeed! bring the booty to my house, and there'll be a double share for every cracksman amongst you."

" Money down, my knowing one?"

" On the nail, Blueskin." The last named put his finger to his nose, and Jonathan gave him a friendly dig in the ribs as they separated.

" I shall hang that fellow one of these days," muttered Wild, " and yet I, to a certainty, have learned a great deal from him. He's a d—d pleasant fellow, no doubt; but one's duty to one's country must be considered : besides, a ' scragging bout ' brings in a matter of forty pounds, and of what consideration is a man's life, I should like to know, against a sum of money like that!"

\*      \*      \*      \*      \*      \*

Close were drawn the curtains in the dining-room of a beautiful mansion in St. James's, that overlooked the park.

A young and beautiful woman reclined upon a sofa, and at her feet sat a handsome youth, with a haggard expression of countenance, regarding the lady.

" And you tell me you have reformed now," Edward Maberley.

" Yes, Eleanor, your teaching has, I think, done me some good."

" And you are not angry with me for it?"

" Angry with you, that is impossible, Eleanor. By the way, I wonder that Rushton is not somewhat jealous."

" Jealous, Edward ! of whom ?"

" Why, of me, to be sure."

The lady started to her feet, and the blood forsook her cheek as she raised her finger, pointing upwards.

" Hush ! do you hear that?"

" That ! what ?"

A low sawing noise was heard, and it was Edward's turn now to rise.

" Eleanor," he whispered, " there are burglars in the house."

But the next chapter must tell us further.

# CHAPTER IX.

### THE BURGLARY AND ITS CONSEQUENCES.

It was just the night for a burglary. There was no moon, and not a star to be seen in all the heavens. A small drizzly rain was falling, and from the park a thick yellow fog ascended, and the oil lamps in the streets struggled through it with their dull light feebly. The pavement was coated with a thick layer of greasy mud, and there were few people to be met with abroad. Already had midnight rung from the churches, and the sleepy old watchmen crept out to call the hour, and then hobbled back, with their Welch wigs pulled down about their ears, and their great collars pulled up to meet them—back to their wooden boxes to snooze again.

Blueskin and two others were in the neighbourhood of Mr. Rushton'residence.

" How many of them is there, Blueskin," inquired one of the cracks-men in a low tone."

" Imprimuis."

" Do what ?"

" That's Latin, you fool."

" Is it ? Then what's the use o' your pattering such lingo to me ? I ain't a Frenchman."

" Go on, Blueskin," whispered the third ruffian, " never mind Choaker —he arn't got no more learning nor a pig."

" Well, then," resumed Blueskin, " there's the old chap and his young wife ; but the old un goes for nothing, because he is laid up with the rheumatism. There's no more men in the crib, 'cept the footman, and as he is a lushy lad, he is made right by one or two at the Cock and Pye, and has enough aboard to make him sleep soundly till morning."

" That wasn't a bad fakement."

" To be sure it wasn't ; but we'd have had him all right, one way or t'other. Why, if it wasn't for dodges with slaveys, what we gets out of 'em over a glass, and how we bribes 'em, and plugs with 'em one way and another, blowed if there wouldn't almost be a stopper put upon us cracksmen altogether."

" Why, blarm my eyes, Blueskin, you don't mean to cast such a hinsult on gemmen of our perfession, as to say there wouldn't be no crib cracked if there warn't no slaveys."

" Who said anything o' the sort ? I only said we owed 'em a good deal, them and the watch together. If people knowed what they was about, there wouldn't be half the burglaries as there is."

" Why not ?"

" Cause they might perwent 'em in a great measure, by keeping in every crib a little dog."

" A little dog ?"

" Yes. What they calls house-dogs is all gammon. We gets over them easy enough ; but when you comes to one o' them little yelping curs as runs about loose in doors—a fellow as is all bark and no bite— as won't come nigh enongh to be caught in a bag, or take no pison, but wakes at a sound, and keeps out o' the way o' mischief—yelp, yelp, fit to bust its little throat—that's the chap to scare away the cracksmen."

" It is to be hoped there's no yelping curs where we are going to-night."

" All right for the matter o' that. Here we are close at hand. Look to the snappers, boys, here in this doorway, and I'll turn the lantern. Oliver [the moon] hasn't shown his mug to-night."

The three men passed under the portico of a large mansion, and examined, by the aid of their dark lanterns, the priming of their pistols. As they did so, Blueskin muttered :

" I hope we shant have to use these things, my rum-culls. Snappers tell tales ; besides, if a man must swing at Tyburn, it is no use to go there with more blood on the mawleys than we can help."

" In course not," agreed one of the fellows, called Bunks, " what do you say, Choaker ?"

" What I says is this here," responded the gentleman appealed to, " when we cracks a crib, what does we go to it for ? Are it for prigging, or are it for t'other thing ? why it is clear. But if there arn't no other way to get out on it—if they will have it, why then I'd give 'em this.." The fellow drew a long clasp knife from his pocket, and opened it with his teeth. " I'd give 'em this, and think no more of slitting their wizens than I would of sticking a pig."

" You're too fast, Choaker ; if you goes on in such a dashing way as that, damned if you'll last over another sessions or two."

" We're wasting time," whispered Blueskin, " come on, and as cautiously as cats."

The burglars crept along a narrow lane that ran between two houses leading down towards the park. Belonging to these mansions were gardens that opened into the most fashionable promenade of that time, and ladies, masked, were in the habit, during the long summer evenings, of leaving their sedans in the public walks, and keeping appointments with their lovers in the green glades. There were no monumental arches, or royal nurseries then—albeit, the place was an aristocratic one—to intrude upon the people's grounds.

"Have you got the sack for the swag, Bunks?"

"It is here."

"Now, then, softly, boys. Over she goes," and Blueskin mounting the low palings, dropped into the gardens of the Rushtons. He was speedily and noiselessly followed by Choaker and Bunks. They walked along the grass-plot and the beds, avoiding the gravel pathway, lest the grating of their shoes should awake attention. As they took their way, with every step on the soft grass, or mould, they purposely widened their footmarks, by working their feet from one side to the other, before lifting them from the ground.

One side of the building came down low, and slantingly, and alongside it ran a leaden water spout, at the far end, scarcely higher from the ground than a man's reach, but running upwards, to the extremest height of the roof. It was by the aid of this pipe that Blueskin was enabled to reach one of the first-floor windows in the rear of the premises.

By swinging to the spout, and working sideways with his hands, he was brought to within a few feet of the window-sill. It was a slow, but dangerous course. The wall being perpendicular, it would have been hazardous to attempt to perch merely upon any jutting point below, and the sill did not protrude more than a few inches from the face of the wall; holding on the pipe by his left hand, he drew from his pocket, with his right, a stout piece of cord, some two yards in length, with a small iron hook firmly fastened at one end. Now he placed the hook in the spout, and, looking in the direction of the window, a little below him, and to the left, he jumped towards it, as well as he could, while, with his right hand, he held by the cord. On the first effort, his foot missed the coping of the window. Again he swung towards it, and this time his foot had nearly dashed in the glass. He looked

No. 5.

above him, and he thought the leaden pipe was yielding with his weight, he muttered an oath, and Choaker, in a whisper, begged him to descend.

" I will do it," said Blueskin, " should I miss my footing, and break my back in the fall."

Once more he swung towards the window, and, by a great effort, he succeeded in obtaining a lodgement for his feet. As he thrust his hand against the sharp corner of the rough wall, to uphold him, his fingers were left torn and bleeding.

To raise the window was a matter of little difficulty, but the shutters were fastened, and it was necessary to use a centre-bit, and circular saw. The bolt that held the shutter, and a round piece of the wood with it, about the size of the crown of a man's hat, was thus cleanly taken out, and all impediment to ingress removed. Blueskin dropped upon the floor as noiselessly as he might, and taking his dark lantern from his pocket with his left hand, while he drew a cocked pistol with his right, crouching somewhat, he flashed the light the length of the passage. That figure, in its wild attitude, masked and armed, would not have afforded a bad study for the modern imitators of the Rembrandt school.

There were several doors opening to the landing whereon the burglar stood, but he had no time to examine more now, further than to see if they were closed, and listen for the sound of any disturbed inmates. All seemed still, so Blueskin darkened again his lantern, and drew two ropes also, with hooks attached to them, which he fastened inside the window, and then throwing out the ends, allowed them to dangle to the ground. Hand over hand came up Choaker, and thought nothing of it, but poor Mr. Bunks, when he got half-way, slipped, and the rope was drawn through his hands with great pain, as he fell to the ground. A muttered imprecation escaped Blueskin, but the burglar below was not to be prevented from again making the attempt. He succeeded better than before, but the palm of his hands were terribly scarified, and it boded badly for any one resisting Bunks that night in the execution of his errand.

" B—t the rope, why didn't we have a ladder? It glided through my hands like a hot saw-edged eel, and took away the the flesh with it."

" A ladder, fool ! and so told everybody upon what lay we

were," replied Blueskin. "Hold your tongue, for you talk like an idiot."

"Which way now, Blueskin?"

"This—follow me."

"Where to?"

"The old man's bed-room—it is on the second floor. Look to your masks."

Gently up that wide old-fashioned staircase the robbers stole, pausing almost at every step, fearful of the old boards, that *would* creak, trod they ever so lightly.

The room was found, the door opened, and the men stood about the bed.

"Why, where's the wife? the old rogue's alone."

"So much the better—here is a gold ticker, chain, and purse. The plate is under the bed—pull out the chest."

"Eh—what—what's the matter?" cried Mr. Rushton, trying to sit up in bed. He heard the click of a pistol, and the next moment the cold round end of the muzzle was pressed against his temple.

"Make the leastest noise, and, God's my judge, I'll plaister your brains upon the pillow."

It was Bunks who threatened the old man.

"Can you find the plate?" whispered Choaker.

"All right," replied Blueskin. "Do you keep watch by the door, while I pick the lock of this old chest; where the devil are the tools?" and the burglar was on his knees beside the bed.

The old man seemed suddenly to understand the scene.

"The plate—the chest—good God! gentlemen, do you mean to rob me?"

"Why, it looks something arter the fashion, don't it?"

"But this must not be; I can't lie here and be robbed—I will call for assistance—thieves! thieves!"

"Cut the beggars tongue out," muttered Choaker.

Bunks pressed the pistol with actual force against Mr. Rushton's bony temple, and hissed in his ears a dreadful threat.

"I will not be still, I must call—Eleanor!"

"Damnation! Is the chest open yet?"

"One moment."

There were footsteps on the stairs.

"Discovered, by G—!" exclaimed Choaker.

Blueskin started to his feet, at the very moment he had wrenched open the lid of the plate chest. Salvers, and cups, and spoons, and valuables of all sorts, in gold and silver, presented themselves to his gaze. He had heard the exclamation of Choaker, but he could not resist the temptation, and he thrust what articles he could into his pockets. The next instant, and Edward Maberley, sword in hand, appeared in the doorway. He made a thrust at Choaker, which the latter parried with his enormous pistol, and then closing, with the heavy butt-end he struck the young man all senseless to the floor. The burglar, jumping over the prostrate body, cried out,

" The house is alarmed. Look to yourselves," as he dashed madly down stairs. He was met by Mrs. Rushton ere he had descended the first flight. She attempted to arrest his progress, but he struck wildly at her, and though she received no hurt, the lamp she held in her hand was knocked down and extinguished. Choaker was escaping; Eleanor rushed on, and her screams for help were loud and piercing.

The old man had flung himself from the bed. Blueskin found two little hands about his throat. It was Eleanor who had grappled with him, crying,

" Villains! murderers! what have you done?"

" Help! help!" cried Rushton.

" My husband!"

" Here, wife, here!"

" Blarm thee, hell-cat!" shouted Bunks, " shoot her, can't you?"

" No, damme, I can't kill a woman in that way, either," replied Blueskin. " Let go, will you?" he added to Mrs. Rushton, " if you don't want me to cut your fingers from my throat."

" Scream! Eleanor, scream!" cried her husband.

There was a pistol fired now, and the old man flew up in the air a good half yard, and then fell upon the floor a huddled heap. A bullet had entered his heart.

With a sudden effort Blueskin flung Mrs. Rushton from him, and the two burglars, scared and alarmed, made for the window by which they had entered. Eleanor had succeeded in reaching the bell-rope, and there was a loud ringing now. The footman ascended the stairs in time to see Bunks fling himself from the window. The man had a loaded gun in his hand, and he discharged it at the escaping thieves. Bunks with a groan fell bleeding to the earth. It was almost like a retributive shot. Blueskin took him up as he would have taken up a child, and bore him, as his life-blood issued from him, across the lawn, and so escaped.

In the great bed-room were many forms and many lights. The servants were bearing away the yet unrevived person of Edward Maberley. The corpse of the old man, who was the master of the house, lay stretched upon the bed, and pale, but still erect, stood Eleanor, and the thought ran through her brain, " I never loved thee living; nay, in my evil heart, I dared to love another. I almost longed for this hour, the hour of thy death, and now the time has come, it brings me no happiness. Happiness! I pined for freedom— I am free—free to mourn thy memory and to be wretched—lost for ever !"

---

## CHAPTER X.

### THE CHARWOMAN—THE INTERVIEW, AND THE RESOLVE.

THE morning after the burglary in St. James's Park, and the murder of Mr. Rushton, Jonathan's manner was uneasy and perturbed, as he partook of breakfast with his wife. He did not know fully how to account for it, but he had that disagreeable presentiment of coming ill, either in the shape of something that might affect himself immediately, or bad news of others, in whom and with whom he was both interested and connected.

" You don't eat your toast with your accustomed relish, my dear," said his wife.

"No, my dear, I don't," answered the gentleman, in a somewhat snappish tone.

" It is buttered on both sides, too, and the crust cut off, just as you like it."

" I can't help it."

" Will you have an egg ?"

" No."

" A bloater?"

" Hang your bloater."

" Well I'm sure, Mr. Wild ; when a woman does all in her power to be civil towards you, you needn't throw dirt in her face in that way."

" Ugh !" Jonathan made no distinct reply, and his wife held her tongue, and poured out the tea, instead of talking, for the next five minutes.   Then she went on again.

" You know Mrs. Bumby, my dear ?"

" Yes, confound her : when that woman's in the house, there's an end of anything like comfort; wet flannels, large lumps of soap, and unwieldly scrubbing brushes meet me at every turn ; besides, she always sticks her pail in dark corners of the stairs, as if she laid traps for the people passing up and down ; I walked into it the last time she was here, and nearly broke my shins."

" She's here to-day, my dear."

" Then she had better keep out of my way, that's all."

" La, Jonathan, I'm sure the poor woman is civil enough, and she gets such early information of matters, I should think you might make her useful to you in the profession.   Now, there was only this morning—"

" What of this morning?"

" Why, there was a burglary last night, at a house close to St. James's Park, and a dreadful murder was committed."

" Murder !" and Jonathan started to his feet, and paced the room uneasily.   He was not yet so steeped in crime as not to start at murder.

He did not doubt but this was the adventure in which Blueskin was engaged, when he encountered him in Smithfield Market.

" Who was murdered?"

" The master of the house, Mrs. Bumby says."

" His name ?"

" Dashton, or Rushforth, or Rushton, I don't know which."

" Is this woman here now?"

" Yes."

" Call her; I will speak to her."

"Before you finish your breakfast ?'

" I have done."

" Mrs. Bumby—Mrs. Bumby !"

" Yes; Mrs. Vild; vat is it !"

" Step up stairs; Mrs. Bumby ; Mr. Wild wants to speak to you."

" Yes, Missis, soon as ever I vipes my hands," screamed Mrs. Bumby below.

" I don't want you ; you may go down stairs."

" But I don't want to go down stairs."

" Then go to the devil. "

" Oh Wild, Wild, is it thus you use me, after the sacrifices I have made for you ?"

" Don't talk any damned nonsense to me, Mrs. Wild, about your sacrifices, for they make me sick.  You sacrificed your liberty for what you wanted—a husband, and I consented to tie a log about my neck, in order to become a free man again.  Strange contradiction! but as for sacrifice, we are equal—"

" And therefore will shake hands upon it," suggested his wife.

" Oh, if you like," and Jonathan shook hands with no particular good grace.

" Won't you kiss me, Johnny, dear ?"

" Now, don't make me sick, pray ; the older you get, the more ridiculous you grow.  Kiss—my grandmother."

" Ah! Jonathan, you didn't talk in that way when first I knew you—"

" Why; if all men talked to their wives all their lives in the same strain as when first they knew them, what would become of the world, and the working-day business of ordinary life ?"

Mrs. Bumby appeared at the door.  Mrs. Bumby was short, spare of figure, and not remarkably pleasant to look upon, inasmuch as she had lost all her teeth, save one in the upper jaw, that stuck out at the side; her nose was cocked and red about the nostrils ; her eyes like two burnt holes in a blanket, with inflamed edges : there were many wrinkles about her crumpet face, and the dirt that was begrimed therein made them look like the black lines in a soiled map.  Mrs. Bumby's style of attire was not calculated to lead the fashion.  She evidently wore a few articles of under-clothing, and what she had hung with tenacity to her thin legs.  She gave you the idea of a straight blot, being the same width all the way down, and the members of the faculty of our own day would have delighted in her, for there can be no doubt she never compressed her delicate waist with the unnatural corset. In conclusion, Mrs. Bumby's age might have been anything between forty and ninety, and it was her peculiarity to be ever redolent of gin. Wild looked at her, and knew her character in a moment.

" Your name's Bumby, I believe."

" Bumby is my name,
 And England is my nation,
London is my dwelling-place,
 And the Lord is my salvation."

" Hum; very explanatory indeed. Mrs. Wild tells me something about a burglary last night : I am sorry to hear of the terrible increase of crime ; but as it is necessary we should all be upon our guard, we ought to learn the particulars of every case."

" In course we ought, vich I always says; if you never vants to be a drunkard, take plenty of gin, and see the fatal consequences thereof, while I begs your parding for being so bold as to hoffer my opinion when not called upon, and creeps into my shell again."

" Mrs. Bumby, I'll trouble you to confine the flowers—"

" Confine vot, sir ?"

" Confine the flowers of your rhetoric, and oblige me by answering my questions only."

" Vich vill alvays be a happiness and a pleasure too, Mr. Vild, and God bless you and Mrs. Vild, vishing you both a family of forty children, and a fortin to keep 'em vith."

" That'll do, that'll do. Now about this burglary."

" The burglary as was taken place last night, atween the hours of eleven and von, ven the family vas up to their heyes in sleep, and never knowed nuffin of vot vas going to happen a more than the unborn babe."

" And the name of this family ?"

" Rushton, Mr. Vild, vich vas a highly respectable gentleman, vith a remarkable nice young voman for a vife, vhere I has often cleaned the paint vith pearl ash and soda, vich makes it come beautiful vhite, and vhere I had two shillings a day, four good meals, and as much as I like to carry avay in a blue and vhite cotton pocket handkicher, vhen I made it right vith the kitchen

maid; three pints of old ale, and a kevarten of the best bingo.
Oh, Mr. Vild, vat a loss society has a sustained in the death of
that ere benewolent indiwidual."

" He was killed, then ?"

" Shot through the small of his back, vith the stone of a harline
plum."

" And the men ?"

" Escuaped immediately arterwards, turning head over heels
out o' vinder, vich they is supposed to have entered in the same
striking hattitudes."

" Good gracious! head over heels, Mrs. Bumby ?" suggested
Mrs. Wild.

" Vich vas the evidence the footman guv his mother, who informed me o' the same, over a leetle drop o' max, this blessed
mornin, vith warious editions, at the ' Cow and Cowcumber,' a
corner o' our street."

" Are there any men suspected in particular ?"

" Not as I knows on; but if it vas made vorth my vhile, and a
wery 'andsome reward vos to be hoffered, vhy, praps I could put
my finger on von or two on 'em, vhen I vanted 'em."

" Indeed! You do not then confine your business to charing,
I see."

" Vhy, I vould, but its an ungrateful perfession ; it von't afford
the devotion it used to, so you see, I ekes it out vith von thing
and t'other. I elps ladies in love matters, runs a herrands, carries
letters, makes appintments, knows a secret or two, and shouldn't
be above bringing a genelman to justice, if I vos only vell enough
paid for it, and the law rekenised it."

" My dear, I congratulate you on the acquisition to your house-
hold of so very valuable a person as Mrs. Bumby, the charwoman,
a very amiable character."

A carrotty serving-wench thrust in her head at the door, and
her huge top-knot looked like a coil of rope on fire.

" There be a gemen below, as want to speak to measter."

" His name ?"

" I wur not to tell it, if any body wur here like ; but it be Blueskin."

" Blueskin !"

And the red rims of Mrs. Bumby's eyes wagged unpleasantly.
Jonathan looked at her, and saw in an instant that the name

was familiar to her.  She seemed to be chewing it between her gums, and the one tooth in the upper jaw stuck out more than ever, and played loosely as the tongue touched it, like one of the broken keys of a pianoforte.

"Idiot," said Wild.  The exclamation having reference to the fiery-headed maid.  Without further speech, Jonathan quitted the room, and the girl closing the door, followed him down stairs.

"Where is this man?"

"In the parlour, measter."

"Didn't he say that you were not to mention his name before anybody?"

"Ees measter, that un did, surely."

"Then, why did you do so just now, before that confounded Mrs. Bumby?"

"Law, measter, what be the harm of that?  I'm sure I do think nothing of her, and missis told me yesterday as how Mrs. Bumby, the charwoman, were just nobody.  Oh, if I thought she were anybody, I wouldn't ha' told the name afore her for the world.  I suppose the genelman's modest like, and sartin sure his bean't a pratty name noways.  Blueskin! eh, eh, eh! Walk up, Measter Blueskin."  And the girl put her hands to her sides, and called the name aloud, and laughed with all her heart.  Wild seized her by the throat, and shook her savagely before he entered the room in which stood the burglar.  Patty the maid clapped her fingers to her throat, and as the tears started to her eyes, she wiped the big drops away with her coarse checked apron, and jogged down the kitchen stairs less briskly than she had clambered up.

"Dash my measter's wig, if his fingers beant regular claws.  I ha' lost more skin than a genelman fox-hunter, and all about a chap wi' a neame like Blueskin.  I will say it as often as I loike. Blueskin, Blueskin, Blueskin : if he had five hundred a-year, and 'ud take me to church to-morrow, he shouldn't come to bed to me wi' a name loike Blueskin."

"Mrs. Vild," said Mrs. Bumby, "its my opinion that if that ere Blueskin had a little salt put on his tail, he'd be cotched, and proved the very bird as is vanted."

"Hark'ee, Mrs. Bumby.  My husband is a very strange man, and if you were for a moment to interfere with any friends of his, or act upon anything you might hear in this house, you will find that you have made the bitterest enemy you ever knew in all your life."

" La, Mrs. Vild, vhere's the harm of a poor voman a giving her opinion. I meant no harm, I'm sure, and I von't say no more about Mr. Blueskin, nor Mr. Vild neither; but I suppose I may jist be allowed to tell you wat Count de la Ruse said about you the other day ?"

" About me, Mrs. Bumby ?"

" Yes, about you, Mrs. Vild. I'm sure you isn't so old nor so ugly, but vat a genelman may admire you, missis."

" Oh, go along, do."

" Vell, then, I von't tell you, that's all. I'll go and seour the back kitching, and never say I opens my mouth nor nobody. I am no tattler, nor my mother afore me.

> " Bumby is my name,
> And England is my nation,
> London is my dwelling place,—"

" I know, I know; but what did the Count say ? Did he really speak of me?"

" Praps he did, and praps he didn't, Mrs. Vild; I don't vish to make your husband the greatest enemy I ever had in my life. Don't say I'm given to chattering; its a kevarter of a pound o' yeller I shall vant, if you please, mum; it'll take a good kevarter to get them boards clean, and have'ee ever a house flannel; mum, this here is quite vored through."

And Mrs. Bumby exposed to light a dilapidated rag, which she wiped her nose with afterwards, and then tucked under her arm, as though that were the proper place to carry such waifs and strays.

" Mrs. Bumby."

" Madam Vild."

" Would you like a little drop of ladies' cordial this morning, Mrs. Bumby?"

" Vell, Mrs. Vild, I never says no to a good thing."

" Then step into my room ; I want something done to the window curtains, and I think I can give you a little drop."

" Bless your heart, Mrs. Vild. Vot a beauty you is ; its no vonder all the men's in love vith you."

And the wily old charwoman followed the shrewd doctress, and cajoled and played with her, and told her more lies in an hour, than she could have stood to in a month, by tickling her vanity, and assailing her on her weak point—the weakness, by the bye, of every pretty woman falling into the sere—jealousy for her waning beauty.

" A bad job this, Blueskin," said Jonathan.

" You have heard, then ?" replied the burglar.

" I have. Is it true—the murder of the old man ?"

" Well, it was an accident ; they didn't go to do it exactually, because, you see, though they had loaded pistols—"

" Of course, of course," interrupted Wild ; " when men commit a burglary, and carry with them loaded pistols, its monstrous clear they can't mean to use them : if they were going to commit murder, they wouldn't load them, would they, with such things as leaden bullets, iron nails, marble stones, and peach kernels. Its quite clear they don't expect the thing, and so they provide for it. A murder's done—you call it an accident, and find friends who say you didn't mean it—it wasn't intended. Very right—its the progress of the age."

" How damned satirical you are this morning, Mr. Wild."

" Who fired the shot ?"

" Bunks !"

" Who else was with you ?"

" Only Choaker, Mr. Wild."

" Did you bring off any swag ?"

" Why, yes, Mr. Wild, and as this bit of an accident is likely to make a fuss, its inconweniently awkard ; what's to be done with the property ? The reglar old fences won't give above an eighth of its vorth, since its safe to be blown in the most frightfullest vay."

" What is there ?"

" Two gold watches, chains, seals, diamond rings, a hundred guineas in gold, eighty pounds worth of bank notes, as many cups and forks and spoons and fish slices and butter knives as I could shove into my pockets ; a silver teapot and a salver as I stuck up between my waistcoat and my shirt behind."

" Was there an alarm raised ?"

" There was."

" Were either of ye hurt ?"

" Bunks was shot about the head and throat. I carried him off."

" Where is he now ?"

" In a little crib of mine, t'other end of the town."

" This is a larger affair than I've mixed in as yet, but if one don't go upon the grand lay," said Jonathan, " a man will never make a fortune; bring me the swag."

" All, Mr. Wild ?"

" All; I'll give ye a better price than you can get elsewhere. The money shall be ready in two hours—bring it here in that time, and I'll send some one to assist you."

" Yes, but, Mr. Wild—"

" What now, Blueskin ?"

" Bunks is getting repentant, and talks of peaching."

" Does he ? he's hardly safe at your place, Blueskin; it isn't safe for you; you might be both bowled out."

" We might, Mr. Wild."

" And so the fellow talks of peaching, does he ?"

" No more nor less, Mr. Wild."

" Bring him here."

" Here, Mr. Wild ?"

" Here, Blueskin."

" And when we have him here, Mr. Wild, what shall we do with him ?"

" This, Blueskin"—our hero put his mouth to the burglar's ear— " dead men tell no tales. Knock his brains out."

---

# CHAPTER XI.

THE THIEFTAKFR'S AUDIENCE. THE PROPOSAL TO ROB ROYALTY.

The conversation between Jonathan and Blueskin was conducted long and earnestly.

At length the latter quitted Wild's house, and, as he strode hastily on his way, there was a firm, but bad expression in his face that told of some fierce inward resolution.

Jonathan himself paced his room moodily, his brows knitted, and his hands folded behind his back, muttering, " 'Tis but a man, after all, and such a man! the world should thank us for tearing such a perambulating wart from Nature's face."

The red-headed serving wench knocked at the door.

" Come in."

" There be a genelman below as do say he want to speak wi' Measter Wild."

" What's his name?"

" Oh, I doan't know; I wouldn't ha' no more o' that; cause, feckins, if I didn't know un, I couldn't tell un."

" Did he explain his business?"

" What, to me, measter? he warn't such a fool; he bean't a Londoner, I can tell 'ee that."

" Indeed!"

" Noa, he got quite a sweet smell loike, and he be a pratty chap, too, but I wouldn't ax him his neame, for all that, tho' I is warrant, if I did, he bean't called by such a handle as Blueskin."

" I will see him here."

The moment the door was shut again Jonathan took from either pocket of his square-cut coat a pistol, and examined the flint and priming. Jonathan's trade was growing dangerous, and as he knew not by whom he was visited, he thought it but right to be armed, and on his guard.

The young man who was now shewn into the apartment by Patty was not calculated, however, to arouse suspicion; he was evidently fresh from the country, of a tall, well-built, manly figure, dressed as a young farmer. Jonathan eyed him, and guessed his business at once.

" Hum! lost a ticker," muttered he; " a greenhorn, by the Lord Harry."

" Mr. Wild, I presume."

" The same, sir."

" I have called upon you, Mr. Wild, on business of an unusual but, to me, important nature."

" It can't be the ticker," thought Jonathan, " there's nothing unusual in that."

" I understand," said the young man, continuing, " that your knowledge of the metropolis is very great; that you have a number of people in your employ, or connected with you, through whom you are enabled to gain information on any necessary matter almost as soon as you dasire it. Have I been correctly informed?"

" Well, sir," replied Jonathan, now eyeing his visitor with some little surprise, " I have means of procuring information certainly, when I choose to employ them; but its not for me to explain my business to every stranger. Tell me what you require, and if I can serve you I will, provided, of course, that you don't object to pay me for the same."

" Fair enough, Mr. Wild. 1 may as well inform you at once of the object of my visit to London."

" Be seated, sir, I beg."

Jonathan Wild was quite courteous in his demeanour: he meant to be paid handsomely for the service he was expected to render.

" My name is Thornton," said the young farmer . " I am from Warwick."

" Warwick?"

" Yes. Were you ever there?"

" I—I—a—I have passed through it," returned Wild coolly.

" It is now, sir, more than twelve months since. On the night of one of our assemblies, the loveliest girl in all that part the—"

" Go on, sir."

" You will excuse me, sir, but I knew her well, and a man is but a man, and can't always controul his feelings. I say, sir, it was that time ago, since this young and only child left her native place, in company with a villain. Her father and friends have never heard of her from that hour, and it is to find the lost one, and if possible, return with her, or at the least, to gain tidings of and maybe speech with her, that I be here in London at this moment—a place I have no great predeliction for, I promise you."

" And through me to ascertain the whereabouts of this young lady, is the object of your visit this morning?"

" It is."

" Hum! are you her brother?"

" I said she was an only child; but you are right enough, Mr. Wild: I am her brother now; I was her lover!"

" I see: till—"

" Till she forgot all but the persuasion of a villain. It is of no use minoing names wi' you; for I be man enough o' the world to know that half confidences leads to no good result. The name of the poor lost girl was Ellen Hodson."

" And her seducer—"

" Captain Austen."

" Austen! Oh! ho!" muttered Jonathan. " I have had more to do already with this matter, my young friend, than you have any notion of. Bark is a good dog, but Holdfast is a better."

" Is the name familiar to you?"

" Well, sir, I can't but say it is; but be kind enough to answer me one question."

" What is it, Mr. Wild?"

" How was the abduction effected."

" The captain obtained disguises, and rode off with the girl from the ball. I intercepted them on the London road, and with my stout cudgel, broke the villain's head; but like a treacherous coward as he was, he fired upon me instantly: I fell to the ground, and he escaped. It was two hours afterwards when I was found on the highway, and carried insensible to Warwick."

" And had you sustained any great injury."

" Enough to make me remember the night, if no other circumstance had stamped it on my heart. My collar-bone was broken —a fever came on, and I was three months, and never left my room."

" And her father. You said the girl had a father?"

" No, don't ask me of him. It unmans me to tell you."

" Then don't do it: it makes little difference."

" Well, Mr. Wild, can you assist me?"

" I can."

" And you will do so; on what terms?"

" Five guineas now, and fifteen more on discovery of the wench."

" That is a large sum."

" If you don't like it, don't pay it. My expenses are very great. It will be necessary for me to employ several people in this business; men will not work without payment. I didn't ask you for the lay."

" Say no more, Mr. Wild. I can't stand haggling about a few guineas, when the object is the recovery of Ellen, perhaps to rescue her from a slough of shame. Here are the five."

" I thank you, sir. Let me give you a receipt;" and Wild,

who, amid all his rascally transactions, prided himself on the conduct
of his business, wrote a receipt accordingly. To so great an extent
did he carry out this spirit in time, that his books were found after
his death to have been kept with all the regularity practised in a
merchant's office, and under their several headings, and as it were,
distinct lines of business; the highwaymen, housebreakers, swindlers,
pickpockets, &c., of his time were duly chronicled, and in a moment to
be found their separate adventures and whereabouts, together with the
amount of property they brought in, being posted daily.

No. 6.

" And now, sir," said Jonathan, " let me see you this day week. I hope by that time to have good tidings for you."

" A week is a long time when a man is anxious, Mr. Wild."

" Yet you have allowed a whole year to pass away, and if I understand rightly from what you have said, made no attempt before to discover her."

" For a long while I was unable, and her father unwilling, to make inquiry. Her mother hoped, day by day and month by month, to hear from her child. They knew not in what quarter to search for information ; but at last it was settled that I should take the matter in hand, for in addition to my great anxiety for Ellen, I had an old score to pay her lover ; I owe him revenge, and as I stand here a living breathing man, I will pay it !"

" That's right !" exclaimed Jonathan ; " I like the feeling ; it does you credit. He broke your collar-bone."

" He did more ; he robbed me of my love, snatched from me the heart that otherwise was mine, and broke it—I am sure of it, Mr. Wild—broke it before he had the time to learn its worth. Not on the head of one victim did his villany fall—not on her—on me alone ; but on her parents and her home, her friends, even her village. We are changed men down there, and we—that be her old father and I are chief farmers in our part of the county—dost think that others cannot feel the blow, because that we be struck—not them. They do feel it— through as it strikes them, and they feel it still."

Thornton rose and walked the room with agitation, while Jonathan regarded him attentively. It was in circumstances like this, and under great excitement, that Thornton spoke with a broad county dialect. Wild was about to practise his favorite game of playing upon the weak points of the man with whom he was brought in contact.

" You could hardly be blamed now were you to go to almost any lengths to revenge yourself upon a scoundrel like Austen."

" Hardly, hardly."

" And you will have this revenge ?"

" I will, if I live."

" You would pay handsomely, doubtless, if a friend were to render you good service in such matter."

" I would, I would."

" Why, then, he must be found."

" He must."

" And brought here."

" Here ? and why here ?"

" Because here we may, unseen "—and Jonathan whispered the finish
of the sentence in the ear of the now excited young countryman.

Thornton drew back, and, with open mouth and ashy face, regarded
Wild.

" Why, thou most cursed villain, wouldst murder the man in cold
blood, trap him like a fox, and torture him to death ? Away, I'll have
nowt to do with you."

Jonathan had gone too far, and he as readily turned back as he
before proceeded on his way.

" Ha, ha, ha, Mr. Thornton ; 'pon my life, I can't help laughing,
though its no bad thing for you I'm such an easy temper. It isn't
every man, I can tell you, would stand such strong language as you
Warwickshire gentlemen command. Lord, man, don't look so fierce,
now," he added, poking Thornton in the ribs as playfully as he might ;
" you didn't think I was in earnest, did you ?"

" Aye, yes."

" You didn't believe for a moment that I meant what I said ?"

" Well, sir, really your tone and manner were such—"

" And you really believed me ! Sir, you must entertain a very poor
opinion of human nature, but I thank Heaven, Mr. Thornton, that
my conscience approves me, and I do not deserve your suspicions. I
may sometimes be engaged with lawless men ; it is my habit sometimes
to indulge in a lawless jest, but my moral and religious nature have not
been wholly neglected. I know my duty to my fellow man, and, in
sober seriousness, I do not believe I could be led into the committal of
a positive dishonest action. You will, sir, I hope, withdraw the unpleasant expressions you have applied to me, and give me credit for
feelings at least as good as those which actuate yourself."

Tom Thornton felt himself rebuked, and hastily apologised to Wild
for his mistake and too great impetuosity. The two men then shook
hands, and the young farmer, promising to call again in a week, bade
our hero good morning.

" A wild spark, that. I thought to have drawn him of a larger
amount, and will do so if I live. I retrieved myself admirably. I owe
that Austen no favor ; if being his enemy will put money in my pocket,
and being his friend will do me no good, I must be a madman to
hesitate. We'll find this girl ; her representation of the captain will
not be the most flattering in the world, depend upon it ; this hatred
of the seducer will then be increased tenfold ; the step he now recoils

at taking he will scarcely pause at then, and the end on't will be that I, Jonathan Wild, shall bamboozle out of half his fortune, this idiot, Thornton, for quietly knocking on the head his rival Austen, and burying his body, by the subdued light of a dark lantern, in my wine cellar. Egad! before I intended, and almost before I thought of it, I'm promised knee-deep in blood. I must go on, or at once retreat; for there's more danger in standing still than aught else. It is but a life or two. Men experience no greater pain in dying than do black beetles; I have crushed the one with my heel, and an unpleasant thrill has run through my frame. I shall live to crush the other, and I doubt me if a more painful feeling follow the consequence." Wild was again interrupted.

"Here be another genelman, sir."

"Another?"

"Ees, sir, and I thinks be a pratty man, if thee loikest, and got a pratty neame too. I axed un his, I did; for I said to myself, says I, thee wonts mind a telling me thy neame, I guess, and sure enough he told me—he be a sweet un, sir, he be."

"What do you mean by a sweet one?"

"That be his neame, and such a soft-spoken genelman I never did see. 'My dear,' says he to me. 'None o' that now,' says I—"

Jonathan stamped his foot somewhat impatiently, but he still allowed the girl to proceed, as she was rather a favorite, and he thought her a bit of a character. He was fond of eccentricity, wherever he found it.

"'None o' that, now,' says I, 'but just 'ee have the goodness to tell us who thee are, and what thee wants, that I may tell measter.' Wi' that he gi' I such a kiss as I ain't had for a year, and 'Sweet 'un,' says he, 'my poppit.' I thought at first he meant the kiss were a sweet 'un, but I found out arterwards it were his neame he meant."

"I know—it is Mr. Sweeting; I will see him directly."

"I thought 'ee would, measter, I knew ye couldn't refuse a pratty fellow loike that. My daisy! what a difference there be between a Sweet'un and a Blueskin."

"Silence."

"Oh, I wouldn't say a word for the world; but only to think, and I can't help laughing all the while at Blueskin—Blueskin—Blueskin."

Mr. Sweeting had been kept waiting in the hall too long to suit his dignity; he had therefore followed the girl, and now, taking her by the shoulders as she stood in the doorway, he whisked her round, saying—

*   " You have announced me, I know, and now, by all the saints in the calendar, I will take upon myself the liberty of further introduction.'

" Good morning, Sweeting."

"*Bon jour*, Mr. Wild."

" What business brings you here."

" An admirable lay, Mr. Wild ; I want twenty pounds to equip me, and then—"

" What then ?"

" I can introduce myself at the next levee at Court, and effect a grand chivalric fakement never yet heard of in the annals of priggism, Mr. Wild."

" Well ; what is it ? "

" I can make five hundred pounds, and all by picking the pocket—'

" Five hundred by a pocket ?"

" Yes, five hundred pounds by picking the pocket of his most Gracious Majesty the King."

---

# CHAPTER XII.

### ST. JAMES'S, AND THE ROBBERY OF THE KING.

IN the neighbourhood of Islington lived a very respectable little Scotchwoman, known to her friends and the world as Mrs. M'Dowall. She had a small income, and traced her descent from Robert Bruce, in a manner which, if not thoroughly satisfactory to every body else, was perfectly clear to the lady herself. Mrs. M'Dowall eked out her means of living by letting a part of her little house.

She had just put up a fresh bill, on the occasion we introduce her to the reader, and now stood behind it, and on tip-toe, in her little parlour, so that her nose just reached above the blind, and her little twinkling eyes and magnificent wig and umbrageous cap were brought to bear with full shock upon the passer by. Like an angler by the

stream, she had baited her hook, and now waited for a nibble.   It wa
not long before she got one.

A lady and gentlemen, of very elegant appearance, paused to contemplate the bill and the top of the landlady.

"Twa on 'em !  and a braw looking couple as a body might wish to
speir," muttered the old lady to herself.

The gentleman smiled, and with his jewelled finger, pointed to the
words,  "Apartments to let;" then drawing a snuff-box from his
waistcoat pocket—a snuff-box that appeared to be composed entirely
of gems, and absolutely blazed and glittered in the sun-light.   A loud
knock at the door followed the approving smile of the lady, who hung
apparently with great affection upon the arm of the exquisite.

"I thought I should not be lang without a lodger ; but I canna say
I thought to have such grandees as these.   Susan, are ye no ears ?
canna ye hear the grand folk knocking ?"

"Perhaps you'll go, mem.  I am up to my elbows in soap-suds, and
ain't fit to be seen."

"Hoot, haw the girl forgets hersel ; but that's just the way with the
English ; they hae nae mair pride than just nothing at all ; to think
that a descendant of Robert Bruce, and a M'Dowall, should come to
answer the door to every loon that knocks : they may just get in for
me as best they can," and Mrs. M'Dowall paced the whole length of
her apartment with great dignity, till she remembered, that if the door
were not opened, the strangers could not enter, and by a parity of reasoning, if they did not come in, they could not see the lodgings ; if
they did not see them, they could not know whether they would suit ;
ergo, the lodgings would remain unlet.

The caution and consideration and love of the siller was stronger
than even the pride of family.   Mrs. M'Dowall opened the door,
secretly determining to discharge her English maid on the first fitting
opportunity.

"Aw—you—a have—apartments to let, my good woman."

Mrs. M'Dowall did not like being called a good woman at all, and
a strange peculiarity it is of her sex ; but none of them do, albeit it
ought to be considered one of the highest compliments that can be
passed.   A good woman is a charmer, indeed !

"Well, sir, and I'm no in the habit o' telling lees, and its stickit up
in the window."

"What rooms are there ?" inquired the lady, a dark dashing
beauty, with magnificent eyes and brilliant teeth ; "we have our

own footman and our maid; you could accommodate them, of course."

" Mrs. M'Dowall intimated that she could find room, and the apartments were forthwith examined; they were considered eligible, and engaged at five guineas a-week.

" When will'ee be coming in, sir?"

" Why—aw—my good woman—"

" I crave pardon, sir; but my name is M'Dowall, and I'm just descended from Robert Bruce, and the M'Dowalls are in some sort related to the great Duke of Argyle, and therefore I'll thank you to call me by the name I'm used to."

" Very good—aw. As to coming in, its not our intention to be going out again."

" Ah, but your servants and your luggage," suggested the prudent Scotchwoman.

" I—a—I shall write to my little place in Surrey for them, and they will be up to-morrow. Of course, we shall pay you in advance. I have no small change; you will take a check."

Mrs. M'Dowall would take anything the gentleman was pleased to give; pen and ink was brought, and the check was written.

" You will not present this for four-and-twenty hours; you will find it quite right, and now, can you recommend me to a tailor; I am going to the levee to-morrow, and—a—I haven't a court suit. I should wish to employ some person of respectability, that you could answer for: I must not be disappointed."

" Sir, there's a countryman o' my ain within a stone's throw will suit your lordship."

" I'm not a lord."

" Craving your pardon, Sir Charles"—

" Nor a baronet. My name is Count de la Titfalarini."

" Hoot, Count; but its ower lang for a body to munch, when the teeth ha' no been used to it; but I'll send for the tailor, and he ll wait upon your Countship. Is there anything else I can do for you at the present."

" Let's have a bottle of Madeira, and take the change out of that."

De la Titfalarini threw a guinea on the table, and the landlady left the room to perform the errand.

" A fuil and his money is soon parted; a bottle o' Cape will be one and ninepence, and a bottle o' Madeira seven shillings. I'll just get a bottle o' Cape, and call it Madeira, and I shall mak five and three pence to the gude; I'll warrant he'll never ken the difference."

The moment the door was closed, Count de la Titfalarini advanced on tip-toes towards it, and put his thumb to his nose, and then extended his four fingers as widely as possible, and exclaimed,

" Flummixed, by jingo; how the old woman bites. Tawny Bess, my spicy mottivo, this lay won't be a bad'un."

Tawny Bess approached the gentleman, and threw her arms about his neck, and gave him a hearty kiss, as she whispered, " You are such a duck, Ned, there isn't a woman in the world could resist you."

" Well, I flatter myself that I have rather an air with me."

" An air, Ned! you ought to have been a royal duke. Nobody would ever believe those elegant legs of yours had ever been crossed on a shop-board; nobody would ever think that filbert nail had been shielded by a thimble; it is beyond the power of belief that you were ever a snip."

" Bess, my love, I will trouble you to forget that little circumstance, and turn your eye to business. Make yourself as agreeable as possible with this old Scotchwoman; worm out of the maid what portable valuables there are about the place, and to-morrow, my love—"

" To-morrow, Ned, you will go to Court, and I shall mizzle in your absence."

" Hush ! the schneider !" and the tailor recommended by Mrs. M'Dowall was ushered into the presence of Ned Sweeting and tawny Bess.

It is the especial privilege of the novelist to annihilate the unities ; therefore we make no apology for at once jumping to the afternoon of the next day.

It is St. James's-street, and the equipages of the most distinguished in the land occupy the road. Along the pavement, an immense number of sedans are borne, and the people crowd the highway and the doorsteps and the windows.

It is the first levee of the season, and statesmen and warriors and nobles are hurrying to pay court to George the First.

As the carriages of popular favourites bowl by, the crowd recognise their idols as they pass, and cheer them with all their might. Sometimes, however, a politician, whose tenets are held to be objectionable in the eyes of the many, is saluted with groans and hisses, and more than one have even been pelted by the mob.

Gaily dressed ladies and gentlemen are spectators of the scene from the windows which they have hired for the show; the latter are explaining, as the carriages pass, the quality of their inmates.

But soft you now! for who rides here? It is no every day lord; who can he be?

His carriage is the most elegant that has been seen to-day; it is drawn by four noble iron-grey horses, and the liveries of the servants are gorgeous. There are three lacqueys clinging behind the carriage, and there are running footmen by the horses and the doors.

Is it a bishop or an ambassador? A little lady, who has come up to London for the first time, from a remote part of Cornwall, suggests the probability of the new comer being the Pope! Happily for the credit of the understandings of those about her, we are enabled to state, on the best authority, that the idea was immediately scouted.

Was it the Stuart driving to St. James's, to give the Hanoverian notice to quit in person? Strange that the Jacobite idea was not less successful than the Jesuitical one.

A ringing cheer burst from the mob, as the carriage was driven down the street. When anything unusual occurs, and a mob is there to witness it, it always cheers as a rule, and the fact applies as well to an execution as a royal passage.

The gentleman in the coach leant forward and handsomely acknowledged the reception with which he was met. He was young and noble looking, magnificently attired, and the smile that sat upon his face when he bowed might really have been worn by one of the Stewarts themselves. A snuff-box glittered in his hand, and his fingers were covered with beautiful rings; the carriage slowly passed onward now, and with a sweep entered the gateway of the palace.

George the First stood on the throne in the reception room. There was an expression of care upon the Royal German's heavy features, which was observed by a noble beside him.

" Your Majesty should sit to receive your subjects."

" Oh, no, my goot Norfolk, dat is not courtesy; what for if I am a king? Shall not my legs do me as much good service as another's?"

George the First had only lately mounted that same throne; the courtesy of the Stewarts was fresh in the remembrance of all; and the German was more amiable from policy than he would ever have been by nature.

" My Got, how hot dis room is; and de people crowd so to-day; I never see so much push."

Each person admitted to the presence of the king passed in front of that throne with a bow from Royalty. Some few who had rendered particular service or were more distinguished than their fellows, had the honor of kissing the king's hand. His Majesty's fingers were begrimed with snuff, which he took from a box that seemed to be formed with one mass of diamonds. The box that had bewildered the gaze of Mrs. M'Dowall was a joke to it.

The stranger who had excited the curiosity of the mob was already in the reception-room, unable to speak a word of English; he was presumed by the attendants, from his splendid appearance, to be nothing less than a new Russian ambassador.

"My Got, who is dat?" cried the king. "Vhere is Norfolk gone? Vhat has become of de Chamberlain?"

Meanwhile the stranger approached in the regular line with that fascinating smile still upon his countenance. His Majesty couldn't resist it. He put his snuff-box in his waistcoat pocket, and slightly bending forward, extended his hand for the other to kiss. The foreign nobleman was at the foot of the throne now, and a sudden awkwardness seemed to possess him; he stumbled as he kissed the king's hand; it was but for an instant, and he was speedily moving onward towards the opposite door with the string.

"Holy Got, how dam hot it is ; I have not had such a day since I have been King of England."

Half an hour afterwards, and the king missed his diamond snuff-box; what on earth had become of it? Conjecture for a while seemed useless till the strange foreigner was remembered. Could it be possible? and a person of such distinction?

Yes, the nobleman with the winning smile was Ned Sweeting the prig; his coachman was a prig ; his lacqueys and his running footmen were all prigs ; and it would be more than the writer would like to do even to answer for the honesty of his horses.

The box which was stolen from King George the First was valued at ten thousand guineas.

## CHAPTER XIII.

### THE THIEFTAKER'S HOUSE—THE SECRET CELLAR.

ALL London was astir. An unparallelled act of daring and atrocity had been committed. His blessed Majesty George the First had been robbed of his briliant snuff-box, and the Ambassadors of Europe had been insulted by the unjustifiable assumption of the august character of one of their body by a London thief. Who was the villain? was the first question. Who could have furnished him with the means of presenting so aristocratic an appearance? the second. It was ridiculous to suppose otherwise than that some moneyed, and, to a certain extent, influential people were at the bottom of it. It would seem that there ought not to have been any great difficulty in tracing these persons out by means of their equipage; but the officers of those days were a different race of men to the detectives of our own time, and though so great a number of people must have been engaged in or known of the affair, and a considerable reward was offered by government, yet nothing like a satisfactory clue was ever obtained. Two or three noblemen were indeed whispered by the mob, and more than one individual connected with the Court were hinted at as knowing more of the matter than they chose to tell; but certainty was as far off as ever. And the King, the Government, and the world in general remained alike ignorant of the projectors and perpetrators of the act.

The business of our hero was wonderfully on the increase. He no longer only helped people to lost papers, favorite purses, old memorandum books, nick-nacks, valuable from being presents, &c., but he carried out his system on a grand scale. He was fast making money.

A few mornings after the day of the levee, he was as busy as he could well desire to be; people were waiting for him in his office, and his lower rooms were crowded, like those of a popular physician, from nine till eleven; and each applicant was obliged to wait his or her turn.

Patty the maid was confined to the duties of the kitchen. A lad with a remarkable head and quick black restless eyes, up-cocked nose, high cheeks, and with nothing at all on his bones but dry skin and hard muscle—a lad called Flash—had supplanted her in the office of porter to the establishment.

Not even Mrs. Wild knew whence Flash came ; he was suddenly popped into the house, as the lady declared, " like a blot of ink on a sheet of white paper," and he was by no means a general favorite. His perception of *meum* and *teum* was remarkably dull ; indeed, *thine* and *mine*, in his vocabulary, meant exactly the same thing when translated to his own advantage.

" I say, Flash, who's with your master ?" asked a gentleman with a patch over one eye who had a very bad cough, and was obliged to go upon crutches, on account of the rheumatism, he said.

" Vell, sir, if I vos to tell you, you vouldn't believe me."

" Why not ?"

" 'Cause people never does ;  they thinks I has a hinterest in deceiving of 'em.   Ven it aint no use to me, vats the good ?"

" Who is it ?"

" Vhy, sir, its a halderman and a justice of the peace come vith the Lady Mayoress's compliments to know if Mr. and Mrs. Vild and their dear little adopted, Master Flash, vill step down to Guildhall this arternoon and take a dish of tea."

" Shall I see Mr. Wild next ?" demanded the man with the black patch.

" You shall if you likes, and thinks you'll be able to get them ere game legs o' yourn upstairs, Mr. Sweeting ;" and the boy whispered in the other's ear.

" D—n !  you know me, then !"

" Vell, sir, in course I seed you before."

" Ah !  where ?"

" At the levee."

" Here, shew me into another room ;  this will never do."

" Lor bless you, Mr. Sweeting, yes it will ;  your own brother vould never know you vith that ere patch, them crutches, and the rheumatiz ;  only you see I has got sich a hye."

And as the accomplished thief looked at Flash, the latter performed a feat on which he prided himself, fixing one eye on the person he addressed, and working the other from side to side, as though it were a piece of human mechanism.

" Let me see Mr. Wild the next."   Sweeting slipped a guinea into the boy's hand.

' Long life to you," said the boy, regarding the coin with great animation. " Now I comes to look at you again, Mr. Sweeting, I am quite certain it wasn't you as I seed at the levee."

" Hark you, my man," said a tall country looking gentleman to Flash; adding in a whisper, " Let me see your master next, and there's a crown piece for you."

" You shall see him directly, sir," replied Flash, making for the door, and muttering to himself, " I am in luck to-day—a guinea before a crown all the vorld over, though it vouldn't do to say as much."

" Little jontleman !" exclaimed a very prim old lady, tapping Flash on the shoulder, before he quitted the waiting-room, " I ha just sax words to say to you."

" 'Es, mum."

" I want a wee bit o' discourse wi the maister; if ye bring me to 't I'll gie ye saxpence noo and saxpence then ;" and she slipped a coin as she spoke into his palm. The boy debated a moment within himself, and then replied—

" Follow me, and I'll show you upstairs as soon as t'other one goes out." So Mrs. M'Dowall, who only gave the boy sixpence, but agreed to pay him another on performance of his promise, took precedence of the thief and the country gentleman who had fee'd the rogue before with a handsome gratuity entire.

Blueskin was closetted with Jonathan Wild.

" And so you tell me this Mrs. Stammers, the fortune-teller, by some means or other has so wormed herself into our business that she knows the particulars of the burglary at Rushton's ?" said our hero.

" Every syllable of it," replied Blueskin. " You see, its jist this way : she's been in the habit of employing coves of all kinds and characters, to pick up information for her in her business, which is just gulling a parcel of fools out of anything she can get. Now, Bunks was von on 'em ; I mean, as she paid, not as paid her, and so you see, he sends to her vhen he gets in this fix, and she, knowing as he'd been useful to her afore, agrees to help him ; but as she heard from the man she sent, who some say is her husband, how badly Bunks was wounded, she vouldn't give him a rap, till he first peached on what lay it was he got knocked about ; the consequence was, the old man got everything out of him, and carried it back to mother Stammers : this I hears from Bunks arterwards."

" And what an idiot must you have been, Blueskin, knowing what you did, to leave this mealy-mouthed cur, Bunks, in the hands of such people."

"But I didn't know it, Mr. Wild. When I found he was shot, I says, 'Where will you go, Bunks?'"

"'To my own crib, Blueskin,' says he; so, thinking he'd be safest there, that's where I takes him. I didn't know he was going for to open his mouth, and when he told me of it—"

"Yes, when he told you of it?"

"I got so blazing wild, I almost thought I should have smothered him in bed where he lay."

"Its a good thing that you did not."

"I think so too, for I should certainty have killed him."

"Hum, that wouldn't have signified, as far as he is concerned, perhaps; but they would have nabbed you to a certainty. He should never have been left about a single moment. As it is, it wouldn't do to bring him here now, for if any thing should happen to him—and although I've never need of them, its astonishing what conveniences I have on these premises for disposing of any awkward people—we should be implicated in the business."

"And did you really think of getting rid of him, Mr. Vild, in sober earnest?" said Blueskin, with some amount of trepidation in his manner.

"My thoughts are my own—my words I have given to you. Make of them what you please."

"My eyes, Mr. Vild, you are a gentleman as it ain't worth every man's while to quarrel with."

"Blueskin, I hate a coward, and it shall go hard; but I will always have my revenge upon a traitor."

"What's best to be done, then, Mr. Vild?"

"Stop; before I answer your question, come with me."

Wild stooped and lifted up a trap-door, which was not observable to every eye, so suddenly at Blueskin's feet, that the latter started involuntarily.

"What's the rig now, Mr. Vild, and for what on earth have you ever had that made? You have made a rapid advance since I made you fly to a few of the ways of the world in the Compter."

"The place was none of my making Blueskin; it was contrived here in the days of William and Mary. This house was the rendezvous of a famous Jacobite club. When I wanted a house, I saw in a moment that it was just the one to suit me, and because it happened to be a little out of repair, I got it on very cheap terms; you are not afraid to descend?"

" Afraid ! no, damn it, Blueskin ain't the man to be afraid, though you have a way of talking with you that mightn't induce every body to be over and above anxious to enter a black hole with you, alone and unarmed, when it leads he don't know where."

" Pshaw !" replied Jonathan, " I will lead the way ; besides, if you doubt me, take my pistols."

" No, I don't want that neither ; I ain't such a cur."

" Take them."

Blueskin did as he was desired, and Jonathan having ignited a torch, which he took from a cupboard close at hand, led the way down the steps, where all was dark. Blueskin followed at his heels.

The apartment in which they now found themselves appeared at one time to have been used as a sort of kitchen ; there was no furniture in it, and it seemed to lead no further, but Jonathan crossed to the wall, which was of stonework, and before Blueskin was aware of it, he had touched a secret doorway that revolved, and led his companion into another division.

It had evidently been used as a cellar, but there were shelves now fitted up in that dark place, and on them piled all sorts of stolen property. From the centre of the floor Jonathan uplifted a huge stone, in which was fixed an iron ring.

The black and fœtid waters of the Fleet Ditch rolled below.

" A good place this, Blueskin, to dispose of those said awkward friends ; eh, Blueskin ? "

" Right, Mr. Vild, but I thought you was too much a man of the world to expose to any one the secrets of your hiding-place—handy crib as it is, and proud as you may well be on it."

The house stood on Saffron-hill.

" I did it, Blueskin, merely to prove my words, and in the full knowledge that by no means you or any one else could reach this place without my knowledge and assistance."

" Suppose we grant that, Mr. Vild, begging your pardon, what a fool you must be to lead the way to this black hole, and leave me to follow with your snappers in my hand. If I chose, now," levelling the pistols at Wild's head, " to shoot as there you stand, at that open trap, pitch your body head foremost into that slimy ditch, and make myself master of what I see, what's to prevent me ?"

" A hundred reasons ; first, that you would be caught in your own trap, and unable to escape, and, secondly, supposing you could so escape, I am of more value to you living than dead ; the other ninety-eight reasons you will, perhaps, excuse me for giving."

" But I might be spurred to it by revenge."

" Examine your pistols," exclaimed Wild.

" Unloaded !" cried Blueskin.

" To be sure they are—d'ye take me for a fool ? You stand there with a brace of empty pistols, but here are loaded ones," producing a pair from his pocket, and levelling them in return at Blueskin, " with which to answer you—ha! ha! beaten on all sides, Blueskin ; and now, having shown you what I can do, let us return," and they went back the way they came ; Blueskin this time bore the torch first, and Jonathan followed.

" Ugh ! it's pleasant to get into daylight again."

" Now," said Jonathan, " I'll answer you the question you put to me before we descended into my surgery below, as I call it, as to what is to be done."

" That's it, Mr. Wild."

" Gather all you can concerning this fortune-teller ; there must be a skeleton concealed somewhere in her house ; let me know where it is ; we must fight her on her own ground. She can know little of us, even with what Bunks has told her, or the creeping rogue, you say, who does her work ; we must repay her in her own coin."

" And the swag, Mr. Wild ?"

" Is gone to the melting-pot ; there are ten guineas apiece for Choaker and yourself."

" No more ?"

" That's more than you could yourselves have realised. Stop, give me a receipt for the amount."

Blueskin did so, and Jonathan continued :

" Let me see you again within eight and forty hours ; we must get this Mother Stammers in our clutches ; I have several below waiting to see me now."

" Good morning, Mr. Wild."

As Blueskin left the room, Jonathan followed him, and bawled to Flash,

" Next visitor."

" Ees, sir. Now then, tumble up, ma'am, this is the way to glory."

Mrs. M'Dowall was introduced, and Flash received sixpence number two, on the old lady's entering the presence of our hero.

" Your business, ma'am," demanded Wild, eyeing his visitor shrewdly.

"I hae just come, Maister Wild, as a body may say, hearing you were so famous in matters o' the kind."

"What kind, ma'am?"

"Just robbery, and murder, aud sic like professional subjects, which you gentlemen o' the law—"

"I am no lawyer ma'am."

"Just so.  May be nae absolute lawyer."

"My time is valuable old lady," interrupted Wild; "therefore,

No. 7

if you have any business to explain to me, or ask my advice upon.    I must trouble you for a fee."

" Wi' all my heart, if ye help me in the matter, I'll gie ye any conscionable fee."

" I must have something at once, or I can't listen to you."

" Hoot, hoot, young man, but you're vary encroaching."

" My rule with strangers."

" I canna say I like the rule, there's no but twa bad payma-ters, he that pays—"

" Yes, yes, half a guinea."

" Half a guinea, laird be gude to me, you canna mean it?"

" For booking your uame and address," said Jonathan, " and the object of your visit."

" Half a guinea!   Why it's ten shillings and saxpence."

" Nothing less ma'am, but, if you keep me more than ten minutes, I charge you double."

" Oh, then, I'll make short work of it; there's the half guinea, and God be wi' it, I'll never see its bonny face again.   There, mon, put it in your pouch, and take down the address, and go to business.

Jonathan did so.

Mrs. M'Dowall proceeded to recount how she had let her lodgings to a dashing lady and gentleman, how the gentleman had given her a check upon a bank where nobody knew him, how she had recommended a countryman who had made him a Court suit, the most splendid thing that ever was seen, and had nearly ruined himself in the purchase of the materials, how the gentleman had paid him with another check, like the first, how the lady had sent her out of the way, a great distance, and then stripped her house of everything portable, or of the slightest value, and how such never could have happened if she had not quarrelled with her English maid. for expecting her, a M'Dowall, and related to the great house of Argyle, to answer the street-door.

Jonathan knew the gentleman, but was not quite so sure of the lady.   Ascertaining that Mrs. M'Dowall would give a good price for the return of her property, he appointed her to call again the next day but one.

As she passed down the stairs she met the gentleman with the black patch and the crutches ; he regarded her with a smile, but she did not recognise him.

# CHAPTER XIII.

## THE FORTUNE-TELLER AND THE SUICIDE.

" How now! who are you ? " cried Jonathan Wild to the figure before him.

" Your humble servant, and Envoy and Ambassador Extraordinary to His Majesty the King of the land unknown," answered the cripple with the patch.

" Ned Sweeting ! "

"The identical Edward that did the trick with the great George, and now stands before you in the best disguise he could assume." And the robber stood erect, and lifting up the patch shewed a couple of unimpaired cunning eyes.

" And the fruit of the adventure, the glorious dust-bin, where is that ? "

" Softly, Master Wild, may I grow grey in a twelvemonth if you are not the quickest gentleman that ever I saw. It isn't for me to stand here answering your questions, but to put new ones to you."

" If we cannot deal with confidence," replied Jonathan, " there's an end of the business, as far as I am concerned."

" You are too hasty, my dear Wild, be Wild by name, but not by nature, you know this lay was not my own, or I should have brought the swag to you direct. I have been employed as the chief executor, and you are to be well paid as an agent in the affair. We did not propose, and could not have carried it out by ourselves. If it had not been for Lord Lisle—"

" I know—I know, but there is no occasion to mention names in an affair of so much importance."

" Very good, so long as we understand each other. This, then, is the way the thing has been done : his lordship, through some people of his own has become acquainted with Mother Stammers, the fortune teller of King's-street."

" Mother Stammers again," interrupted Jonathan, "this woman crosses me at every turn. How has she gained such wonderful ascendancy ?"

" In the old-fashioned way, Master Wild, by preying on the credulity and follies of those with whom she is connected—but to the point the box is nimmed but not disposed of."

" They suppose it cannot be done in safety in this country?"

" Certainly not, and somebody must be emplowed who has connections abroad ; you are the man chosen, can you carry it out?"

" I can, but the article itself must be entrusted into my hands."

" That may be effected, but the persons who bring it to you will not lose sight of it while it is in your possession, or until they have received an equivalent, or some sort of guarantee."

" How damned logically you talk ; you must have received your lesson beforehand—it's not your own style."

" Why—aw—my dear Wild—"

" That's it, that's more like yourself ; you need not say another word.  I see you are to be the puppet, and Jonathan the tool, but I must be well paid for it."

" If you effect the negociation, I am authorised to inform you—"

·" There you go again, those words ; why don't you speak naturally?"

" Well—aw—if you does thing clean, you'll have five hundred pounds for your trouble."

" Speaking like a man of the world ; and you, what is to be your share?"

" A like sum ; which will enable me to give up prigery and enter into business."

" Turning fashionable tailor, discounting young swells' bills, giving three years' credit, and being content with cent per cent profit."

" Oh, I see, same thing in the end, only another system of robbery ; well, I think I may spare you, on condition I receive one hundred out of the five for my good will."

" Your good will, Wild? why; what in the devil's name do you mean by that, how can you interfere with me, and what is the use of your good will as yeu call it?"

" I'll tell you.  If I don't choose to allow you to turn honest, as you call it, you shall not, or my name's other than it is.  You are in my possession ; your life, and your means of living ; I can cut off one as I could the other."

·· You are joking now, Mr. Wild.

" Am I?  By the Lord, if I am not paid that hundred pounds, you'll find, Ned Sweeting, how dear a joke it is for you."  Jonathan hammered the table as he spoke, and leaned forward, and looked up into the other's face, and Sweeting did not doubt that he was in earnest.

"We shall not quarrel, Mr. Wild, I'll be bound. We are both of us—aw—men of the world."

"To be sure; now, when am I to see this box?"

"When you know how to dispose of it?"

"Good! Be with me to night at ten o'clock, bring the box, and some other person with you, and I'll take you and him to the east end of the town, to the house of a friend of mine, where the business can be done."

"A bargain, Mr. Wild," and Sweeting turned to depart.

"Oh, and Ned, by the way—"

"Yes, Mr. Wild—"

"Ascertain for me what you can of the doings of this fortune-teller, and it shall be worth your while."

"Agreed, Mr. Wild." And the robber departed as a crippl with a patch over his eye.

"A very pretty affair this is likely to turn out." muttered Jonathan when alone. "Now, Mother Stammers, I shall be even with you, or there must be some devilry at work more than I am acquainted with."

Now, then, sir, here you are; didn't I tell you I'd introduce you the next, and no mistake, for the beautiful crown you gave me, and ain't I as good as my word? Rely upon it, sir." added Flash, in a whisper, to the country gentleman who had given him the crown piece, "there is nothing like paying liberally for what you vants, but if you'll take my advice, you'll not pay the whole amount aforehand; it makes even the wery best on us a little bit careless, 'cause we ain't no longer interested in the wictim. does you twig, sir?" and Flash opened the door of the audience chamber for the admission of the young farmer.

"Good morning, Mr. Thornton."

"I am here, you see, Mr. Wild, true to my appointment; the anxious time that I have passed since I saw you it is useless for me to recount—have you any news for me?"

"I have not, I regret to say. I have been wholly unsuccessful in my endeavours, and I am afraid, sir, that I cannot now promise you, in good faith, much assistance. I have set several of the most knowing of the fraternity to work on the matter, and, though I promised them liberal payment if they obtained me the information I desired, I have learned nothing more than you know already; you see it isn't exactly in our way of business, though my connection is daily increasing, and

before you or I are many year older I will undertake to say that there
will ot be an eventful circumstance in any known family of respectability ill London that I shall not,   if I  choose, obtain minute particulars of."

"I am very sorry to hear this, sir; I told you how interested I
was in the young girl's fate."

"And I, too, Mr. Thornton, am interested, more than the mere
money I shall receive from you will warrant, perhaps, but the truth
is I had a relative living in Warwick, at the time this abduction took
place, and, since I saw you, I have heard from him the particulars of
the affair.  I am not in the habit of returning money; indeed, more
than I have received from you, I have already expended in the case,
but I will not ask you for more, as I do not think that I shall be
honestly able to furdher your views."

"This is, indeed, a sad disappointment."  The features of Thornton shewed the working of the feelings within, while he added:

"You can think then of no plan?"

"None," replied Jonathan, "more than we have already employed; we may yet hear, and you had better furnish me with your
address.  Yet, stay—" he exclaimed, as a sudden thought seemed to
strike him, "there is one other way in which you can assist yourself
however, as well as through my agency; enquire out Mrs. Stammers,
a professed fortune-teller in King's-street."

"A fortune-teller!" cried Thorntan, for what do you take me, a
superstitious fool, Mr. Wild?"

"No, Mr. Thornton; but a man ready to profit by every advantage
that may present itself.  This woman, in the practice of her trade,
and to carry out the chicanery of her calling, is acquainted with the
ways and means of more persons in the metropolis than you would
perhaps dream of.  Go to her, tell her plainly what it is you want,
let her understand that you do not believe in her gift of dieination,
but only in her great knowledge and information; offer her liberally,
provided she effect what you desire, and the chances are that you will
be successful."

"A thousand thanks, Mr. Wild; should that be the case, I shall
not forget it was by your means that I obtained my object."

Thornton took his leave of Jonathan Wild, and repaired towards
King's-street.

When Jonathan was left alone the thought that pervaded his mind
to the absorbtion of all others was this :—

" The fortune-teller appears to be mixed up more or less with every piece of business in which I move. I must see and know something of this extraordinary woman."

It was growing dark when Tom Thornton sought out Mrs. Stammers. With very little difficulty he found her rooms.

Old Martin received him at the door, and, in answer to his inquiry, bade him enter. The old man then caught up his hat, and went out upon the stairs. He lighted a short pipe now, and sat down upon the black boards, and swayed his body backwards and forwards—to and fro—to and fro—while broken sentences, that sounded like muttered imprecations, escaped his toothless mouth, and he beguiled the time picking out a particular knot in the oaken floor some few steps below him, and spitting in an imaginary circle round it.

Mrs. Stammers was prepared for the reception of visitors.

" Your purpose, sir? "

" Is to be informed of the present, not of the future."

" I do not keep a news office.

" But you are a woman of the world, and have means of information at your command, inaccessible to the public generally. I am willing to pay you handsomely if you can help me."

Mother Stammers eyed her visitor attentively, and then, with less of mystery in her manner than she usually adopted, said :

" You speak sensibly, sir, and it may be in my power to help you, as you say. You are not of this town, sir ? "

" No, 1 come from Warwick."

" And inquire for—"

" Ellen Hodson, the farmer's daughter."

" I know you now, sir, your name is Thornton."

" Good God !" exclaimed the young farmer, " then you know her too, tell me, tell me all."

" Softly, sir ; you are younger than I and proceed at too swift a pace for me to keep up with you. My hand must be crossed with gold if you would mend my march."

Thornton hastily put a guinea in the fortune-tellers palm.

" Now, ask me the questions you demand."

" Where is Ellen ? "

" In poverty and an obscure lodging near union street in the borough." She lives then—is she well—is she—"

" Seek her yourself, here is the address." And she wrote it with a pencil on the fly-leaf of a pocket-book."

" And he, what has become of him ? "

" You are not ripe yet to hear that answer, when you have seen her, and heard her tale, come to me again ; bring more gold with you, and revenge shall be yours."

Thornton scarcely waited to hear this speech, but hurried from the room.

Old Martin was roused from his reverie by the footstep of the farmer ; starting up, he caught Thornton by the coat, and importuned him for money.

" I've nothing," said the old man in his broken tone, " nothing to buy a bit of bacca with, or a drop of drink these cold nights. She's a tyrant to me, and I'm only her dog, only her dog."

Thornton gave him a shilling to get rid of him, and hastily passed out.

" Ugh ! you fool," while he eyed the shilling, then spat upon it, and shook it between the hollows of his closed palms, " to be plucked so easily ; why, anybody may have your money, only you pay with this difference—with this difference—gold for lies, silver for truth—ho, ho, ho," and the old man laughed himself into a fit of coughing which threatened to carry him off at every gasp, and he then returned to the chamber of his wife."

Later in the evening now, and the thick fog obscures the shops and the houses of the citizens, and hangs heavily about the few dull oil lamps that light the way. There ir a drizzling rain, and few passengers are abroad, save those whom business compels. The streets are greasy with mud, and tears of trickling damp are upon every stone, and wall, and woodwork. Tom Thornton is making his way towards London-bridge. He does not cross the bridge, he will take a boat at the stairs ; he is told that they can take him nearer to the point he is desirous of reaching. A bargain is easily made, and they push off.

The darkness of the streets is broad daylight to the depth of murky shadows falling on the bridge—Old London Bridge, not the present beautiful structure—and there are red flames, and fires, and forges to be seen on the opposite shore, while a few dull lanterns, here and there hung to the craft on the river, serve only to make the darkness seem more dark. They are in the middle of the river. Now, suddenly a scream is heard, and then an indistinct dark outline cuts the air. A heavy plash, and a body has fallen into the water.

" Great Heaven ! what can that be ? "

" Another on 'em, master ; they often does it in this part. Are you in a hurry, or shall we pull to the place ? "

" Pull, pull, by all means—oh, think, we may yet save life." A few strokes of the oar, and they were there. With straining eyeballs Thornton pierced into the black stream.

" There—there—with your boat-hook you may reach it ; " and, in the attempt to gain a hold of the form, Thornton, with both arms stretching forth over the side of the boat, and head and body now bent down, nearly plunged himself into the Thames. " See—see—'tis a woman. Great God! she sinks, and for the last time." He stretches forwards to his utmost power, he grasps at the clothes of the victim, they elude his touch ; now his hand is twined around a mass of fallen hair—the suicide is dragged into the boat.

Thornton sits beside the senseless form, and puts the wet hair from the cold face, and tries to look into the closed eyes of the lost creature.

Tom Thornton knows her now—it is Ellen Hodson.

---

## CHAPTER XV.

### THE LOST LAMB RESTORED TO THE FOLD—THE FIRST APPEARANCE OF A NEW PERFORMER.

WHEN Tom Thornton discovered who it was that he had snatched from the river, his very heart seemed to grow cold within him ; the men beside him could not, of course, enter into his feelings ; they gaped with astonishment to see him pressing in his arms the senseless form of the suicide.

" Which way, your honor, now ? "

" In shore directly, to the nearest point—no matter where."

" There's a public-house called ' The Rummer,' your honor ; that's where they takes most of this sort, for the crowners to sit upon."

" Is there a surgeon's near?"

" Plenty sir ; where there is accidents there is always crowners, and where there is likely to be danger there is sure to be doctors."

Ellen betrayed no signs of life, unless in the muscular twitching of the eyes ; he could not hear her breathe, and the action of her heart to him seemed suspended.   He was in despair.

" Pull, pull, for God's sake pull, or the poor girl will surely die."

" I was afraid she were dead already, sir, such a leap as that is enough to kill a dozen little things like her ; hold her up by the heels, sir, and let the water run out of her mouth."

" Do you think I'm mad?"

" I don't know about that, sir, but it is what a great many does, when they picks up a half dead 'un."

" It is a vulgar error, and a most dangerous one.   Be silent and pull."

When they reached the shore, Thornton sprang up hurriedly, and with his burden in his arms, jumped on to the pebbles, and ran onward, though knee-deep in water for awhile ; he inquired of the first persons he met the way to the house in question, and received from them proper directions in reply.   Many of them catching a glimpse of the lifeless figure in his arms, whilst the water ran in narrow streams from the saturated clothes of Ellen, turned, and led the way towards the house themselves.

There, as the waterman had said, they were no strangers to such cases, and the bed, and the hot blankets, and all the necessary assistance they speedily procured.   When the Doctor came Tom Thornton grasped him by the hand, but could not speak.   Silently he pointed upward to the room in which lay all he loved.   The man of healing sought his patient, and the young farmer pressed his hot brow against the cold marble of the high old-fashioned mantel-piece of the room, at the door of which he had received the doctor.   Now he stood erect again, and listened for the sligthest sound.   No moan, no breath came to tell him that she lived. And yet, how should he hear it there? And the circumstances of that night turned his brain.   He would listen no more ; he paced the floor with rapid strides ; and, fearing now to hear the sounds he had before desired, he thrust his fingers in his fingers in his ears lest a single groan should break upon them.

A quarter of an hour—half an hour—an hour passed away, and he could only hear the sound of footsteps overhead.   It was an hour of intense anxiety, if not agony of mind ; he prayed to hear, at last, should it even prove the worst ; his hand was on the door, and he was going up to learn the truth, when the medical man entered the room.

" Oh, tell me, sir ; she is—"

" Safe," replied the doctor.

" Thank God!" cried Thornton, fervently ; "and I thank you too sir, for your readiness and skill.   Your fee will be—"

" One guinea ; but I have no claim upon you—I understand from the waterman, that you picked up the girl by accident in the river ; can it be possible that you know her ? "

" I do, sir, I know her and her parents well—I've been brought up with her, all my life."

" Pardon me, sir, I have no further curiosity, I do not seek to know any more," interrupted the doctor.   " I am only glad that I have been enabled to render aid."

" May she be removed from here, and how soon ? "

" In the morning, provided that proper care and attention be shown with her."

" I thank you ; good night."

" Good night," and the two shook hands and parted.

Thornton did not then see Ellen, but he wrote her a note in which while he did not allude to her late attempt, he told her that Providence seemed to lead him to her now, to assure her of the kind reception she would meet with in her home ; and that he would be ready to accompany her in the morning to Warwickshire.

He received in reply a piece of paper whereon was written, in fain and somewhat illegible characters,

" I will go with you.   God bless you.

" ELLEN."

It was early in the morning when a hired carriage stood at the door of " The Rummer," to convey away young Thornton, and the poor girl whom misery had tempted to her own destruction.   It was known only to a few the circumstances attending that attempt, and the intended journey ; hence, when Tom Thornton led her tenderly to the carriage, and after she was seated and with pillows propped up, by the assistance of the good landlady took his seat beside her, beyond the servants of the house they excited little attention.

Scarcley a word, as yet, more than " Dear Ellen," or " Good Tom," had passed between Miss Hodson and the young farmer ; and it was not until they had left the town behind them that there was anything like conversation.

" Is this the road to—"

" To Warwickshire, you would ask,"

" Yes," said Ellen, "but the word faltered on my tongue. Can I ever face my dear father?"

" You have no cause to fear him."

" Oh, no, not fear—it is not that, but—and then, my mother."

" She will receive you with open arms."

" And the world—the little world I used to know, about my home—how shall I endure the whispered scorn, the smile of derision, when they see the yeoman's daughter—that went away to be a lady—return a wicked, bowed-down, broken outcast."

The tears flowed abundantly from the eyes of Ellen, and Thornton almost feared his power to console her.

" But this will not be so Ellen. You have committed folly—evil, it is true, but you now repent, and where shall repentance fly, if not to the home it knew before the sad one was a sinner ? "

" Oh! yes, repent. My God ! how bitterly I feel it ! and were it any other sin I mourned, I would raise my eyes to Heaven, and ask it to forgive me—humbleness in my voice, grief and penitence in my heart. But to love—to trust in man and be deceived, though God may—humanity will never—pardon. But, were it only this—but it is not! I have committed a higher crime—I have tried to cast away that which was not mine own. He who gave me life could have alone the right to take it. Oh, indeed, indeed I have been very wicked," and she wept more bitterly than before. Thornton put his arm round her waist to support her, and she bowed her head upon his shoulder, and her bright hair hung over it and his sleeve, and they and his hand were wet with her tears.

" You mustn't be wholly downcast ; your own argument should be your greatest comfort. Your biggest sin is done to Heaven, and Heaven forgives where man does not. Armed with that beautiful support, you would be enabled to bear with resignation the whips of the world ; and, perhaps, Ellen, a brighter time may yet come—a time when he who led you into error shall be forgotten, and you are enabled to find, in the honest protection of an affectionate husband—"

" Don't talk in that way, Tom, I shall be very ill if you do—worse at thought of that, than all beside, except—except my father. Did he suffer much ? "

" I cannot tell you he did not ? "

" And my mother ? "

" She suffered too, but differently."

" And when you came to London the object of your visit was—" '

" To seek out you."

" And at their desire ? "

" At their desire and my own."

Ellen now fell into a long train of thought, and Thornton would not disturb her. It was a delicacy not often manifesting itself, even among the most refined and intellectual classes of society, that prevented him from alluding to the cause or subject of her past grief or crime. He spoke of the weather, pointed out beauties in the scenes they passed through, described the manufactures of the principal towns, spoke of the interests and gaieties of the great metropolis itself, but never once alluded to that which had led her there. Kind, soothing, and attentive, like some affectionate brother, he tried to make the way smooth, and the journey pleasant to her, while, all the time, his heart was bursting with grief and indignation at the course to which she had been driven. The surface was calm, but the under-current raged and boiled and bubbled.

By short stages, for the health of Ellen was still delicate, that journey was taken. As on the third day they neared to Warwick, the trepidation and uneasiness of the poor betrayed girl very considerably increased. She knew the road—the hedges, the ditches, the trees—the very songs of the birds seemed the same to her she had so often heard before ; but oh! all were changed now, the face of nature wore a cloud, or when she smiled it seemed to wound our Ellen most ; the singing of the birds was more plaintive than it used to be, and in everything above, around, and about her, she fancied she heard, or saw, or drank in some evidence of her own guilt. It needed all Tom's persuasion now to console her—but he used it gently as a woman, wisely as a sage.

" Let me take you to the ' George.' I will see your father first, and bring him to you ; it will be better, less abrupt than your going at once to the farm."

" No," replied Ellen, " it would be an insult to my father's mercy, an injustice to the parent roof. I have erred, am guilty ; I am penitent: at once, and on the threshold of my father's door, he shall bless me with forgiveness, or spurn me from him for ever ; no public halting-place shall intervene."

Thornton gave directions to the driver, and for nearly an hour now they went on without a word. Ellen lay back in one corner of the carriage, and her handkerchief and her two hands were before her eyes.

Tom laid his fingers gently on her shoulder, and whispered,

"We are at the corner of the old lane now, we will leave the carriage here, let us walk."

The carriage stopped, they descended, and the young farmer supported her in her every step.

The Elizabethan chimneys of the red farm house were now caught rising from the dell, and the smoke curling upward told that there was life, and light, and warmth within.

Taking a sequestered path that led through a cornfield, and across a meadow, they reached the farm yard of Mr. Hodson. A little garden abutted on it, and, opening the wicket, they passed through it. No soul was to be seen. It was the dinner-hour, and the labourers were away from the farm yard, and the neighbouring fields.

To the old rustic porch, more modern than the rest of the house, and overhung with woodbine and honeysuckles, stole the young man's charge. Ellen needed all the help now that Tom could give her; he stood in the porch-way, and shouted out,

"Farmer, Farmer Hodson, 'tis I, Tom Thornton, come back from London with good news for you."

The old man came running out, and his wife closely followed him. It was to welcome their youthful friend; they knew not of the meeting that was in store for them. The father threw up his hands, and only one word, "Ellen," came broken from his lips, but the mother cried out, all joyously,

"My child—my dear child—my pretty one!" and struggled to reach her.

Ellen withdrew herself now from Tom's support, and tried to rush on without. A faint scream escaped her, "Father! Mother!" forced themselves through a passage of sobs and tears, and, staggering forward, Ellen, in the endeavour to fall upon her parent's breast, sunk at her father's foot, and clasped her round the knee. The old man raised his eyes and murmured,

"Heaven pardon thee, as I do, my child!" then lifted her in his arms, and bore her, like a baby to her little bed above stairs. When she awoke she was in the well-remembered room that had been hers a child, and that she had only left a few short months. How all unchanged it was—and yet how changed was she!

She was better now, and her little hand was in the affectionate grasp of her mother, who wept over her and smiled, and wept again, and even laughed ; then, with the same kerchief, wiped her daughter's, eyes, and said, "God knew how happy she was that her lost one had returned.

     \*       \*      \*      \*      \*      \*

Jonathan Wild was in his office a month or two after the occurrences we have narrated, when Flash brought him a letter which had arrived by that day's general post  It bore the Warwick post-mark, and was from Tom Thornton, informing Wild how he had succeeded in discovering the object of his search, and that the young lady was now happily situated with her friends at home, and recovering that health which she had lately lost.   It contained no farther intelligence, but a bank note for five pounds was enclosed.

"And my gallant friend Captain Austen," thought our hero, "what the devil has become of him ?   He will never marry the girl, that is certain ; and so I suppose she will forget her fine lover in time, and this young farmer will forgive her her sins, and make her his wife. An easy world this—but I must to business.   Bunks is to be hanged to-morrow at eight, along with Bob Booty and half a dozen other fellows; Mrs. B. wants to draw a little cash on account of his blood-money ; Tawney Bess is to be here at twelve for her share of the last lodgings she robbed, Ned Sweeting is waiting his instructions before he starts into the north—I can't help laughing to think how I knocked that 'honest' scheme of his, of going into business as a schneider, on the head—and Blueskin wants me to procure an *alibi* for his friend Choaker, who has got into trouble again, and wont be content till he swings."

Tap, tap—a smart knock at the door with the knuckles.

"Come in."

"I asks yout perdingn, Mister Vild, and I knows I shall be forguv, and a great many years of happiness is what I wishes you, for it is a proud gentleman as you is, and you ought to be."   It was Mrs. Bumsly the charwoman, who, wiping her hands with her apron, and then rubbing her nose violently in the bend of her scraggy arm, took up her position with more than her accostomed courage.

"What the deuce do you want, woman ? I am busy."

"I vants nothing, though I vouldn't be rude enough to refuse a little drop of anything you was to be pleased to offer me—I is a humble person, as I shows you."

"Mrs. Bumsly is my name,
  And England is my nation ;
London is my dwelling-place—"

"Get out," growled Jonathan, and he seized the charwoman by the
arm, and was about to expel her forcibly, when Flash dashed into the
room crying,

"Hurrah! master—dont be afraid—it's all right."

"What's all right, you confounded idiot?"

"Missis is brought to bed of a little girl, and it's a squeaking avay
like a good 'un—"

"Vich is vot I comed for to tell you," added Mrs. Bumsly, "to be
aforehand vith the nus, ven I gits struck for my trouble, and eggspos_
tulation arn't of the leastest awail." Jonathan did not stop for
further parley, but hurried from the room, and mounted to his wife's
chamber.

"Mister Flash."

"Mrs Bumsly."

"You is a rising young youth, you is, as ever I see, and my adwice
to you, Mister Flash, is—to onor your father and mother, and everybody else as is older nor yourself—eggspecially charwomen; they is
not recognised as a body by hact o' parliament, but they has their
fancies and their weaknesses—does you know vhere the key o' the
cupboard is, for I'd give the vorld for a thimblefull o' blue ruin?"

When Jonathan entered the bedroom the nurse popped a baby girl
into his arms, and said, as she made him a curtsey,

"Give 'ee joy—the finest little thing that ever I nussed."

"And the mother?" whispered Jonathan.

"Going on quite nicely, sir ; indeed, I may say, 'as well as can be
expected.'"

With which very original remark the nurse drew back the curtains,
and showed him Mrs. Wild, whose hand lay above the coverlet,
waiting for her husbands grasp.

————————

## CHAPTER XVI.

### THE BURGLAR'S ARREST—THE LAST SCENE AT THE FORTUNE-TELLER'S.

BUNKS, the man who had shot Mr. Rushton, was sitting on his truckle-bed, and buttoning the knees of his breeches over his worsted stockings, while Blueskin and Choaker, from opposite sides of the fire-place, watched the progress of the other's dressing.

No. 8.

The appearance of Bunks, which had been at no time prepossessing was now rendered worse by the excessive whitness of his face, his long unshaven beard, his hair matted with blood, and the bandages about his head.

"You mean to say," said Blueskin, " you mean to say, then, that Stammers isn't her name after all."

" No more than it is mine ; her name is Dormer," answered Bunks, " and that little old fellow's her husband ; it don't matter to you how I knowed it, but know it I does, and that's enough for what you wants. A great many years ago that ere fortune-teller was a beautiful young girl as got seduced by an Irish nobleman, who, just as you might expect, wasn't going to marry her nohow, but he had a valet—a chap that used to help him in all his dirty tricks, and would do anything for money ; well, this Mother Stammers, as she calls herself, or Margaret as she used to be called, was, much against her inclination, married to this man, who received two or three hundred pounds to take her off his lordship's hands.   When the money was spent, which didn't take long, he wanted her to go on anyhow, and want so far as to introduce gentlemen to her, and would have sold her over and over again if he could.   She was bad enough, but she chose to be bad her own way, and she hated this Dormer with all her heart—"

" My eyes! what a long yarn, Bunks ; cut it short."

" Did you ever hear of a crown-piece that weren' no bigger nor a shilling ? "

" No."

" Nor a gallon o' beer as would go into a pint mug, did you ? "

" No."

" Then don't you expect me to do what's unpossible either."

"Go on, Bunks," said Blueskin, " never mind Choaker, he's nobody."

" I don't mind him.   You asked me to tell you what I knowed, and I'm telling on you.   Well, when things got desperate with the Dormers, what does Martin, the man, do, but forges the name of the nobleman as his wife had lived with, to a cheque for a hundred and fifty pounds.   They paid him at the bank, but it was found out soon afterwards, and old Martin was given into custody ; however, his wife went to the nob, and made the thing square, and when Martin was brought up, there wasn't a prosecutor.   From that day to this she's kept him under her thumb, and he daren't so much as say his soul is his own. She has regularly took out her revenge on him, and tells him every day it's in her power to hang him ; he believes her, and fears and hates her like the devil.   I don't know any more."

" Quite enough too, Bunks, for the purpose I wants."

" Hark ! didn't you think you heard some one on the stairs ?"

Choaker had started up, and dashed his pipe in the grate.

Blueskin, too, was in the attitude of listening, while Bunks stayed his fingers, which were in the act of fastening some unseen string.

" Look to the door," cried Bunks, in a loud whisper, and Choaker sprang towards it, and turned the lock, and set his back against it.

" Open," cried a rough voice from without.   There was no answer returned.   Blueskin was at the window, examining the distance from the ground.   It was too high to hope for escape by that means.

" Idiots that we are," said he, " to be caught like so many rats in a trap ; curses on it ; but I knew this was an unsafe crib from the first."

" Open in the King's name," cried the officers, for such they were ; " open, or we shall force the door."

" It's all up," cried Bunks.

" And we shall swing at Tyburn," added Choaker.

" That be hanged," growled Blueskin, " we'll make a fight of it, at all events, and act like men."

Bunks caught up the poker, while Choaker drew a long knife, and prepared for a desperate resistance.   Blueskin was the only one of the three armed with pistols; he held both the weapons in his left hand, for a moment, while he unlocked the door, which opened into the room. Standing on that side on which were the panels, as he turned the lock, and drew back the door as far as it would go, it necessarily screened him while he did so from the view of those who were entering.

There were but two officers, and they expected only to find Bunks, but they were armed for an encounter.

As they sprang forward with a shout the two thieves prepared to meet them ; the officers were, however, powerful men, and thought but little of the weapons to which they were opposed.   Before the up-raised arm and poker of Bunks could fall upon the head for which it was intended, the ruffian's wrist was caught midway in the air, and his throat tightly grasped by the disengaged hand of the foremost of the two constables.

Bunks was hurled back, and almost immediately overpowered.

The antagonist of Choaker was not so successful.   On entering the room he had flown at his man, and, truncheon in hand, had endeavoured to strike the knife from the fellow's clutch.

He received a slight wound in the attempt, but also pinned his man. Now Choaker roared—

" Fire away, Blueskin, fire, and be d—d to you! "

The officers were not aware of the presence of a third party, and so stood with their backs to Blueskin, the one holding his man against the wall, the other kneeling on his prisoner's chest on the floor.

Blueskin doubted not that he should effect his own escape : he looked round for a moment, and then taking aim at the broadest part of the constable before him, cried out,

" It's all over with Bunks ; Choaker, look to yourself. The shot was fired, and Blueskin dashed down the stairs into the street. The unfortunate constable dropped his truncheon, while a shriek of agony escaped him, and he clapped down both his hands to the wounded part behind him.

Choaker had now little difficulty in knocking him backwards, jumping over the prostrate officer, and following his companion Blueskin, Bunks alone was secured a prisoner.

While this scene was being enacted, another, at which we must assist, was going on in King's-street.

Old Martin, goaded to revenge by the long series of tyrannies and insults that his wife had for years heaped upon him, in what she conceived a just spirit of retribution, had determined, at length, upon executing revenge. It was generally believed that the fortune-teller had amassed considerable property ; but, as usual, rumour had exaggerated it to a very great extent.

Martin knew, however, that she was possessed of money, though he did not think it could be any very large sum : he calculated that he so could use it, as to better his own condition during his remaining years. He had never entertained the slightest affection for the fortune-teller ; his marriage, as we have seen—for the statement of Bunks was substantially correct—was a convenience for which he was paid after his own terms ; and from the hour when, by the committal of the forgery, he put himself wholly in the power of his wife, who wielded it to her own purposes, he hated her with a hate that never knew abatement. He would have left her long since, but that he feared her, and knew that she had means of ferreting him out from any hiding-place in all England ; besides, how was he to live, never having in his possession more than a few pence at a time, and it was wholly impossible for him to return to the trade with which he had begun life—that of a horse-couper.

Then, if he left her, and found the means to eke out existence without her, what became of the hopeful feeling of revenge that had solaced him in his trouble—soothed him when he smarted under indignity—that he had hugged in the very depths of his grovelling misery!

Mrs. Stammers had latterly increased her persecutions. It might have been that her trade began somewhat to fall off, and her temper, at all times bad, had grown more violent than ever. Martin thought this, and thought also, if he delayed too long the day of *reprisals*, the business decreasing, they would have to live upon the savings, and as his wife was an extravagant woman, and ate and drank of the best, and spent money, or rather caused it to be spent, notwithstanding she was bed-ridden, almost as fast as a fine lady, he concluded that the time was ripe for carrying his murderous schemes into execution. He had no fear of punishment in this world for the crime he purposed; he thought to elude justice here, and his mind could not grasp an hereafter.

He was seated, as we first saw him in an early chapter, rocking himself in a low chair before the fire, and his lips continued moving and moving, as it were, at the coals, though no sound escaped them. Once or twice, he turned his face towards the bed behind him, and cast a furtive glance at the fortune-teller, who seemed to be asleep.

We have said he did not speak, but these were the thoughts that passed through his brain :—

"By this time to-morrow, and I shall not only know exactly how much money there is in that trunk under the bed, but I shall have the golden yellow-boys in my possession, and you—ugh! how I hate you— you will have paid the penalty for all that you have made me endure for so many years past. I can't be found out—oh no, I can't be discovered. I have provided too well for that, and to think how easily I can do it. I could laugh, I could, it is such a jest; but I won't, I won't."

A fit of coughing seized the old scoundrel, and again he looked towards the bed, to see if he had awakened his wife.

She still seemed to sleep, and cautiously now, and slowly too he drew a small phial from his waistcoat pocket, and held it before him, and looked at it by the red fire-light. The self-satisfaction he felt at possessing in that little bottle the means of a hundred deaths so tickled the fancy of old Martin, that a low chuckle burst from him in spite of himself.

The sleeper moved, and he hastily concealed the bottle.

"What are you doing there, driveller?"

"Nothing, my dear." Could she have seen that phial; could she have read its label—"Poison." No : she would have spoken differently;

for though she used the term of insult by which she had habituated herself to address him, her tone was less harsh than usual.

"Martin"—the old man was very much surprised at this—"Martin, where is the brandy?"

"In the cupboard, my dear; shall I give it you?"

"No; mix me some in this teacup."

"It is not clean."

"Then wash it at the stand; there are jug, basin, and a cloth."

He took the cup, and crossed with it to the wash-hand stand.

"Now," thought he, "now the time is come: now, when she cannot see me, I will do it." With his back nearly wholly turned, he dropped a small portion of the contents of the phial into the bottom of the cup, and then returned the bottle to his pocket. "It has no taste, they tell me, and she cannot have seen me; I was too quick."

But suspicious eyes are ever restless, and those of Mother Stammers were like the lightning in their glance.

"You've washed the cup, Martin?"

"Yes, Mrs. Stammers; yes, my dear."

"Then half fill it with brandy, and let the water be hot from the kettle."

Old Martin did as he was desired, and poured in the brandy, and mixed with it the boiling water, in full sight of his wife. He thought she could not suspect him now. As he handed it to her, he shook a little, and went a trifle paler than before. Her eyes rested keenly on him, but it was for a moment only.

She took the cup from him, and raised it to her lip. A demoniacal expression passed over the withered face of the revengeful wretch before her.

"I will put it down; it is too hot," and she placed the cup untasted on the chair beside her. Revenge was disappointed; it was not yet baffled.

"Let me put more brandy with it to cool it," said her husband.

"That will make it too strong—taste it yourself." Again the fortune-teller fixed those glowing eyes upon the shrunken man, and for an instant he almost fancied that she had seen him drop in the poison; but she removed her glance so carelessly, and said (for her) so pleasantly, "Or, perhaps you had better mix another glass for yourself," that Martin was quite satisfied, and only wondered a good deal that she was thus agreeable. It was, indeed, an extraordinary and unusual circumstance.

"I will drink to her pleasant journey," thought he, "to the unknown country she is going to visit: it was thoughtful of me to give it her in something that will keep the cold out."

He brewed for himself now, and sat down in the chair by the fire as before, except that he turned it round, and faced his wife.

"This is what I call comfortable—comfortable," repeated the old man. "Now you're in a good temper, and we can spend a pleasant evening together, for the first time for—"

"Many long, long years."

"Not my fault, you know, Peggy; not my fault."

"It is hardly worth talking about that now: do you think it is, Martin?"

"Perhaps not, perhaps not, my dear. Your better health, my dear, and"—the old man's eyes twinkled as he spoke—"and long life to us both, eh! Mrs. Stammers?"

"Ah! Martin," said the fortune-teller, in a tone of apparent tenderness, "you will outlive me."

"What, and I so much older? No, no, that won't do for me, that won't neither. Now, do you know, Peggy, I say, do you know, though we have lived such a cat-and-dog life—cat-and-dog's the word"—Mrs. Stammers nodded—"I hope that when your time comes, it may be mine too. Indeed, I'd rather die before you, d'ye hear, Peggy, die before you." The last words were almost inarticulate from the ill-suppressed chuckle and the fit of coughing that accompanied them.

"Your health, Martin," said Mrs. Stammers, and again she raised the cup, but held it from her while she said, "By the bye, is there a biscuit in that cupboard?"

The old man went to see.

"No; you have had the last."

"I can't drink this without something to eat; I have had some brandy before. Go and get me a few at the corner, Martin; it is not far: there are some halfpence on the mantel-shelf."

He was not accustomed to be asked; he was usually told to do a thing. He took the money, and went quite cheerfully. When he had quitted the room, he muttered—

"She hasn't a notion of the poison; her devil's temper would have broke out immediately, and if she hadn't killed me at once, by flinging something at my skull, she'd have alarmed the house, and given me into custody; and then how civil she has been to-night! She has a motive in that: I know her so well. She wants me to do some dirty work for her, dirtier than usual; but she's mistaken for once, ho! ho! how sadly she's mistaken, to be sure," and he went on his way to buy the biscuits, chuckling, as usual, till he coughed.

As the door closed, up started the wild form of the fortune-teller. She flung back her red hood, and her iron-grey hair hung in elf-like locks about her shoulders. Now she listened: she heard only the retreating footsteps of the old man, as he descended the creaking stairs—the old man, her husband, who had devised and carried into execution the means of murdering her, his wife.

She threw down the clothes, and scrambling to the foot, threw herself out upon the floor. Like a coiled-up, broken mass, for almost a minute there she lay motionless. Could they have heard her in the floor below?—they might, but they would not think it was her—the bed-ridden fortune-teller. On all fours—yet, by the aid chiefly of the power in her hands and arms, for her legs, well-nigh useless, she dragged, and from side to side, but still forward, flung them after her, she reached the table whereon stood the brandy the old man had mixed for himself. Clutching the table with her two hands, she raised her head above it, and then seized the cup, while a shrill laugh broke from her lips, that she tried in vain to suppress. She put the cup upon the floor, and pushed it step by step before her, as she made her way back to the bedside. By the same action she had employed when removing it from the table, she now placed it on the chair by the truckle.

*And there were the two cups.*

Suddenly came the thought and stabbed her brain—she knew not which was the poisoned one! In her excitement she had forgotten to to note which was last placed there.

She saw at once how necessary it was to collect herself. She did so by an effort, and she remembered that the tea-cup which Martin had given her was, within the rim, a little chipped. It was that one now she took, and placing it as she had placed its fellow on the floor, pushed it back as she went to the table by the fire. Again she raised herself, and now she put it where the other had been.

*She had exchanged the cups.*

Back she crept, and crawled, and swung—there was a footstep on the stairs. She caught by the bed-clothes at the foot and they yielded to her grasp.

If he should come in and find her there upon the floor he would comprehend all—might he not beat out her brains?

Again she caught at the bed—she raised herself now—the footsteps were growing nearer. She was on the bed, and his hand was on the look. She dragged the clothes over her head, and he entered the room. " I've brought the biscuits, my dear; I haven't been gone long— have I ?"

" Eh ?"

" I haven't been long gone, I say."

" I don't know, I thought you had. I think I must have been asleep."

The fortune-teller rubbed her eyes and yawned as naturally as possible, while her husband cast a quick and searching glance round the apartment.

All appeared exactly as he had left them.

" Ah, no," thought he; " she suspects nothing, she has really been dozing."

The fortune-teller took the biscuits, and broke one of them, and began to eat. Presently she lifted the cup beside her, and took a long drink. The old man leant forward, and looked with straining eyes into the countenance of his wife: he could only read a smile about her mouth. A fit of trembling seized him suddenly, and he snatched up the cup from the table, and drained it at a draught. The victim of his own villany, he had himself taken the poison which he had prepared for his wife.

Now they sat facing each other, and not a word was spoken by either. A more fearful picture cannot be conceived : man and wife each eagerly watching for the other's death—silently gazing for the working of the murder.

Old Martin regarded his wife with so fixed an expression of countenance, that she was fain to withdraw her gaze a little ; she drank the rest of the brandy, and then raised herself upon her elbow and renewed her watching.

" Why do you look at me so strangely—eh, Peggy ?"

" I do not look strangely at you."

" You do—remove your eyes—they hurt me—hurt me."

He reclined back in the chair now, and spoke with greater difficulty. Still she watched him.

He moved not—spoke not. Another hour passed by, and the fortune-teller could hardly keep herself awake. His breathing was regular, there was no change in him.

By and bye her eyelids drooped, and her head nodded: the brandy was operating in spite of the excitement. She tried to rouse herself, and watched her husband as before. It seemed to her that he was dozing now. After a minute or two, again her lids fell down, and her head nodded, and by violent jerks only did she recover herself. Half an hour more, and her elbow slid a little on one side, and her cheek still resting on her palm was brought on a level with the pillow: she was asleep.

The muscles of her face worked strangely: she was dreaming horribly. She struck out her hand, as if to ward off a blow, and she swept down the lighted candle. A groan broke from her, and unconsciously she turned.

A little while, and there was a dreadful smoke in the chamber—a heavy, suffocating smoke from a smouldering burning. The people in the house discovered it, and were soon astir: but the old man and his wife were still as the grave.

Now there was a knocking at the door—a tramping of many feet, and loud cries of "Fire! fire!"

The door was burst open, and a dense volume of smoke rushed out, and the wind fanned the smouldering fire into red curling flames, and drove the people back. The inhabitants were removing their goods into the street: the engines had arrived, and a huge mob collected.

Two hours sped on, and the house was gutted; a little longer, and it was levelled with the ground; all, save the outer walls.

The remains of the fortune-teller and her husband were found among the ruins, charred, blackened, and burnt.

---

## CHAPTER XVII.

### THE HOUSE OF SHADRACH, THE JEW.

At the hour appointed that evening, Ned Sweeting and another rapped at the door of Jonathan Wild.

Sweeting had thrown off the disguise in which he had appeared during the morning, and now, with the addition only of a long black wig and moustache, looked sufficiently changed to defy recognition.

A huge cloak enveloped his figure, and his companion wore another, of similar size and shape. They appeared to be two foreigners of middle class respectability.

The door was answered by Patty, the maid, Flash being at the moment out of the way.

"Your master at home, my dear?" demanded Sweeting in an assumed deep voice.

The night was very dark, as we have before had occasion to describe, and when Patty, opening the door but a little way, and holding up the candle to look upon the visitor, met the white face, large eyes, black hair, and long moustache of the cloaked figure bent down a little to a level with herself, she almost shrieked with fright, so horrid did it seem. She had been sitting in the kitchen, discoursing with Mrs. Bumsly on the probability of ghosts. Sweeting was obliged to repeat his question before she could stammer forth a reply in the affirmative.

"Who shall I tell him it is?" asked the trembling Patty.

"The devil and Doctor Faustus," replied the robber, as he and his companion stepped into the hall.

No sooner had the words escaped his lips, than Patty let fall the light directly, screamed violently, and dropped down on the door-mat. Sweeting had taken care to close the latch.

"How could you be such an idiot?" whispered the companion of the thief. "She will alarm the neighbourhood, and all through your cursed folly."

"Hush, my lord," replied the other. There were lights moving above stairs and below; the voices of Jonathan and Mrs. Bumsly were heard at the same moment, though they accorded but poorly together.

"What, in the devil's name, means this disturbance?"

"If so be you has caught a ghost, Patty, hold it till I bring a light."

"Who the devil is there, Patty?" shouted Jonathan.

Patty, by a great effort, made reply—

"The gentleman as you be speaking of, sir, and he's brought his doctor wi 'un."

Jonathan now descended the stairs, and Sweeting and his friend advanced to meet him. He recognised them in a moment, and bade them follow him.

Pat was left in a lump upon the mat, upon the floor, and in the dark.

"Loard ha' mercy on us if I doan't go back to t'auld place again. I'll be clawed to pieces one of these nights, and only my effigies sent whoam to my friends; that ever I should live to see Old Nick and Doctor Crostus call on my master in a friendly way, quite."

"Patty, my blessed, is you there?"

"Don't 'ee come anist me, I smell strong enough of sulphur to knock you down."

Mrs. Bumsly appeared with the kitchen candle by this time, and helped the bewildered Patty to the regions below.

"Vell, now, and is you certain it was Old Nick, arter all?" inquired the charwoman.

"Sartain, sure; when I opened the door his two great eyes glared at me like furnaces, and his breath came hot, and quite brimstone-loike, it almost knocked me backards, and when I said, ' What be thee neame, sir?' and he said ' The devil and Doctor Tossetus.' I looked at his horns, and at sight of 'em I tumbled down dead; though now I'm a bit better loike, I only wish I'd axed un to lend me his tail."

Jonathan and his visitors stayed but little time before their departure.

The snuff-box was produced, and given by the stranger, who accompanied Sweeting, into the hands of Wild; the former, while he searched for it in the breast-pocket of his coat, revealed a glimpse of a brace of large pistols, and a dirk in his belt. Our hero smiled when he saw these precautions, but he made no remark. It was not his part to play otherwise than a fair game. The three understood each other, and a hackney coach being, by this time, procured by Flash, who had returned from an errand, they started on their way to Houndsditch, to the house of Shadrach, the jew. They left the vehicle at some distance from the residence they were seeking out, and then turned down a bye street, and, led by Jonathan, pursued their course through a low and wretched neighbourhood.

At length they came to a large and old-fashioned wooden building. Jonathan stopped before it.

"Good Heavens! it cannot be here," exclaimed the stranger, who had brought the box.

"And why not?" demanded Jonathan; "have I brought you this devil's dance, think you, for nothing?"

Sweeting and his companion backed out into the road, if the narrow gutter that ran between the houses was deserving of that name, and looked up at the large desolate building before which they stood. It was rapidly sinking to decay; the glass was gone from many of the windows, others were boarded up, and here and there, a great patch of brown paper, insecurely fastened, flapped to and fro, as the wind drove by the place in gusts. Not a light was to be seen in any one of those chambers. It seemed to have been long since left, the habitation of rats.

"And can this possibly be the residence of a man with the means of obtaining the common necessaries of life, much less one in possession of any large sums of money?"

"You shall see," replied Wild, and approaching the doorway, he pulled a bell by means of an unseen string. For some time there was no answer, and the three stood under the great wooden portico, speaking only in anxious whisperings. Again Jonathan rung, and this time the summons was answered by the deep baying of a dog.

Presently a light was seen to dance from window to window, and then a shuffling noise was heard, and the baying of the dog was nearer. A little wicket in the solid door was now removed, and through the close iron bars a feeble voice muttered,

"Mine Got, who is dare at this time of the night, and vat you vant?"

"Lemishades," replied Jonathan, in a subdued tone.

"Lemishades it is, and the pathway of the moon is vet."

"With the tears of Abraham," continued Jonathan.

"Abraham is blessed, and you are?"

"Jonathan Wild."

"And your companions?"

"Good men and true; Lemishades both."

The Jew appeared to hesitate only for a moment, and then the wicket was closed again, but the great door was unbarred, and the strangers stood in the hall of that ruined building.

While the old Jew was fastening up the door again, they had time to contemplate the figure before them, and the place in which they stood.

The man was Shadrach himself, and appeared to be bending under the weight of age and infirmities; he wore a long black gown that came quite to his heels, but, being open in front, displayed, as he moved, his lower limbs, the breeches and red stockings in which they were encased. His long white beard fell almost to his waist, and his silvered hair stole out and hung down in straight lines from either side of the small black velvet cap he wore upon his head.

A striking peculiarity in the pale and shrunken visage of this aged

man was the black, and ever restless undimmed eyes that shot out
fierce glances from underneath a pair of thickly-overhanging, shaggy
brows.   By the side of Shadrach stood a huge black wolf dog, whose
coat seemed to have been singed and torn, but whose powerful limbs,
fiery eyes, and the glimpses of the long white teeth that he constantly
revealed, as he glared at the strangers, told how good a protector he
could prove to his master.

The hall in which they stood had undoubtedly once been handsome,
the marble flooring was now black and broken, and the ornaments,
that had once been gilded, were rotting with damp, and the spider
spun his web from the carving on the beams.

" You are very late," said Shadrach, " vat is it that you vant ?"

" We cant talk here," replied Wild ; " take us to your sanctum."

The old man looked from face to face, as in a moment of doubt, but
our hero broke in with—

" Tut, Shadrach, don't be a fool ; have not I been here before, and
do I not know the ways of the old place ?  Need you fear to trust us ?"

Shadrach again observed them with the most searching minuteness,
and then stooped down a little, and whispered to the wolf-dog; the
beast put up his head into his master's withered hand, and eyed the
strangers fixedly ; then, when Shadrach had removed his mouth from
the animal's ear, and stood up again, the dog seemed to answer the
whispered speech of his master, and growled with savageness in reply.

" Yes, yes," muttered the old Jew with a chuckle, " I don't think
I have much to fear ;  dis vay, shentlemen, dis vay."

The Jew went first, Wild and his companions followed, and the
great dog brought up the rear.   From the hall they passed into a long
passage, and thence climbed a broken staircase.   The stairs were of
wood, and as they put their feet upon the steps, they creaked, and
seemed to yield, and little clouds of dust flew up, and threatened them
with choking.

" A queer den this of yours, Shadrach ; not a bad place for a ghost
story."

" Dere is von, I have heard, Mr. Vild; I vill tell it you some day."

" When we have less busines to transact than at present."

" Dat is right, Mr. Vild."

The Jew had led the way into a chamber now, that seemed to be
the sanctum named by Jonathan.   There was a strange assortment of
furniture in that little room, and this German Jew would seem, among
his other pursuits, to follow that of chemistry.

There was a furnace in one corner, with its paraphernalia of bellows, crucibles, metal-pots, and iron instruments; in another, hanging against the wall, were human skeletons, and the bones of larger animals; great books were there in heaps upon the floor, while small, but rare specimens of sculpture were huddled together, or flung carelessly aside. There were stuffed birds, and great snakes, and strange fishes about the place; the chairs and tables were so crowded that it was with difficulty our adventurers found seats. The old Jew cleared them places on a great chest.

" God knows what you are sitting over," whispered Jonathan, while the Jew tended his fire; " the rotting bones of manly strength and womanly beauty, the things that have been, or the things that are ; the records of the dead, or the trappings of the living ; the finery of a past day, or the mockery of this."

" Now zen to business," said the German Jew.

Jonathan produced the snuff-box of the king.

" I require for this eight thousand pounds."

" My Got! eight thousand—you take away my breath—vhere should a man get eight thousand pounds in these days ? "

" I know not, neither do I care ; but look at the brilliants, examine the workmanship."

Shadrach took it in his trembling hands, and his eyes sparkled involuntarily as he gazed upon the diamonds:

" These are very beautiful, certainly."

" Beautiful! they are worth a king's ransom."

" They are not worth so much as you say. I shall give five thousand in a sheque."

" Bah! hand me back the box."

" Not so fast, my friend—you forget I am a poor old Jew ; I have not got ze money."

" Then give us back the bauble, and let us go."

" Abraham ! I vill give you six thousand."

" Not a penny under eight—you will send it to Russia and get twelve."

Jonathan nodded assent. The Jew placed the box at his feet; in a moment it had descended, and no one saw how; then the old man laughed and said—

" Now zen vhere is your box—oh, noses ! if I do not give you a farthing."

The three men started to their feet, and Jonathan cried out—

"Villanous Shadrach, we will throttle you as you stand before us!"

But the Jew only laughed the more, and called the wolf-dog to his side.   He had no thought of jugglery, however, for he pulled a sort of bell-rope in the ceiling, and straight a small box of iron came gradually to his hand.   He took notes from it to the amount of eight thousand pounds, and sent it to its place again, while he handed the papers to Jonathan.

The interview was over.

When they gained the street again, Sweeting muttered—

"How d——d extraordinary this old Crœsus is not robbed and murdered!"

"He will be, one of those days," replied Jonathan Wild in a similar under-tone.

## CHAPTER XVIII.

WE must now suppose that eighteen years have elapsed since the events of the last chapter.

Eighteen years! there is a lingering sound in the words.   Applied to the future it seems almost like an interminable vista of time, and anything promised to us at such a distance, however good, appears but a shadowy benefit.  The mountain is so high we lose its apex in the clouds; it is a long and thorny way to climb, and there are many dangers in the path.  But, having made some small advance, how rapidly do we seem to be moving onward, and when we arrive at the end of our limited journey, it appears but yesterday we began it.

Eighteen years had made no very striking change in Jonathan Wild. He had grown stouter, and his features were sterner than they used to be; the animal had come out more in the jaw, the brows were shaggier, and wore a more habitual scowl, while the rat-like expression of the eye seemed to have been increased by the feeding of the spirit.

But if Jonathan had not improved in person, he was considerably

bettered in pocket since we last heard of him. His business had become enormous, and he now styled himself "Thieftaker General of Great Britain and Ireland."

It is no romance, but a matter of history, how he was a receiver of stolen goods to an unparallelled extent; how, when almost anything of value was missed, he was applied to immediately by the wealthy and the great, as often as by those in a middle sphere; how if he had not got the article sought for, he always knew where to find it, and could and would procure it by a given time; how all the thieves

No. 9.

of London regarded him as their chief and patron, and how he hanged or saved them at his pleasure; how he influenced even the judges of the land, and was tolerated, if not absolutely assisted, for his utility, by the Government.

When he could not effect his purposes in one way, as far as tampering with justice was concerned, he tried another, and the following account from a contemporary life of the arch rogue is both interesting and amusing :—

" By ingenious quirks, or by managing the juries or evidences, he has brought off some of his favorites who had been taken in the very facts for which they were committed, as he did once by two fellows who, having committed a robbery on the highway, and several persons, well mounted and armed, happening to come by immediately, they were pursued, and taken, with the gentlemen's rings and watches about them; and, being forthwith carried before the Justice of Peace, were committed to Newgate.

" Within a day or two of the Sessions, Jonathan, whose wit seldom ailed him at a pinch, inquiring the names of the prosecutors, went to them, and, asking them if they had not been robbed by such and such fellows, now in Newgate, the gentlemen answered they had.

" Jonathan pretended a great spleen to those fellows, who, he said, were the greatest rogues in the whole world, and that he would have hanged them long ago if he could have found them; and, therefore, begged of the gentlemen that he might assist them in managing the prosecution, and he would engage the rascals should not escape. The gentlemen, very willing to have part of the trouble taken off their hands, accepted his offer, knowing Mr. Wild to be a person very well skilled in those affairs.

" Accordingly, they appointed to meet at a tavern in the Old Bailey, on the morning which was appointed for the trial of these highwaymen.

" When they met, Jonathan told them there was a great crowd in the court, and that they had better stay there till the trial should begin; which he said would not be till about three o'clock in the afternoon. In the meantime a dinner was bespoke, to be ready at one; and Jonathan sent a man to the court, with orders to call them when the trial came on. Jonathan made such good use of his time, that, whether by putting something into the liquor, or by fair drinking, is not known, but it is certain he made the gentlemen very drunk, who passed away the time till evening without thinking of the matter, at which time one of them, wondering that their messenger had not called them, they sent to the court to know what was doing there, when they found the court was broken up, and the two highwaymen were discharged, there having no evidence appeared against them."

Jonathan lived now in good style; he not only kept on his house in the city which we have before in part described, but he had also a country residence at Kilburn, and kept his carriage. Mrs. Wild now seldom went abroad without her footman at her heels—in a word, our hero had now attained the apex of his fortunes.

In the man himself, however, there was but little change; certainly no improvement. We cannot touch pitch and avoid defilement: Jonathan's long association with crime of every shade, his admixture with criminals of every degree, had brought him to contemplate the blackest acts as matters of every-day occurrence, in which he objected only to take an active part when the danger was very apparent. It should be added that the impunity with which he had practised the most daring villanies made him less cautious than he used to be, and the toleration with which the justices appeared to regard him, induced him in his vanity to suppose that he was a necessary officer of the Executive Government.

When we again want our hero we find him, as of old, at his books in the office—by books must be understood his day-book and ledger, for Jonathan was not of a literary turn.

"And so," said he, looking up from his accounts to the youth who stood opposite him; "and so, Jack, you did the trick well?"

"Well! Mr. Wild, I did it like an angel—an angel of darkness I mean, sir, of course."

"You must give up burglary, Jack, and take to the high toby spice. You are too dashing a fellow for a milken; but tell me all about it."

"You see, Mr. Wild, it happened in this way: I heard of a set of tradesmen of the city who meet every Wednesday night at 'The Cock,' in Bartholomew Close, to smoke pipes, drink grog, and talk eternally about bell-ringing."

"Ha, ha, ha! ninnies—but go on, Jack."

"Well, sir, one Wednesday night, what does I do, but get a handsome wig and suit, that made me look several years older, and pretending to be a young squire from the country, I introduced myself to the company, and, the moment they began to talk about bell-ringing, seemed greatly interested  We had a long discourse upon the matter— I making them believe that I was very clever at the game myself, and if I was allowed to find five other young gentlemen out of my part of the country, we would ring them for two hundred guineas. After a time the match was agreed upon, and the day settled for it to come off, under a forfeiture of half the money on either side. There was a good deal of talk as to where it should be, but, at last, Lincoln was chosen, because that city has, as they said, the sweetest set of bells in all England. Well, Mr. Wild, when the time came off, we started, and so did the cits, every man of them, not only with his share of the two hundred guineas, but pocket-money besides, to defray his expenses from home. When we got to the cathedral, these gentlemen were all in a hurry to try the bells, and wondrous eager for the matter to come off. So they began to strip themselves forthwith, and put on their ringing-dresses, which were nothing more than flannel drawers and jackets made of the same—when I come to this part of the story, I can't help laughing, Mr. Wild, because there's an end of it; for all we had to do to win the two hundred guineas was, to walk off with their breeches, in which we found other money, watches, snuff-boxes, &c. enough to make it a very pretty adventure."

"Ha, ha! quite an amusing little affair; and who is to render an account to me of the joke in a commercial view?"

"What do you mean, Mr. Wild?"

"Who's to bring me my regulars? for though I did not propose the lay, I must have my share of it, and that you know."

"Certainly, Mr. Wild, every man of us understands that, and Blueskin is to be with you this afternoon with the swag."

"Right; and now, Jack, I have a job for you. You know, my lad, I took a great fancy to you, years ago, and I always promised your mother I'd make something of you."

"You certainly have been very kind to me, Mr. Wild."

"Kind to you, my boy—there are few things I would not do to serve you."

"Oh, sir, if I only dared hope—"

"Hope, eh, hope what?"

"You'll be angry, sir, if I tell you."

"Not I—what is it?"

"Why, sir, since you have so often expressed yourself thus kindly towards me, I'll venture to tell you. Miss Fanny, sir—"

"What of her?"

"I—a—I hope you won't be angry—but I'm very much in love with her, sir."

" Ha, ha!" roared Jonathan, though it was anything but a pleasant laugh to hear; " you in love with my daughter? Hound! son of a thief! your utter and damnable ignorance is your only excuse."

The young man was so surprised by this sudden and unexpected outbreak, that he could find no words in reply, but, speechless, sat and, gaped at the great thieftaker, who seemed to foam with rage and wounded dignity.

At this moment there was a gentle tap at the door, and a sweet musical voice was heard to say without,

" May I come in, papa ?"

And an assent having been given, the thieftaker's daughter entered the apartment.

" Come here, Fan," cried Jonathan to the beautiful intruder who sailed over the floor like a duchess on a court birthday, " and give your own answer to the suit that is preferred; this young gentleman is in love with you. Let us hear the reply that Fanny Wild will make to Jack Sheppard."

There could not well be a greater contrast than was afforded in that little group. Jack had risen as the young lady made her appearance, and now stood leaning against the back of the chair in which he had been seated. He was some nineteen or twenty years of age; dark in face, and wiry, but short in figure ; but he needs no long description, for his portrait has been often painted. Not so with Fanny Wild.

Tall, slight, and of graceful, supple figure, it was the extreme elegance of her carriage, and naturally aristocratic mien, which first struck attention. Then you looked into her face, and it was so youthful, so sweetly fresh and fair, you wondered how you could have gazed on her and noted aught else.

Her features were very regular ; but her eyes were so surpassingly beautiful, that they seemed to absorb admiration : blue as the wild harebell, and fringed with the longest, silkiest, and blackest lashes that ever cast a gentle shadow upon peach-like cheeks, they played and languished, and laughed, or killed, or seemed to do whatever most they pleased.

Her mouth was ripe and ruddy, and curtly formed, and parted upon a set of brilliant teeth, while every dimple that sat about her mouth and rounded little chin, seemed to invite a separate love to its soft resting-place. Her powdered wig heightened the effect of her gloriously transparent complexion, and the little black velvet hat she wore above it was ornamented with a sweeping ostrich feather, and looped with a diamond buckle, that gave her an elegant finish. The dress of her day became her, and she wore it after the most approved mode.

" Am I answerable, papa, for the folly of this, or any other gentleman?"

" Not answerable *for* it, miss," said Jack; " but you may vouchsafe to reply *to* it, presumptuous as it may seem."

" It is not my intention, papa, to wed any gentleman in trade, and if I object to one thing more than another, it is chips."

" Chips, Miss Fanny !" and poor Jack keenly felt the retort.

" You have had your answer, sir," said Jonathan; " now never dare, by hint of word or look, to allude to this subject again, or I'll clap you in the stone box, pass you over to the next sessions, and hang you at Tyburn before you have an idea of it."

" Sir, I meant no offence."

" Bah ! forget it. Fan, my girl, you have no business here while your father is engaged in his professional pursuits; but there, never mind, now you are here, you need not go; I have no secrets to talk of, though it might happen otherwise. Sheppard, I want you to be at the ' Bowl and Trencher,' in the Mint, to-night, at nine o'clock. You will see a young pale-faced man, in a light green suit; get into conversation with him, and keep him there till I join you."

" It shall be done, Mr. Wild."

" And hark you, Jack—"

" Yes, sir."

" No more nonsense, Jack ; you understand."

Jack coloured, and his eyes were fixed on the ground as he walked towards the door.

" Jack," said the prettiest voice in all the world, " I'm not angry with you, but don't make a fool of yourself again; there's a good fellow," and Fanny, who was cuddling her father's arm, and just swaying herself in the most coquettish and elegant manner possible, extended her hand, adding, " You may kiss the tip."

Jack availed himself of the lady's condescension, and quitted the room.

" Well, miss, and what's brought you here, pray ?"

" Why, papa, mamma was coming into town—and, as I wanted a few things from Houndsditch and Little Britain, in the way of laces and gold thread, I took a seat in the carriage with her, and while mamma was shopping, I walked on here, having bought what I wanted, and I expect she will be here in a few minutes herself. I could not come to town, pupsey-pa," and she kissed her yellow-faced and pock-marked parent in such a way as would have driven any young man mad to see; " I could not come to town without giving you a call, and I'll be bound you have something nice for lunch in that great cupboard.'

" No, my dear, I've nothing—there is nothing there, I assure you."

" Oh, but I will see ; the key is in the door, and I will see."

And before Jonathan could prevent her, she tripped across, and threw open the cupboard.

The next instant a piercing scream escaped her, the blood fled from her cheeks, and all insensible and white, she fell into her father's arms.

Three human heads, on a bloody cloth, were there upon the shelf; the eyes starting, and the mouth, drawn away from the teeth, grinning horribly. It was a sight to startle even stronger nerves than those of a young lady of eighteen.

"Curses on it!" muttered Wild, " I did not know the rascals' heads were there ; but one has such terrible sacrifices to make in the cause of science and friendship—damn you," he added, as he shook his fist at the three heads, " to frighten my girl in that way ; how should she know that we all had a pipe together the night before last, and you were only worked off at Tyburn yesterday morning ?"

He managed to close the cupboard, and ring a bell for assistance. It was not answered immediately by a servant, but a young gentleman of very elegant appearance entered the room.

" Why the devil didn't you—I beg pardon, my lord, but I had rung for assistance, and—a—"

" You very naturally took me for one of the servants—no apology, I beg. I have been waiting in your visiting-room for some time, and did not care to dance attendance any longer, so walked straight here, knowing the way—but, dear me, what is the matter ?" and the young nobleman advancing, his eyes fell upon the sweet countenance and graceful figure of the thief taker's daughter.

" Nothing of any moment, my lord; my little Fanny here has been frightened, that's all."

" Your little Fanny, Mr. Wild ?"

" Yes, my lord ; my Fan—my girl—my child—is there any law why I should not be a father ?"

The young nobleman did not seem to be listening to this, so wrapt was he in contemplation of the fainting maid before him.

" How beautiful! how heavenly beautiful ! " escaped him.

Jonathan Wild turned and fixed his savage eyes upon the handsome intruder, and then burst out in a loud hoarse tone—

"What do you mean, my lord? who do you call beautiful? I'd have you to know that this is no demirep, to listen to your lordship's mock heroics, but a plain man's plain and honest child, who, when her time comes, will marry, in a plain and prosy way, some plain fellow, who will love her, and whom she will love. You must not think her beautiful, my lord, or, if you do, think at the same time of the ugliness, the villany, the might, the power, and the strong right arm of her father, the thief taker general."

Mrs. Wild now came to Jonathan's help, and a deaf old crone made her appearance in answer to the bell. As the mother bore her daughter from the office, Fanny, for the first time since she had seen that which had alarmed her, unclosed her eyes, and her gaze met the handsome features of the young nobleman. Her heart received the impression of his manly beauty, and a single glance had engraven it there for ever.

"Sit down, my lord, sit down; excuse my haste just now, but you will forgive me, I know; I have only one, sir, and all my affection is centered in that little girl; you can't think how much I love her; I am jealous of the wind when it blows upon her. Hark you," he added to the old woman, "if you don't get over that deafness of yours, I shall send you back to the workhouse again."

The reply was inaudible, but all the way down stairs the crone kept muttering to herself—

"The workus, eh? in course it's the workus, when we is old, which-so-be 'tis, there's nothink but the workus. Ah! the world has no gratitude, 'specially to charwomen; it briles and griddles, and briles and griddles again, and you only loses your fat the more you flares up. How 'tis altered, to be sure; nobody as seed me now would think I was the same woman; howsoever,

> "Bumby is my name,
> 　　England is my nation,
> 　London is my dwelling-place,
> 　　And the Lord is my salvation."

## CHAPTER XIX.

### FANNY WILD'S FIRST LOVE.

FANNY WILD had ascertained that the young gentleman she had seen in her father's office was called Lord Lisle. He was the nephew of the nobleman of that name mentioned in the earlier portion of this work; the late celebrated Lord Lisle had died abroad, and this youth succeeded to the title while yet a minor, and at college. The business that had taken him upon more than one occasion to the house of Jonathan Wild is easily explained. Our hero very often inducted aristocratic youths into the dark scenes of London life, and with that curiosity which is so common and pardonable in youth. Lord Lisle had commenced the initiative process with some eagerness.

Madam and Miss Wild returned to Kilburn soon after the recovery of the latter lady. Her mother had explained to her that what she had seen was only some of her father's nonsense, as she called it, but which it was very wrong of him to leave about: but there, that was always his way, when he hanged a friend he would always have his head afterwards. To be sure, it was a very gratifying thing to the poor gentleman who was going to suffer, to know his head-piece would be preserved in spirits, or his skull handsomely polished, and stuck in a glass case, side by side with the fatal rope; but if her father would persist in these little attentions, complimentary as they might be to the deceased, and gratifying to the collector, he ought, at least, to keep his cupboards locked before the nasty things were fit to be seen.

The late doctress was less sensitive than her charming daughter.

Now, the young lady had a waiting-woman named Nancy; and a very model of a waiting-maid she was; much perter, and much more natural than any of the young ladies in the same station of life we so often find ourselves introduced to by the modern dramatist.

" Nancy," said her young mistress, when she reached her bed-room " Nancy, I am very unwell, and I want you to be very clever immediately."

" Good gracious, Miss Fanny, why what do you take me for—you don't think I am a M.D. in petticoats, do you? If you are very bad,

Miss Fanny, I'll go for the doctor, but I won't recommend anything myself."

" You are a fool."

" Thank you, miss."

" I am very well; go away, I'll dress myself—I don't want you."

" Yes, miss."

Nancy went to the door, and her fingers were on the handle when Fanny stamped her little foot in a fury, and cried out—

" Where are you going? Come back—how dare you leave me?"

" Didn't you say I was to go, miss?"

" And you had the impudence to take me at my word! there, get along, do."

These contrary directions for the moment puzzled the maid, but she was used to the airs and graces of the spoiled beauty, and she thought she knew how to manage her. She returned to the chair in which the other was sitting, and said—

" You look vastly pretty to-day, Miss Fanny; you have such a charming color that—"

" If you flatter me in that ridiculous way, I'll tell mamma to give you a month in advance, and order your boxes to be put on the step of the door immediately."

" Somebody has been vexing you, miss."

" No, they haven't."

" Something has happened unpleasant."

" No, there hasn't."

" Then you must be ill."

" No, I'm not."

" Then I have it, Miss Fan, and you were right at first, and I will be your doctor. I know the disease quite well; I brought two young ladies through it, and a maiden aunt—though I shan't be three and twenty till next birthday. You are in love."

" Eh?"

" Don't deny it, miss; I can take my oath to it. You have exhibited what my first master, Doctor Diddlewig, used to call the promonitory symptom—you are as cross as two sticks."

" Nancy!"

" Oh, now I know you are. I don't mind what you say, for I can bring you through it quicker than the meazles; if you were to tell me to go directly, I wouldn't do it, now I know what is the matter with you. Who is the gentleman?"

" He isn't a gentleman at all, Nancy."

" Good gracious! he isn't a sweep, I'm sure.  Oh, 1 hope to good-ness you wouldn't think of doing anything of that kind.  I am not a rich thieftaker's daughter, and I'm not a beauty, but I wouldn't have a chummy if there wasn't another man in existence."

" What are you talking of?"

" You said he wasn't a gentleman, miss, and anybody beneath a gentleman is a sweep."

" He is a nobleman, Nancy."

" A what?"

" A nobleman."

" You take away my breath."

" Is there anything extraordinary in a young nobleman falling in love with me? am I so old, or so ugly, girl?"

" Certainly not, miss."

" And it is not because I am the daughter of the great Wild, in-stead of the great Marlborough, or the great anybody else, that I am not to be loved."

" Of course not."

" Very well ; then there is nothing out of the way in my marrying a lord," and the young lady gave a series of double knocks upon the floor, with one foot crossed over the other, in it's high-heeled satin shoe, and with the little diamond buckle just showing in front.

" And what's the nobleman's name, miss?"

" Viscount Lisle."

" O Gemini! I am so glad."

" Why ?"

" Because a friend of mine, Miss Wickshift, has a mamma for a housekeeper there."

" Do you mean, Nancy, that your friend's mother is Lord Lisle's housekeeper?"

" I do, miss, and through her I shall be able to get you any infor-mation, at any time, you require."

" Nancy."

" Yes, miss."

" There is a grand masquerade to night, at the Pantheon : it is said that many of the young nobility will be there."

" I see it in a moment, Miss Fan ; Lord Lisle will be there, and so must we."

" What do you say ?"

" I say we must go."

" But what would be the use of our going, if we did not discover those we went to see.   You know perfectly well that everybody will be masked, and supposing that his lordship goes, unless we know his dress, we shall be unable to find him."

ι  " I'll bet my head  that he goes," said Nancy quite confidently, " and as to his dress, why I can  discover that by the means I speak of."

" And what excuse can we possibly make to get away?"

" None, Miss Fan ; its of no use making excuses to get away.  You must have  a  head-ache, and that will be your excuse to get to bed early.   You can  bid  your  mamma good night, and then easily slip down from your  room with me.   You can as easily now send me to London, and I can procure you the information you require, and bring back the dresses for us.   Your  mamma will not want me in the mean time."

" But there's no stage running now."

" I have only to go to the ' Barley Mow,' and young Will Cooper will find me a conveyance to take me there and back, in less time than the stage would run one way."

" You conquer difficulties easily."

" When it is an errand of love."

" And nothing seems to daunt you, Nancy."

" I am your waiting-maid, miss."

It was  forthwith arranged  between them, that Nancy should go to London, ascertain all the particulars that she could glean, and settle matters accordingly.

Away she went, under the direction of Will Cooper, and leaving the conveyance at some distance from the residence of Lord Lisle, which was at the west end of London, as that part on the Holborn side of Tottenham  Court-road was then called, she dropped in upon the mother of her friend, as she said to the old lady, " quite promiscuously."

" Bless me, and I am so glad to see you," exclaimed Mrs. Wickshift ; " I'm not at all busy to-day, and can sit and chatter with you for an hour or two with pleasure, for we have no company to-day, and that makes all the  difference : his lordship is going to the masquerade to-night."

" Oh, oh," thought Nancy, " so far, so good ; then I have learned something, at all events."

In the course of their interview, his lordship's valet, Mr. Watson, was introduced, and between Mr. Watson and Miss Nancy, a pleasant little flirtation was established. The valet informed the chambermaid as a matter of great secrecy, that he intended to go too, and his master was to wear a green domino, trimmed with gold, while he meant to disport himself in blue and silver. Then the chambermaid informed him in secret also, that her young mistress, the great thieftaker's daughter, was over head and ears in love with Lord Lisle, and meant to visit the Pantheon, for the purpose of meeting the object of her love, and she, Miss Nancy, was to be the partner of her adventure. In a whisper, now, as Mrs. Wickshift entered the room with one of the under servants and the tea equipage, she told him how both he and his master would recognise them by their dresses.

Mr. Watson was delighted; he had not encountered such a charming *Grisette* as Miss Nancy for many a day; but he thought to himself, at the same time, what a capital thing it would be for him, if he could, by any good fortune, secure for himself the approving admiration of a young lady, reported to be at once so wealthy and beautiful as Miss Wild. Miss Nancy, on her part, was infatuated with Mr. Watson; but she could not help imagining to herself how much more delightful it would be, if she could only ensnare the Viscount.

" To trap an heiress," thought Watson.

" To catch a Viscount," mentally ejaculated Nancy. And the two hugged themselves in the luxury of their two separate ideas.

As early as she could with decency, the chambermaid left, and having gained the vehicle, sought out a *costumier's*, and procured two dresses for herself and mistress, exactly alike. When she had arrived at Kilburn, she had not been away longer than the time she stated she should be when she started. Fanny was much pleased with the diligence of her waiting woman, who omitted, however, the full particulars of the episode of the valet. Mr. Wild, who returned home at all hours of the night, had one key of the street door, and the latch was always arranged for him. Now there was another key, and to procure this was no great difficulty. Nancy agreed to manage that part of the business, her young mistress having approved of the dresses selected.

All that evening, Fanny was very poorly, and her mother suggested various remedies for the head-ache of her daughter. Nothing would do, however, but going to bed, and as Madame Wild said she should not sit up late herself, she the more readily consented to Fanny's early retiring.

" Good night, my dear."

" God bless you, mamma." And Nancy, looking as demure as a
Methodist parson, lighted her young lady up to bed. The maid's own
room was an inner one, communicating with Fanny's. Instead of
undressing, the two girls began to array themselves as daintily as
might be, and in the middle of their toilet, heard Mrs. Wild retire to
her own room, which was, fortunately, at the back of the house,
where she could not hear the latching of the street door.

In the course of an hour from that time, when the house was supposed to be at rest, Fanny and her maid tripped lightly down the
stairs, and got safely into the garden.

At the turning of the lane, Will Cooper was stationed with the
vehicle, as agreed upon between him and Nancy, and the tickets had
been purchased where the dresses were hired, and ere midnight, our
young adventuresses were in the gaily-lighted promenade of the
Pantheon.

## CHAPTER XX.

### THE MASQUERADE AT THE PANTHEON.

NOTWITHSTANDING Mr. Watson's intention, if possible, to carry off
the thieftaker's daughter, he still thought it necessary to the proper
developemnt of his scheme, that he should inform his master of that
young lady's weakness in his favor, and her intention to be at the
masquerade.

He also stated that her maid would accompany her ; through whom
he had learned the intelligence. This led to the point that Mr.
Watson was fishing for, his master's authorizing him to be present at
the masquerade. His lordship was delighted most unexpectedly ; it
was beyond his most sanguine hope that the charming creature whom
he had encountered, for the first time, that morning, in her father's
office, and whom to look at, in Jonathan's eyes, was almost an offence,
should reciprocate his sudden passion. It was rather startling, too ;

the young lady had merely caught one glimpse of his person, gone home, and loved, and now proposed to meet him at a place of public entertainment. It was sharper practice than his lordship had been used to, and, despite of his sudden love, he could not help deeming her conduct somewhat unmaidenly. Before he condemned her, however, he was particular in his inquiries of Watson, and when he heard that the chambermaid had delivered no message from her mistress, but, indeed, as it appeared, broken the confidence with which she had been entrusted, he no longer regarded Miss Fanny as guilty of any flagrant impropriety.

"And now, Watson, let me see the dresses, that I am to choose from."

"There are only two, my lord, two dominoes, the one green, and the other blue; the green one is the handsomer—your lordship will wear that, of course."

"I don't know; let me see them both."

Contrary to Mr. Watson's anticipation Lord Lisle chose the blue and silver, and told him to wear the green and gold.

"Egad!" thought the valet, "I was not so sharp as I ought to have been; yet my luck jumps with my wishes, I ought to have told the girl the wrong suit, and so it appears I have; although I didn't mean it. Miss Wild will expect his lordship in the green and gold, and I shall be a happy fellow."

Midnight at a masquerade in the old Pantheon! A rare scene of life and light, and brilliant fashion, aristocratic depravity, money assumption, and vulgar buffonery. In the public assembly of that day there was a much greater admixture of classes than in our own time. It would puzzle a conjuror to find the wife or daughter of a nobleman among the characters in the promenade at one of Jullien's *Bals Masque*, but it was not so rare a circumstance, the attendance of aristocratic dames at the like entertainments of a century, or a century and a half ago. Stiff and formal, and precise as appear the starched portraits of our grandmothers—though it may sound like high treason to say as much—there's very little doubt that those respectable old ladies with their white wigs, and paint, powder, and patches, their high heels, their short petticoats, and their remarkably low dresses, were not a bit better, but, indeed, somewhat worse than the present feminine generation. They gave their time quite as much to flirtation and scan-mag, more to the vapours and strong waters, while fans and masks have brought untold miseries upon deceived fathers and cornuted husbands.

The old Pantheon was one of the most spacious, as it was the best frequented of any other public place in London. It was especially so in the winter time, when out-of-door entertainments were less to be enjoyed. The balls and masquerades there held were, as we have before said, attended both by beauty and fashion, and upon the night of which we write, there was a large assemblage of both. Conspicuous among many, both from the elegance of their attire, and the gracefulness with which they moved in the stately cotillion, were the charming figures of two young ladies, who wore over their full evening costume dominoes that completely enveloped them, fastened only at the throat, and which were sometimes waved aside in the dance, and wore made of white watered silk, edged all round with a fluting of pale pink satin. The girls were so nearly of a height, and apparently so much of an age, that several of the visitors concluded them to be sisters. To a close observer, however, notwithstanding the manner in which one of them imitated the other, it was easy to distinguish the superior grace of her companion.

The one was Fanny Wild—the other Nancy, her waiting-maid. They were unattended by any gentleman, but they found themselves eagerly sought after as partners in the dance. The cotillion was over; the gallants with whom our maidens had danced had promenaded them through the rooms, and led them to seats. They took an early opportunity of whispering each other.

" It is growing very late, Nancy, and I see nothing of his lordship : are you sure you were correct in the description?"

" I am sure, Miss Fanny, that I remember correctly what I was told; but of course, I cannot tell how true Mr. Watson's statement was."

" Dear me! Nancy, but if you were not quite sure, it was very ridiculous to bring me here. What did you say he was to wear?"

" Mr. Watson, Miss?"

" Mr. Watson—Mr. Fiddlestick! No, wench, not Mr. Watson, or any such trumpery person, but the young and elegant Lord Lisle."

" Green and gold, miss."

" There is a green and gold domino at this moment entering the room, and see, attended by another in blue and silver."

" Our gentlemen, Miss Fanny, as I live. Bless us and save us, how my heart leaps !"

" Your heart ! Why you are not in love with his lordship too ?"

" Certainly not. I know my place, Miss Fan, but a body may

have her feelings, if she is not a young lady herself, only a young lady's lady."

"And for whom, pray, are your feelings interested?"

"Mr. Watson, Miss Fanny, is the nicest gentleman I have seen for many a day," responded Nancy, with a simper.

"Oho! are you there, my girl?—with all my heart," laughed Fanny, in return.

"I was a fool," thought the maid, "not to tell her it was her lover in the blue and silver, and then I might have secured this lordship;

No. 10.

but I suppose they would have found each other out, so it is best as it is."

The new comers had remarked our maidens almost as soon as they were themselves observed.

" They are there, Watson, by all that's fortunate," exclaimed his lordship, who was attired in the blue and silver which he had chosen, while his man wore the green and gold ; but who the deuce is to know the mistress from the maid—their dresses are exactly alike ?"

" We shall easily discover that, my lord, though our *inamoratas* are, apparently, twins."

" Our what ?" inquired the young nobleman, haughtily.

" Our *inamoratas*, my lord."

" Why, you scoundrel, you haven't presumed to fall in love with Miss Wild ?"

" Certainly not, my lord ; but a man may be allowed his feelings, if he is only a gentleman's gentleman."

" And to whom have you engaged them, sir ?"

" Miss Nancy, the waiting-woman, my lord, is one of the sweetest creatures I ever encountered," said the valet.

" Aha ! is that the case ?—well, I have no objection, I promise you."

Strange, how the thoughts, and even the words of people, will accord at times !

The nobleman and his valet now approached where the young girls were sitting, the Viscount whispering Watson to keep close beside him, and engage the maid in conversation.

" .Can it be possible," said his lordship, advancing, " that so much grace is suffered to repose in idleness, instead of lending additional charms to the dance ?"

This was a speech vapid enough, in all conscience, but it was in the over-strained fashion of the day, and Lord Lisle must not, therefore, be regarded the worse for it.

" That's Mr. Watson," whispered Nancy, " by the blue and silver."

" He is a very impertinent fellow," hastily replied Fanny, " and I wonder that his lordship should encourage him. We are not over-looked, sir," she rejoined, " and it's our own pleasure if we do not dance every time."

" That's the maid," said his lordship, aside, to Watson, " that's your beauty, from the pertness of her reply ; draw her off, Watson, as decently as you can manage it."

Watson accordingly stationed himself beside Fanny, while his lordship addressed himself to Nancy.

" The rooms are very crowded ; are they not?" suggested the valet.

" What a very natural and beautiful remark," thought Fanny ; " how easy it is to distinguish between a nobleman and his valet."

" Very crowded indeed, my lord."

Miss Wild, be it remembered, had never heard the voice of Lord Lisle.

" Egad ! it is all right," mentally ejaculated Watson; " there must be something devilish distinguished about me, that she takes me for the Viscount at the first start off, but I'll profit by it at all events ; I hope his lordship won't discover that he has got hold of the maid instead of the mistress."

All this passed through the fellow's mind at a glance, while he replied—

" My lord ! you know me, then?"

" Ah ! we who are not in the habit of daily meeting with noblemen, do not fail to recognise those whom we have once seen."

" And you are, then ?"

" Nay, it is not because I know you, my lord, that you are so easily to discover me ; it is the privilege of the mask to preserve the incog.; I am here to night to see and judge of others, not to be known and judged myself."

" Then I must let you know that we noblemen cannot encounter beauty without its impression remaining with us, as the impression of nobility remains with you, and I must tell you who you are."

The valet was beginning to talk unmeaning compliment with almost the ease of a fine gentleman.

" Your lordship surely cannot know that," said Fanny, with some degree of trepidation; for, in sending Nancy to the house of his lordship, and, afterwards, going herself to the masquerade, she had no intention of compromising herself—at all events, for some time to come—by letting the Viscount know as much.

" Do you think that I should have seen you only this morning, and forgotten you so soon ?—you are Miss Wild."

And the valet seized her hand.

" Oh, heavens! my lord!" said Fanny, rising ; " let me go. Now I see the folly of my act—what will you think of me ? Let me go. Nancy, we must return, and instantly."

But Nancy was nowhere to be seen. In company with the blue and silver domino she was in another part of the rooms.

"You see your maid has left you, but do not be alarmed—my—hem! my fellow will take care of her."

Fanny knew not how to act, and, for a moment stood irresolute; then Watson, taking her little hand, drew her arm through his, and led her down the room.

To return to Lord Lisle and the waiting-maid:

"As Miss Wild is not attended by any other than her servant, she will, perhaps, allow a friend of her father's to show her any courtesy in his power."

"Stars and garters!" thought Nancy, "he takes me for my young lady! and I shall be a viscountess in my own right."

"My father has many friends—how shall I call you."

"The world calls me Lisle; I saw you this morning, when you were very far from well; let me hope that you sustained no very ill effects from the alarm you experienced."

"You see me here to-night, and that is an argument in my favor."

"And your father, do you expect him here?"

"No; the old gentleman has not a notion but what I am at home and asleep, in my own little bed—and that's no word of a story," added Nancy to herself with a smile.

"You have been tempted then from the retirement and monotony of your father's house at Kilburn, to enjoy an hour at the masquerade, in the old Pantheon?"

"Since so well-informed and gay a gentleman as yourself, my lord—for you see I remember your title—can be drawn here, you must not wonder that a poor weak girl, who never sees anything, should be tempted for once to play truant; but, perhaps, my lord, it was not the mere masquerade alone that lured me here."

"What else could it be?"

"Oh, my lord, that would be too much to confess," and there was that in the manner of the waiting maid, that conveyed a great deal more than her words. Coupling these with the statement of his valet, the Viscount might be pardoned the vanity of supposing himself beloved by the thieftaker's daughter.

"Miss Wild, forgive me," said he, "I know not when an opportunity may again occur in which to declare to you the passion of my heart; until to-night I have seen you but once, and those few moments were to me whole years of love, believe me—"

"Oh, my lord, I know you don't mean it, and you are a terrible gentleman to flatter."

This, which was said with a half giggle, and simper, brought Lord Lisle from his seventh heaven to earth again; but Nancy, who was an adept in such matters, perceived, at once, as much, by his attitude, though she could not see his face.

Our quartette of lovers retained their masks while they played at cross purposes; Nancy, therefore, threw all the pathos of which she was capable into her voice, and murmured with so much fascination and simplicity—

"Ah, my lord, what answer shall a weak and innocent girl make to a great nobleman when he declares that he loves her ?"

"This: that difference of station cannot affect true love, and she places her faith in the honor of the man who woos her."

"She does," replied Nancy, in a low, trembling voice, and Lord Lisle drew her to him, and these two also passed down the room.

An hour afterwards, and in one of the ante-rooms might have been heard whispering voices.

"Confound it," said somebody, "I am convinced that my wife is here, and I will find it out. It isn't because she is old that she has given up the flirtations of her youth. I am not very young myself, but I feel the blood sparkling in me still, sometimes; that was a charming little creature dressed as a Tyrolese peasant; I never saw such a charming pair of ancles in my life, fairy ladders, leading up to—well, never mind."

This old gentleman, who had a fancy for talking to himself in the dark, for the room was nearly so, hearing somebody approach, crept into a corner, while two of the masqueraders entered the place.

"Do not hesitate, dearest," said Lord Lisle, for he it was ; "the carriage is at at the door ; love and happiness await us."

The answer of his companion was inaudible to the old gentleman, across whose brain came the thought, while he stood in a fever behind the door—"that's my wife, and that is a young rake persuading her to elope with him; but I'll have my revenge."

"Hush !" whispered Lord Lisle ; "hush, darling Fanny—keep close to me; somebody else is in the room."

"There can't be a doubt about it ; he called her Fanny, and that settles the thing," thought the husband on the prowl.

"I know that he is here," said an old lady to herself, as she felt her way in ; "though he did tell me he was not coming, but I knew better, and, old as he is, his age did not prevent him from following that little girl about with the very short petticoats ; he little thinks

I am here, but I shall catch him." Man and wife had probably caught the habit of muttering their thoughts, the one from the other.

"That's Fanny's voice," said the husband, "though I can't make out what she says."

"That is my villain," said the old woman, "mumbling somewhere, though I can't tell what he is doing here in the dark."

"Remain here a moment," whispered Lord Lisle to his companion, "I will return directly I have ordered the carriage ; take off your mask, you will find it too warm else."

He found his way to the door and was gone.

There was another couple now in that little ante-room.

"My lord, I implore of you to let me return. Give me a year— a month—but one short week—I must go home, where is my servant ?"

"I will find her for you, sweet Fanny."

"That fellow is Fannying my wife again," mumbled the old husband.

"There is my old fool of a hubby," returned the old wife.

"Hark !" said Fanny to Watson, "don't you hear somebody ?"

"No one that will interfere with us ; stay here a few moments while I see to the carriage, and find your waiting-woman. You can unloose your mask here, and breathe more freely."

Watson, the assumed lord, had followed in the steps of his master.

"I'll be shot if I don't find her," said the old gentleman, feeling his way, for it was not to be seen at all plainly. "Hist! Fanny!" whispered he.

There were three whispered "Yesses," in reply ; one from old Fanny, another from young Fanny, and a third from the pretended Fanny, neither of whom could, of course, recognise a voice, in that hushed tone of inquiry. Six hands were extended, and, as fate would have it, the ancient caught between his own the little palm of Miss Wild.

"Heavens ! how quick you have been."

"Did you think I should not find you ?" muttered the other.

"Hist, Fanny, Fanny."

Again those three "Yesses," were heard to respond, as Lord Lisle caught old Fanny with ardour by the wrist.

"I heard you at once, darling, but come, let us not delay. Oh, believe how much I love you," and he covered her hand with kisses.

"That's not my hubby," thought the old wife, "but if he is such a villain as to run after Tyrolese peasant girls, it would be flying in the face of Providence for me to be angry with a young gentleman for kissing my hand in the dark."

A third time, and "Fanny" was called, as softly as before, and the three "Yesses," were returned in different tones; old Fanny's was languishing, young Fanny's was pettish, and the pretendeded Fanny's was surprised.

She, the only one without a partner, was least confused, and heard the other two Fannys with wonder. Now, however, her hand was eagerly seized, and Watson implored her to lose no further time.

"How changed your voice, my lord, since you went out you have taken cold," said Miss Wild. "Now pray lead me to the coach, and we may meet Nancy as we pass through the rooms."

"My lord—the coach—Nancy!" cried the old husband, "why, what on earth does all this mean? You are not my wife."

A little scream broke from the lips of Fanny, and, at the same moment, almost the echo of it seemed to be heard in two places in the room.

"But you are young, by your voice, pretty by your figure," and the old fellow threw his arms about her waist, adding, as he attempted to kiss her, "and yielding, by your speech."

At this moment was heard the sound of people approaching, and a voice crying out,

"Come along, friends; let us throw a light upon the scene. They have been hopping about in the dark for the last half hour, like a parcel of cats in a cellar."

Now a gentleman, bearing a lighted candle in either hand, and followed by a laughing crowd of masqueraders, entered the room.

When a light was thrown upon the scene, and Fanny Wild looked up, and saw the puckered, bloated countenance of a white-headed old man, dressed as a youthful shepherd, and knew that he it was who had so lately wound his arms about her, and struggled hard to kiss her lips, she shrieked loudly, and rushing to the doorway, so sudden were her movements, that she made good her escape: a moment later and she might not have effected it.

If the surprise and horror of Fanny Wild were great, equally amazed felt Lord Lisle, and chagrined a thousand times more, when he beheld the thin and withered face of the old man's wife. He started from her, as he saw the thieftaker's daughter make good her exit, and attempted to follow her; the laughing mischief-makers with the lights prevented his egress.

The blood mounted within him, and he drew his sword, and exclaimed passionately, " Stand back, gentlemen: the man who stays me asks his own death."

They fell away a little on either side, and the passage was opened. The valet and chambermaid, their hands still affectionately intertwined, regarded each other with momentary surprise.

Mr. Watson was the first to recover his equanimity, as he whispered to Nancy—

" We have played the wrong cards; but the game isn't a bad one as it stands. Shall we remain partners, my dear?"

" I can only follow suit."

" Then come along, my poppet." The valet drew her arm through his, and walked towards the door.

" Make way, gentlemen, for man and wife."

" Lover and mistress, now, you mean," said the foremost who opposed them; " but as you may be the other hereafter, we won't prevent you going the same way, for one of the few times in your lives."

Watson and Nancy passed out with a slight cheer and the compliments of the party. Of our three pair of masqueraders, only one was left. With no loving eyes did they regard each other; but the old woman was, perhaps, the more politic of the two. She crossed to her husband, and said, so as not to be heard by the group,

" Had we not better do as they have done before us. You know that gentleman kissed me by mistake, and if you hold your tongue, and take me home directly, I'll say nothing about the Tyrolese peasant-girl, or the minx you were cuddling just now."

" Ugh !" growled the old man, " I knew you would be here, and its my belief you were going off with that young fellow."

" And if you come to that, you had an appointment with short-petticoats, and I knew you were coming."

" I was determined to find you out," said the husband.

" I was resolved to discover your iniquity."

" Heyday, and the devil rides upon a fiddle-stick," cried the leader of the masqueraders : " here is a genuine case of matrimony, my lads ; here are a couple, sparring and spitting to your hearts' content. I consider it is our duty to make them friends again."

" Ha, ha, bravo ! make the old people friends again."

" To effect which, my dear fellows," continued the leading rake, " we must make them dance a fandango together. Ho ! musicians, a fandango there."

" The musicians are putting away their instruments, sir," said a waiter, " and most of the company are gone."

" Fetch me a fiddler; I'll be damned if I go, or anybody else shall stir, till Darby and Joan here have had a fandango—a guinea for a fiddler."

" A fiddler! a fiddler! a fandango!" roared the crowd; and a fiddler was found to obey, for a gold-piece, the commands of the young bloods. The doors were shut; no soul was allowed to stir, and the old man and wife, hating, and almost spitting at each other, were compelled to take hands, and, to the laughter and amusement of the roysterers, perform the dance in hand, while they formed a ring about them. Nothing can well be conceived more grotesque than the forced capers of these vain and quarrelsome old fools. The lookers on roared themselves hoarse, and some began to caper too, catching the excitement from the dancers, who were spurred on, and not allowed to rest. At this moment, one who had, perhaps, taken too much wine, tripped, and measuring his length on the floor, knocked over both the candles, the only lights in the room.

There was darkness now upon the scene—let us draw a veil before the rest.

----

## CHAPTER XXI.

WHEN our heroine, for such is Fanny Wild in this portion of our story, at least, rushed from the ante-room, her immediate object was to seek the vehicle that had conveyed thither her maid and herself, and return forthwith to Kilburn. When she had once escaped the men who guarded the first doorway, she had no difficulty in reaching the outer entrance in the Oxford-road; but there she stood upon the steps, and the cold wind blew upon her, and she knew not how to proceed, saluted, as she was, with the cries " Chair, chair, my lady?— fetch your ladyship's carriage any part, your ladyship?—link boy, marm ?" &c. She was distracted by the many voices, the glare of torches, and the trampling of feet. She knew not where to find the particular vehicle which had brought her there.

" What is the name, miss ?" said an old linkman in attendance.

" Wild," replied Fanny, mechanically.

" Miss Wild's carriage," ran along the line, and was repeated by fifty voices.

At length there was a movement, and " Miss Wild's carriage stops the way," was heard, as the lumbering coach was guided to the door. She ran towards it, and was speedily seated within.

" Where to, ma'am ?"

" Oh, anywhere away from this."

" Now then, Jarvy, you are to drive anywhere, and the lady will pay the turnpikes."

A shout of laughter broke from those rude men, and recalled Fanny's scattered ideas.

" Home, home," she said.

" Your ladyship's linkman," said one man, thrusting in his head for a gratuity.

" I fetched the coach, miss," said another, poking in his head from an opposite window.

" And I called him, miss," cried a third.

" Oh, do go away—I haven't any money—please," and Fanny threw herself back upon the seat, and put her two hands before her face.

Will Cooper, who acted as coachman, threw a couple of shillings upon the pavement, after this dreadful confession was repeated by the swarm about, and drove off as well as he could. At first he had no easy matter to wend his way out of the crowd of conveyances, but Will accomplished it at length, and, pursuing his way along the Oxford-road, a little before they arrived at Tyburn, he turned off into the open country on the right. Now that they had passed from the bustle and turmoil, the shouts of men, the stamping of horses, the dull flare of oil lamps, and many torches, the thought stole suddenly that she had left her companion, Nancy, behind her. What should she do—go back ? Should she find her in that vast crowd ?—it was too late to think of it. What then was to be done ? She must go on without her, and Nancy, finding that she was gone, would, doubtless, follow her, without losing an instant ; she could experience no diffi-culty in obtaining a vehicle from such a place, and Fanny was pleased to think that before they started she had given her maid her purse. Over all the events, and even the words of that night, she pondered, and when she arrived at the turning of the lane by her father's house, the way had seemed so short, wrapt in thought as she had been, that she could hardly believe she had reached her destination. Telling Will Cooper that she was now at home, and lest the wheels of the carriage might be heard, she bade him " good night."

Responding to her wish he left her. Now she drew her little dress hood over her head and shoulders, and ran towards the garden. The gate yielded to her touch. Suddenly as though a pistol had been held to her heart, she recoiled. She remembered that she had not the key with which to re-enter the house. Her heart sank within her; she had dismissed the carriage; she was alone. It was nearly four o'clock in the morning. What should she do? The bright stars were yet in the heavens, but day would break soon; she looked to the east, and there was a little patch of grey, and a long thin line of faint light. Cold came the wind, and her teeth chattered as she stood there. Was her father at home?—if she were to knock he would know of it. She would not that he should become acquainted with her indiscretion of that night for the world. She would wait; Nancy must come soon. She crouched down upon the cold stone step of that wooden gateway, and the wall, and there she sat, hopeful for awh'', and though the morning air was cold, and chilled her to the bone, her thoughts were not of it. Now she heard a noise—a distant sound, it was true—but it seemed like a gallop of a horse in the distance. Nearer and nearer, now it came, alas! to die away—it was only the wind that rushed and swept over the high ground, and lost itself in the rustled branches of the trees.

Where was she?—had any mischance occured to her?—if so, good God! why she was the cause. Bitterly, oh, how bitterly, did she repent the folly of that night—folly, did she call it? it was worse, it was a crime. She saw it all, now; she would have given her right hand—her hopes—her life—to have recalled the last few hours. She wished that she was dead. Again the wind uprose, and caught her savagely, dashed her in the face, and beat about her rudely.

It was morning now, and in the light she looked down upon her dress of the masquerade; that dress which had so pleased her—which had won so much admiration for her, while she trod the gay and crowded hall. She could remain there no longer; she would drown herself in the fish-pond: she even went so far as to look at the water.

speedily discovered with whom, yet even in her confusion she did not think it necessary to mention the name of Lord Lisle. Jonathan was very harsh with her at first; but when she cried, and clung to him, and asked him to forgive her, he could not withstand her tears and entreaties, but took her in his arms and kissed her, and had her put to bed.

Now her room, usually so neat and well arranged, looked like the chamber of some careless female rake. Here on the toilet-table, amid scents and cosmetics, and powder-puffs, and little black patches, lay the huge powdered wig, and ribbons and laces, gold trinkets and paste. Upon one chair was cast the dress of the evening, and on another had been thrown the elegant white and pink domino, worn with so much pride over night. It had fallen from its place, and lay a little heap upon the floor.

Pale, but beautiful in her languor, she now reposed in bed. Her mother went to her, and tended her with all care.

"My father, my dear father; I must see him, mamma. I have something to ask of him which he must grant."

"A bad time, my dear, to ask your father anything. I would put it off, if I were you, for a few days."

"O, but I can't do anything of the kind, mamma, and papa will do it I know, for I shall put my arms about his neck and kiss him, and then whisper in his ear—he must."

"I think, Fanny dear, you will have but a poor chance with him this morning; he will never do it."

"How do you know that, ma'am?" said Jonathan, entering his daughter's room at the moment, his memorandum-book still in his hand; "how do you know what I shall grant my girl?"

"You will, papa, I know you will."

"Is it anything very unreasonable?"

"O no, not at all unreasonable," replied Fanny; "but I won't tell you a word about it till you promise me first." She held her father's great horny fist in her white little hand, and looked up at him so beseechingly, and with such fondness, that the rough nature of the bloodthirsty thieftaker was not proof against the coaxing of his only child.

"What is it, Fan? What is it, my girl?"

"Nancy—"

"What of her?" And the shadows fell darker on Jonathan's face at the mention of the waiting-woman's name.

"She is not so guilty as I am, papa; she has committed no dishonesty; she only obeyed my orders. You have forgiven me; you will forgive her too?"

"Eh? Why, confound the wench, I don't know what answer to make you. The girl has never been back all night; I can't get over that."

"But you would forgive her if she had: if, not daring to face you or mamma, she had stolen to me, and I had promised to intercede for her, and not turn her lost and characterless upon the world?"

Jonathan could make her no reply; he only pressed her hand.

"You may come in, Nancy, now," cried Fanny, and the waiting-maid made her appearance from the inner room, looking as smart and as pretty, and almost as perky as ever.

You would not have thought to see her there, after the games she had played over night. When Jonathan went to London that morning, he said to himself,

"It is a puzzle to me sometimes, how an ugly, villanous rascal like myself ever came to be father to such a good and pretty, loving and loveable little thing as my Fan."

The thieftaker's affection for his child was the redeeming evidence that Divine Nature wrote upon the man, endorsing him with his Creator's hand.

## CHAPTER XXII.

IN a small dark room, in a low neighbourhood, sat Blueskin and Jack Sheppard, smoking and conversing together.

"Queer crib this of yours, Blueskin—I can't say much for it."

"I don't want you, my lad; you see it suits me—very little rent to pay, and I does as I likes; I get two or three of these dog holes in different parts of the town, and I find them handy at times, besides, Jack, my lad, you need not be afraid of any one overhearing you, so tell us all about it, my boy, and what Jonathan wanted you for last night."

" Nothing particular, Blueskin, a little of his usual business, that's all. I told him you had to be in the Mint, and get into conversation with a cove, whose name I afterwards found out was Dibbs the cheese-monger. It seems his business had been going all wrong lately, for he was fond of sporting and gambling, and all sorts of things of that kind, and never looked after the shop. Well, Mr. Wild had heard of him—"

" As he hears of everything, Jack, but go on."

" Well, and having heard of him, he determined to make him answer his purpose; so, after putting two or three on to the cheesemonger, to pluck him as cleanly as they could, he meets the poor devil by acci-dent, at a tavern, as it would seem, and pretends to be very much con-cerned for him, and promises to see him again last night, at a house in the Mint, and think over something for his good meanwhile. I was sent first to sound this Dibbs, and preach up what a great man Wild was. I did it, Blueskin, but I didn't like it; it seemed like baiting a trap for the man."

" Why, so it was."

" That's how I looked at it; however, he bit, and when Jonathan came, the butterman was as down on his luck and as humble as a chap could well be. Jonathan pretended to pity him, and treating him to drink, sat down, as he said, to advise with him. There was Dibbs between the two of us, for, of course, I was to echo all that Wild said. A great many schemes were proposed for the flat's benefit, and of course, none of them would do: at last, when the fellow was quite desperate, Jonathan, slapping him upon the shoulder, said, ' Zounds, if you can't do anything else, why don't such a big dashing fellow as yourself take to the road?' ' How can I?' answered the poor devil, ' without a rap in the world, even if I were so inclined. Where's the horse and the snappers to come from.' This was just what Jonathan wanted, so he put some fly to hiring everything in a minute, and telling him there was none of his people out on the Edgware-road, and that I would see him properly mounted, starts him off at once on that lay, and so the cheesemonger was turned into a gentleman. Well, as we heard afterwards, when he had loitered about the road for some time, he saw one man on horseback coming towards him, without any servants or attendants, which proved to be a peaceable citizen. Dibbs ventured to stop him, and commanding him to deliver, the citizen sur-rendered all the money he had without any words, which proved to be

nine guineas; then Dibbs made the best of his way home to the Mint, where he found us ready to receive him. He gave us an account of what he had done, and what he had got, and all the circumstances, thinking he had behaved himself very handsomely for a beginner. Jonathan praised him too, and for his encouragement, took from him—how many guineas, do you suppose, Blueskin, out of the nine?"

"Why, I know he's a d—d unconscionable dog, Jack; say five."

"He kept seven for himself, and gave the cheesemonger two as a mark of his favour."

No. 11.

"Confound the fellow: why, what did Dibbs say, eh Jack?"

"Why, he said, very naturally, Blueskin, that this dividend, as he called it, was a little unequal, and that he, who ventured all, should have had the greatest share of the booty; but Jonathan told the poor butterman, now that he was initiated, that he had become his subject, nay, his slave; that he had power of life and death over him, and that so far from murmuring at what he took from him, that it was his opinion he should think himself very much obliged, winding up by saying loudly, this was the way he was always served by a parcel of ungrateful rascals, after he had put bread in their mouths."

"Ha, ha! I can't help laughing, Jack, though I pities the poor *Romanee* from the wery bottom of my buzzum; I can't help laughing, I say, at the great man's impudence; take my word for it, Jack, I have lived longer in the world than you, my man, and this sort of thing can't go on. I don't mean little puddling things like the cheesemonger's and his nine guineas; I mean the villany that keeps them going."

"Why, what do you think, then, Blueskin, that Jonathan will ever come to be hanged?"

"As certain as you are sitting there; unless one of the boys interferes with the law, and drives a knife into him beforehand."

"But he has so much power—such friends among the lawyers, and justices, and great folks."

"They can't stand too much, Jack; there is such a thing as going too far in this world. A little frog may blow himself out till he fancies himself a wery fine figure; and wery well he may look, for a time; but, if he blows beyond that ere pint, he'll bust; now that's just where Mr. Wild is."

"I used to think he'd been very kind to me,' said Jack, "and that I was much indebted to him, but I see now that it was only done to serve himself. I'm sure I've no cause to love him, and his treatment of me yesterday morning."

"Eh—what? did he ill-treat you yesterday morning? then how comed you to forget it last night?"

"I did not forget it, Blueskin; I have not forgotten; it I shall never forget it," and the blood showed in Jack's dark face, and his eyes lighted up instantly.

"Why, I have not heard of this, Jack."

"Why, it was about Fanny; for, to tell you the truth, I can't help loving that girl, though she did not treat me much better than her father."

" Then why don't you have your revenge, Jack ?"

" How ?"

" Carry the girl off in spite of him."

" Will you help me ?"

" With all my heart ; and you can help me, too, if you will. There is a bit of a burglary to-night, only in the small way, but you are such a light and dapper figure for crib-cracking, while, you see, I am five and twenty years older nor you, and getting fat, and stiff in the joints. I ain't so nimble at that game as I used to be."

" Where is it ?"

" At a poor place, the house of a doctor, who has just had some cash paid him, though I don't kdow how much ; but most likely fifty or a hundred, at least. I heard it through a friend of mine that's courting a girl who lives dolly-mop to the young lady as the doctor is to marry ; so you see the information is first-rate."

" When does it come off ?"

" To- night."

" I'll assist you, Blueskin ; and Fanny Wild—"

" Shall be yours, my boy."

" But the danger of it—I am no coward, but Jonathan, from mere revenge, will hang us both, to a certainty."

" Lor bless your pretty little heart, what a baby you is, to be sure ! Quite redifferent, I assure you. Once he finds you have run away with his daughter, he's so fond of her that he couldn't bear to have her out of his sight for four and twenty hours together ; so he's sure to make it up with you; and then he'll make your fortune, for her sake, that she may have a rory-tory cove fit for the thieftaker's daughter."

" You paint it fairly, Blueskin ; but, as I love Fanny, and would gladly risk my life to call her mine, I will think as you say."

" In course you vill ; and when your fortune's made, Jack Sheppard, you won't forget to make the fortune too of your friend and pal, poor old Blueskin."

## CHAPTER XXIII.

### THE DOCTOR AND THE WEDDING PORTION.

It was the afternoon of the same day when three persons sat at tea; who they were, and what was said must be recorded to help our story. The trio was composed of a young man and maiden, and an elderly lady, the mother of the latter. Mrs. Purvis was the widow of a highly-respectable gentleman, who had died, leaving her an only daughter, and a very limited income. Laura Purviss was, at the period we introduce her to the reader, some nineteen years of age, and, of her style of beauty, a rare specimen. Pale, fair, and delicate, she might have been supposed already in the first stage of a consumption; but that her spirits and her health appeared equally good—fragile as was her form, beyond a doubt.

She was engaged to the gentleman who sat opposite to her, one Dr. Horton, a very young practitioner, not yet sufficiently established to think himself warranted in taking home a wife. The engagement had existed between this youthful couple for more than two years, and it was only the straitened means of the surgeon which had prevented their marriage.

He found it a hard struggle to make his way in the world, without money or connection, and oftentimes did the knowledge that poverty alone stood between him and happiness with his Laura, render him bitter against the world in thought and spirit.

His was a high and intellectual, but contradictory nature; he was capable of mastering great abstract principles, and following the minute windings, even to their furthest course, of science and philosophy; but he did it step by step, the result of a reflective process, and not at once, as most men grasp their little span of knowledge, through the perceptive faculties.

He was tall and thin; his face, too, was lean, but the broad and polished forehead, and the clear bright grey eye removed it from the mass of ordinary countenances, too many of which, indeed, look as if " natures journeymen had made them, and not made them well, they imitate humanity so abominably."

Now Mrs. Purvis, who was quite an every day personage, but of whom we shall have more to say hereafter, went out after tea, for a walk, and left our lovers to themselves.

" Another month, dear Laura, and I hope to welcome you to my own home ; heaven knows it wants a lady's presence to cheer it, for it is dull enough in all conscience."

" You a student, Robert, and complain of dullness, but I am not sorry to hear you say your house is lonely, for you will see the great difference quicker, after I become its mistress ; I'll have no rusty, musty, dusty, books, and instruments of torture, and I don't know what besides, in every corner of my house, I can tell you, sir. You must confine all such matters to your laboratory, Mr. Robert. Fancy my turning the corner unexpectedly, in the dark, and bouncing up against a great skeleton, that pokes his arms out when he is touched ; I have heard of these things."

" I have one ; but I always keep a green curtain before it ; so that, unless an unwarrantable curiosity be exhibited, no stranger will ever be alarmed."

" And when are you to receive this handsome sum of money, Robert, that is to enable you to accomplish such wonders."

" Handsome Laura it is but fifty pounds. '

" Fifty pounds ! that is a great deal of money."

" And I am going to put it to an admirable purpose—to render my home in some degree fit for the reception of my wife."

" What an expensive thing marriage must be, Robert."

" Why so, Laura ?"

" Oh, I know not," answered the young lady, laughing ; " only you seem to think it necessary to have such a bank to start with."

" Is that intended for a reproach, Laura, because I have not earlier fulfilled my engagement ?"

And the brow of the young surgeon was flushed.

" Why should you think me of so unmaidenly a thought ? You are too quick, Robert."

" It is my poverty that makes me so ; the painfully narrow means, within which I have been compelled to struggle, and make the appearance of a gentleman, have rendered me irritable ; the knowledge that those limited means have debarred me from the happiness of making you my wife, has, at times, almost driven me mad, and I have fretted my heart out against the bars of my poverty, and hated the world."

" But you tell me that your practice is increasing, that you are making friends, and, more than all that, you are going to have fifty pounds ; now, I never saw so much money as fifty pounds, Robert, in all my life, and my wishes are very humble, and mamma, you know, has her own income, and I am quite sure that we shall do very well, and before the fifty pounds are spent, I have no doubt but you will get another fifty pounds, and so we shall go on, quite rich; by the by, what are you to have that fifty pounds for ?"

" That is a secret, Laura."

" But you ought not to have any secrets from me."

" It is not my own, or I would willingly inform you of it, it belongs to a family of influence, and I have sworn not to reveal it."

" It must be something very terrible indeed, since it was necessary to bind you by an oath ; and I am sorry for it."

There was a shade of melancholy upon the face of Laura Purviss, that, after a moment, by sympathy, communicated itself to the surgeon's. He endeavoured, however, to cast off all appearance of sadness, but it was a long time before he succeeded."

That evening passed less pleasantly to Laura than any she had known for some time. Mrs. Purviss returned at an early hour, and at ten o'clock Horton took his leave. After he had left the house, the maid-servant who had shown him out, standing looking after him, on the door-step, and then up and down the street, as is the custom with maid-servants on occasions, muttered to herself—

" There you go, for a shabby skinflint. He is here five evenings out of six, and I haven't seen the colour of his money. There is a mystery somewhere. I thought, when I told Tom, that he had got his lump of money as he was to have ; however, I don't think so now, or they'd be married at once, but lor, when all we knows of the goings on of a family we picks up at key-holes, we can't be expected to take our davey of every particular."

Slowly and sadly the young doctor made his way home. He was not satisfied with himself. It was not that he had any cause to complain of his own industry, and if fortune frowned upon him, how could he prevent that ? but he had engaged himself in a transaction which, as an honourable man, he could not, at the best, but regard with a most suspicious eye. The means that act would bring him, though they would secure him his wife, he could not help looking on with loathing, as the price of his own unscrupulous conduct. He fell back upon his poverty, but, to his reason, it pleaded only with a poor argument, and in faint tones.

When he gained his home, situate at the corner of a street then leading into the Edgware-road, he found the boy whom he had left in charge of his surgery asleep at his post.

" How's this, Mike—asleep, eh ?" and he shook him with some degree of violence ; his self-examination had made him dissatisfied with everybody and everybody and everything.

" There has been nobody here, sir, and there would not be, if I was to keep awake for a month."

" How do you know that sir ? how dare you take upon yourself to judge who should and who should not come here ?"

" I takes nothing on myself ; if you don't like it, pay me my wages and let me go."

Horton was humbled immediately. He had to pay the boy but a few shillings a week, and yet he was a month in arrear, and had not the wherewithal in his house to get out of the boy's debt. He was obliged to lower himself in his own opinion, and in that of his scrub, by succumbing to the necessity that would not permit him to kick the little brute out of doors.

" There—I did not mean to be angry with you—I shall not want you any more to-night ; I'll attend to the shop myself. Get your supper and go."

" Supper !" muttered the boy ; but it was in a low tone, for he saw that his master was in no humour to be further crossed. " A lot of supper there is for a cove in a place like this, where there ain't half enough for the rats. I knows, when I can't see them, they sits and looks at me with eyes of envy when I gets a bit of mouldy grub. Supper ! If master is going to bring a wife home here, blest if she had not better bring her wittals with her, or it's Captain Short she'll come here."

The boy made a survey of the cupboard, and must evidently have found enough ; for what he could not eat he put into his handkerchief, and, rolling that up, tucked it into his three-cornered hat, and bidding his master a good night, jogged whistling on his way.

" How mortifying, how cruelly mortifying, are these daily insults, in the shape of reminders of one's straitened means !" said Horton, plunging himself into his old arm-chair, that stood within the little study beyond the surgery. He dragged down a great book, and placed it on his knee ; and, having trimmed his lamp, tried to study. But his thoughts were far removed from the work of art before him ; he had no crushing weight of unhappiness to bear, yet was he wretched.

He was young, well-learned in his profession, a man with good and comprehensive reasoning powers, he loved, and was beloved by a beautiful and intelligent girl of pure and gentle mind. What was there in professional and domestic life he might not hope for. Alas! he knew that he should gain the stepping-stone to all this good by a compromise with honour. But the stride was not yet taken ; he might pause, fall back upon his fortune, and yet go on an and prosper. He would reject the temptation that was offered. He would—but how should he meet Laura and her mother? The day of marriage was already named—there would be expenses attending it, and could he bring his wife to a home like this. Time wore away, and he heard the clock strike twelve, a moment after, and there was a knock at his private door—the boy had sut up the surgery before he left. Horton was in a deep reverie, and started at the sound, while a deeper paleness marked his face.

" He has come again," he cried, and I am wanted ; now Heaven give me resolution."

He went to the door, and inquired the name of his visitor at that late hour; he knew the voice that made answer, and he admitted a man of more than ordinary height, whose figure was completely enveloped in a huge blue cloak.

" Come in, general," said he ; and the stranger followed him into his study. " Be seated, I beg."

The new arrival was a military-looking man, of some fifty summers with the sternest possible expression of countenance.

" Dr. Horton," said he, as he took a seat opposite the master of the house, " for you are, I believe, a physician, as well as surgeon— It is now nearly the time that I shall require your services."

" Is the lady ill, then ?"

" She is, and your speedy attendance would be advisable. Is all prepared ?" said his visitor, " and is the child sufficiently young ?"

The doctor looked strangely confused, and the gentleman repeated his question.

" Oh, quite—quite, General Austen."

" And you have arranged it with the mother ?"

" I have," replied the other; but there was a strange indecision in his tone—he knew that he was stating an untruth, that he had not anticipated the time so close, that he had made no preparations at all, that he had even sometimes contemplated, as we have seen, receding from his bargain.

General Austen did not seem to notice this, but went on to say—

"Should the child—the child of my wife, Lady Diana, prove a boy, then the property will be retained in the family without the necessity of the *ruse* we have agreed, between us, to practise; but if, on the other hand, it should be a girl, then the change will be required that you will effect. This—concluding that your scruples in such a matter would not be excessive, and being assured that you were a man of talent—induced me to retain your services for the *accouchenr* of my wife. I have promised you, in any case, fifty guineas—I shall have a handsome compensation to make the nurse in addition to yourself, but I will increase your fee to a hundred."

"A hundred, general."

"A hundred, sir." And General Austen—he who was the captain of our early history, the seducer of Ellen Hodson—took from his breast a pocket-book, containing many notes. "On second consideration," he added, "I have received a large sum of money in gold to-day, from abroad; you will, perhaps, not object to receive the sum from that," and the general placed upon the table two canvas bags, containing, at least, three hundred guines each.

"Are you not afraid, general, to carry so much money on your person as that?" asked the young doctor, with hungry eyes, as he surveyed the glittering gold on the untying of one of the bags.

"Afraid! no. I have been used, all my life, young man, to real dangers, without stopping to make false ones."

Horton had risen, and, with his back to the table, stooped to stir the embers in the grate. As he bent down his face before the fire there was a strange bad expresssion in his countenance lit up by the red flare; he raised the heavy poker, as though to insert it between the bars, but, in an instant he swung it above his head, and as he turned half round it fell with tremendous effect upon the temple of the general; the weapon dropped from his hand as his visitor fell upon the floor. A hundred thoughts now swept with lightning speed across his brain! in that little moment he lived whole years. His act had been wholly unpremeditated—it had seemed to spring not from himself but from some devil tempting him within. With a strange revulsion of feeling he caught up his lancet with one hand from the mantel-shelf, and, with his lamp in the other palm, he stooped down to judge of the effect of that tremendous blow. Could he number them he would give a thousand years of life to come to recall but one for his victim—a year—a month—a week—an hour—a minute. All was fruitless, life had fled; and with that stroke a soul had winged its flight.

Now Horton rose again, but, stupified and aghast, looked upon the murdered body of his victim; so late erect, so full of life, and power, and pride.

Slowly and mechanically he turned his gaze upon the table; there lay the canvass bags, and the half-spilled gold. What should he do? He gazed in speechless horror—not that he thought anything of his contiguity to a corpse; with Lady Macbeth, he thought—

" The sleeping and the dead are but as pictures;
It is the eye of childhood fears a painted devil."

But, then, the lifeless mass before him was of his making. Hush! Holy Father! what was that? A low sound was heard, like the drawing of fingers on wet glass; for a moment the surgeon was paralysed, but, hearing a window raised, he was, as suddenly, himself again. He advanced a step in the direction of the stairs that came directly down into his room, and from the first landing emanated the sound; forgetting, in the new surprise, the event of the few minutes before, when his foot struck the yet unstiffened body of his victim, impeding his course. He recoiled—he had no power to advance, and that in his way.

Now a heavy footfall was heard on the landing, and then another, and two men, with masks on their faces, and pistols in their hands, dashed down the staircase into the room. The bigger man of the two passed to Horton, and presenting a pistol at his head, bade him offer no resistance The other stopped before the prostrate figure of the murdered man, and, stooping down, put his hand upon the cheek of the dead.

" Good God," he cried, " here has been murder, and but a few minutes since; do you not see, Blueskin, that this damned doctor has killed this gentleman for his gold ?"

Blueskin looked round, and was surprised at the sight that met his eye. On entering the room he had caught only the figure of Horton, as the one endowed with life, and, therefore, the power of resistance— he had seen nothing else—not even the gold.

" Are you sure he is dead ?" he replied. " Undo his dress, place your hand upon his heart."

" He is dead."

But few more words passed between them; Horton was almost

passive in their hands. They bound him with a rope in his arm chair—a rope which Jack Sheppard produced from his pocket—and seizing the gold upon the table without attempting to examine the property about the corpse, they fled hastily by the window they had entered.

Face to face were the murderer and the murdered, and there was little difference in the whiteness of either cheek. Horton would have fled, but he had no power to move he was so tightly bound to that huge arm chair. He would have pressed his hands to his eyes, but his wrists were lashed together and behind him. He tried to close his eyes, but they would keep open, and fixed themselves on the dead man's face.

He thought of Laura—of all that he might have been—of what he was! A murderer! a foolish, baulked, insensate murderer. Setting aside the honor of his crime, behold the retribution! and the gold—the gold that had led to it—was wrested from him ere it was well his.

From side to side he moved his head, and would have given the world to beat his brains out against the marble mantel-piece. He tightly clenched his hands—were he free, he knew that he should have courage to do it—he swayed his head again, and, in fancy, thought that he was beating it against the marble.

The light went out. In the darkness of that chamber he was alone with his victim, he could not close his eyes—they were still fixed there—there, in that direction. Now he thought he heard a low breathing—he might not be dead, after all! He thought that the murdered figure was creeping towards him—he thrust his back further, deeper, into that leathern chair. Now there seemed a hand upon his knee, now the figure uprose, and his throat was tightly grasped in the icy claws of the other. He tried to cry out—but he could not. At length, a wild, unnatural howl broke from his lips, and his enemy seemed to fall.

In the morning, when the boy came as usual, he could not get in, but the neighbours being summoned—the door was, after a time, broken open. The dead body of the late General Austen was found upon the floor, and, opposite to him, sat his murderer—a raging lunatic.

# CHAPTER XXIV.

### THE DRAPER'S SHOP AND THE ABDUCTION.

FANNY WILD, be it remembered, had not set eyes upon the face of Lord Lisle since the morning when she looked upon him for a moment in her father's office, on recovering from the fainting fit into which she had been thrown by the appearance of the three heads in the cupboard.

On the night of the masquerade, from the first moment when the green and gold, and the blue and silver dominoes approached her and her maid, she had associated the viscount with the former colours, and during the time that she remained under the escort of the valet she never discovered her error.

Let not the reader think worse of the judgment and delicacy of our heroine because she could not distinguish in that one interview the difference between the true gold and the spurious metal. Fanny Wild had seen very little of the world, and Mr. Watson, in his way, a great deal. It is true that the first impression created by the young nobleman, was not strengthened by the valet's representation of his master, and now, as she thought of the viscount, it was only in that moment when she opened her eyes to look upon him in her father's house.

She had removed her mask in the ante-room, as her companion suggested, and when the lights were brought she looked, naturally enough, only to the unmasked man who held her in his grasp—the old husband, who was seeking his old wife. When she remembered this part of her adventure, and how she fled, with a scream, immediately on the discovery, without turning, either to the right or to the left, she sometimes thought whether the whole had not been a deception and a cheat, and if, on that occasion, she had seen Lord Lisle at all.

A few weeks after the night of the masquerade she was engaged one afternoon, towards dusk shopping in the city, when she observed that she was followed very closely by a man of gentlemanly appearance, whose face she did not know, but who, by crossing and re-crossing before her, seemed to take every opportunity of throwing himself in her way. She was accompanied by her footman, and, therefore, felt but little alarm. At length, she entered a mercer's shop, and while her servant remained at the door, the gentleman followed her in. When she had given some of her orders at the counter, to her amazement, on turning, she found the stranger beside her,

" I did not think, Miss Wild," said he, " you would have been so unkind as not to afford me an opportunity of speaking to you."

" Oh, Heavens!" she mentally exclaimed, " who can this man be ?"

She knew the voice again, it was the same that had talked to her all that evening.

" Do you so soon forget ? Am I not he with whom you danced, who told you of his love, who hoped that he had won some little love from you in return?"

Watson had been reading some of the old-fashioned romances, and preparing this speech at each corner.

" Who are you sir ? You are a very bold, impudent man, and not the person that I took you for. My servant is at the door, the people of this shop know me, and I have a great mind to have you ducked for an impostor—if I were to tell my father—"

" And if I were to tell your father, Miss Wild, what would he say to his daughter, who made an appointment with a rakish young nobleman, at a masquerade, and, but for an accident, would have been carried off by another ?"

" 'Tis false, sir, whoever you are !" said Fanny, with some of her father's blood roused in her now; " I dare you to do, or say, what you please—you are a miserable trickster, and, if you do not leave this shop instantly, I must request the people to put you in the kennel."

" I am not to be frightened, Miss Wild, by the airs of a young lady."

" Indeed !" replied Fanny. " Mr. Silkskin was very proud of his customer, and knew Miss Wild and her father well; advancing with perfect politeness, for though he was rather a big man, and, like most of his class, he was a bit of a buck, in his way, he put his hand upon the collar of the intruder, right in the back of the neck, and the assailed, who was necessarily obliged to run crouchingly, gained the door.

" John," said Mr. Silkskin, " this man has insulted your mistress."

" Has he, by George! Mr. Silkskin? I am much obliged to you," and John seized the poor devil as the mercer removed his grasp, and being also of a powerful make, with one hand lifted him a little off the ground; then raising his knee to assist the impetus, he caught him in the lowest and broadest part of his back, and sent the unfortunate gentleman on to his nose in the gutter. When he rose again he was covered with mud, and there was a little crowd on the pavement. The yell of the boys was almost as annoying to Mr. Watson as his ignominious expulsion."

" What has he been a doing of?"   " What is it then ?"   What are you taking home the streets for ?"   " That ere mud ain't yours !" and a host of such expressions greeted him.   There was quite an excitement.   The valet was about to sneak off, when when a voice whispered in his ear—

" Why don't you have your revenge ?   We'll take your part— don't give it up like a cur."

There were several arguments now, pro and con.   Nobody rightly understood the cause of quarrel, and everybody began to talk about it.   Some were taking one side, some the other.   Watson made a statement to those about him that was very far from the truth ; the footman himself did not condescend to give any explanation at all, but stood with his back against the closed shop-door, ready to defend himself in case of an attack.   There were two persons in the mob that tried to incite the rest.   They failed to establish a riot, and there were few people about the door when Fanny desired, for it was now dark, that a coach should be brought.   One was found at the corner of the street, Mr. Silkskin saw her to the door, the steps were down, and her footman held the hand-rope while somebody else stood on the opposite side.   The next instant she was seated in the vehicle, and the mercer was re-entering his shop.   In a trice the steps were up, the door shut, and the coach which contained Fanny Wild was driven off at a rapid pace.   She had not seen what had happened to her servant, and she did not know but that he occupied his seat upon the box.

Now it seemed to her that she had been driven a considerable distance, but as the night was so dark, and the streets were so ill-lighted she could not tell where she was.   She put her head out of the window, and called to the driver to know in what direction he was going ; he answered, to her father's house at Kilburn, as be had been told.

" But this is not the road to Kilburn."

" Oh, yes, miss ; not the road you come, perhaps ; but it is the best."

" But John—where is the footman ?"

" He said he should be home, miss, as soon as you ;  he had a little business to do somewhere in London."

" But this is all very strange; stop the coach—I will go no further."

" It is a very little way miss, now; don't be frightened," and the driver lashed his horse.

Fanny tried to see who was on the box, but she could only make out that there were two men there; she could not see their faces, and their voices were strange to her.

She was growing very frightened.

She thought to scream, but she knew by the sound and motion of the wheels that she was in the country now, and there would be no one to hear her; but her fears crowded rapidly upon her, and to scream she was forced.

It had only the effect of causing the driver to lash his horse the more.

Onward and onward, through dark lanes and slushy roads, and rutty ways they drove her, shaking her from side to side as they went ou their uneven course.

Once she thought of opening the coach door, and precipitating herself into the road, but it seemed so high, and the vehicle was going at such a rate she feared to be dashed to pieces. Presently she saw a little light in the distance; it seemed to belong to some house by the roadside; she would concentrate all her energies when they neared that place, in the hope that some one would hear her.

She was already prepared to shriek when the vehicle took a sudden turn, and entered the grounds of the very place from which she had seen the light. It was a small neat cottage that stood some five and twenty yards from the road, and there was a carriage-way that led to it. The coach was stopped before the door of the house which was now opened, and ere she knew where she was, or had time to recover herself even sufficiently to speak, she she was handed from the vehicle into the little hall, and thence into a sitting-room of small dimensions, but respectably furnished.

An old lady in a widow's cap advanced to meet Fanny.

" I am very happy indeed to see you, miss; my son will be here soon, and then he will welcome you. It was very kind of you to come and stay with us like this."

Our heroine opened her great blue eyes wider than usual—what on earth did all this mean? was she dreaming, or was this old woman mad? " Very kind of her to come and stay like that!" Fanny had no words for reply, and the lady in the widow's cap went on to say—

" I'll be bound you're a good deal tired, and a cup of something ma'm will do you good; I'll go and get it ready for you directly," The old woman accordingly left the room, and Fanny was left alone in speechless astonishment. She crossed the room, and tried to fathom the mystery; the more she thought the greater was the puzzle, and, at last, she sat down, mechanically facing the door, and wondered what was next to happen. Presently she heard the sound of approaching footsteps, the handle of the door was turned, and Jack Sheppard entered the room. He was very differently dressed from the last time that Fanny saw him, the same morning she encountered Lord Lisle.

"I am very glad to see you, Jack; you, perhaps, can inform me why I have been brought here?"

"I can, miss: in obedience to my orders."

"Your orders, Jack—are you mad? Your orders! and who are you, to tear away a young lady from her home, and friends, and bring her she knows not where—for what purpose, I say, has this been done, and how will you answer this to my father?"

"Your father, Fanny, is not all powerful, though you and he may think so; other and younger men may yet hold as much importance in the world as he does."

"Whose house is this Sheppard?"

"Mine."

"Yours! I knew not that you had the means—"

"No matter; while I live in it, this cottage is mine—or, rather, my mother's—I took it for her."

"And why am I brought here?"

"Can you not guess, dearest?"

"How dare you call me by such an epithet; you know I hate you.'

"No, not so bad as that, miss, neither," replied Jack, who had made himself very dashing indeed, in a scarlet coat, trimmed with gold lace, white kerseymere breeches, silk stockings, with elegant clocks, high old-fashioned shoes, and brilliant buckles. He now threw himself into a seat with quite an air, and went on to say—

"Not so bad as that; you don't, perhaps love me over-much, yet; you have been accustomed to look down upon me, and hear of me as a carpenter's wild apprentice, as the scrubbed boy that did your father's dirty work, and as you told me lately, at the best, you hated chips; but things are altered with me, now—I am a gentleman; I love you most consumedly, and you must and shall be mine."

Fanny listened with forced calmness to the whole of this speech;

but now she crossed to Jack, tapped him on the shoulder and drew her
figure erect, and looked at him with a fierce glance in her large blue
eye, and her nostrils were dilated with passion.

"Are you drunk, Sheppard, or have you been taking lessons in stage
foolery? Do you know who you are, and to whom you speak?"

"I do; I am called Jack Sheppard."

" "The burglar."

"Oh! the burglar if you will—and you are Fanny Wild, the
daughter of a thieftaker, and an itinerant doctress. Come, what is
the difference in our position?"

No. 12.

" Insulting fool ! but your audacity is only equalled by your madness.   Order the vehicle to be brought me here instantly to the door,
and let it take me in safety to Kilburn, and upon the despatch with
which you execute my commands depends my overlooking your inso-
lence, and saving you from ruin with my father.   Come, sir, it is time
this jest was at an end.   You see I am not frightened ; your folly
only makes me angry—quick, Jack, quick."

" How little do you know me !" returned Jack.   " Once for all, I
am independent of your father, and care not for him ; but I love you,
Fanny, with all my heart.   I have been at great trouble and some
risk to bring you here ; and do not mean to part with you, I promise
you." _

" Not part with me !   What then will you do with me ?"

" Make you Mrs. John Sheppard, my dear, and a happy woman for
the rest of your life."

" I would hang you in a week, and spit at you ere I left the church."

" Then we would not go to church at all, my love, but perform the
ceremony by hopping over the broomstick."

" I will appeal to your mother."

" My mother does my bidding."

" I will escape."

" You will not have an opportunity."

" I will murder you."

" Then there will be a double murder, for I shall kill you with
kindness."

" Jack Sheppard, I hate you."

" Fanny Wild, you are the darling of my heart."

" Stand off, sir, or I'll shriek."

" Oh, we'll have no shrieking here, my pretty one ; our plan is to
stop the mouth with kisses."

" You shall stop my breath, first."

Jack had thrown his arms round our heroine, but she had escaped
from his clasp, and her hand was already on the bell, when a loud
knocking at the house-door stayed them both.

There was a violent altercation without, and then Jonathan and
others with him, entered the apartment.

Mrs. Sheppard, at the same time, joined the group.

" My father, my dear father," and Fanny had rushed to the thieftaker.

" Bar the doors there, let no one escape."

" You will find no one in this house, sir, except my mother, and myself, with a crazy old servant ; but by what right do you enter here—this is my house, and without a warrant you have no right to force your way in."

" Don't talk to me of right, don't speak to me at all, Jack Sheppard, for fear my rage should master me, and I put a bullet through your head, as there you stand before me."

" Jack, my dear Jack," cried Mrs. Sheppard, throwing her arms about her son's neck, " how could you be so foolish as to provoke this bad man's anger. Oh! miss, if you really love my son, as he tells me you do—"

" I love him, ma'am? I hate him !"

" Oh, Jack, Jack ! you'll break your mother's heart,"

" He will, ma'am," said Jonathan, " if his death will hurt you ; for this insult and violence to my child, I will hang him at Tyburn-tree within twelve months, or my name is not Jonathan Wild."

" Bad, black-hearted man, have you no mercy ?"

" Ask him, madam—ask your elegant son, there, where would have been his mercy with my child, my Fan, my own little girl here ?"

" He would have made her his wife."

" His wife? the wife of the burglar Sheppard—I would sooner see her dead at my feet, and the dogs feeding on her dainty flesh. His wife!"

" Come Wild," cried Jack, " I'm not a bad-tempered fellow, but I can't stand too much, and I won't try. I didn't mean to harm Miss Fanny there ; I would have married her like a gentleman, and trusted to her loving me afterwards ; but since she says she hates me, why, my pride won't allow me to pursue her any further—though I shall always love her. As for you and your threats, Mr. Wild, I'm out of leading-strings now, and care nothing for you."

" You have had a slice of luck, lately, my young friend ; but the swag won't last for ever, mark you that—my trapping you to-night for all your cleverness, should be a proof to you how vain is the attempt to keep anything from my knowledge. Good night, Mrs. Sheppard ; don't forget my words ; a few more sessions and I shall hang your son, out of the way. Marry my daughter—marry my beautiful Fanny ! Zounds ! the fellow's only fit for St. Lnke's.

Jonathan accompanied by his myrmidons, led his treasure from the house.

## CHAPTER XXV.

### THE LUNATIC ASYLUM—THE MANIAC—THE GRAVE.

A hired vehicle entered the gateway of a large house that stood in its own grounds some ten miles from the metropolis. From the coach descended an elderly lady and a young one; the first named passed up the steps without looking either to the right or to the left, but the younger, gazing upwards and about her, saw that the house was an old-fashioned red-brick building of the heavy architrcture of the second James, or the time of William and Mary. The windows were heavily barred, iron spikes spouted up from every sill, and the gardens, were enclosed with high walls, above which were spikes again, that made them impossible for a man to surmount. Before the visitors were admitted, their approach was known, and there was a great clanging of bolts, and bars, and locks. A respectable-looking man, out of livery, received them, and, without waiting to hear their errand, ushered them into a well-furnished room on the ground-floor. Here they took their seats in silence, regarding everything with attention, but apparently too much occupied with thought to speak.

Presently a door was opened that communicated, and a bald and benevolent-looking gentleman, somewhat shabbily attired, entered. The visitors rose as he approached them.

"My dear madam," said he, shaking hands with the elder lady, "this is very kind of you, I am delighted to see you."

"We thought it our duty, my dear sir, to call, on the score of long friendship, as also for another reason, which you will readily guess at, without any particular allusion on my part."

"Certainly, madam, certainly; I appreciate your motives—have you brought the instruments?"

"Instruments, sir, we did not know anything about them; we received no instructions—are you obliged to use instruments?"

"Good God! madam, are you a natural philosopher or not?"

"Very little indeed, sir."

"Then, madam, I must tell you that natural philosophy has all to do with it; mineralogy and so has geology, but natural philosophy is at the bottom."

" If you had said chemistry, I should not be so much surprised because that is a branch of medical practise, and might, from too deep study, have produced the effect.''

" Deep study—deep grandmother, ma'am!  Can't you comprehend that the primary cause is the pump-handle.''

" Pump-handle!" exclaimed Mrs. Purvis, for she it was, do you mean to say that the case of poor Doctor Horton's malady is a pump-handle ?''

" Doctor Horton, you old fool.''

" Old fool!'' and the winow drew herself up, while Laura, who accompanied her, was considerably startled.

" No, ma'am, not Doctor Horton, but me, ma'am—my malady, ma'am.  Has not Louis the Fourteenth, in his damnable tyranny, combining with the Pope of Rome, and the grand Turk, made me swallow a pump-handle, originally no bigger than a tin-tack, which has grown in my stomach, in the shape of a lion's tail curling upwards, three yards and a half long, without the tip.''

" Poor gentleman, then you are—''

" The man in the iron mask, condemned to perpetual imprisonment for my tail—did you ever see my tail?''   And forthwith the poor lunatic began to unbutton his coat and waistcoat, and threatened, if he went on at that rate completely to denude himself in the course of a very few minutes.  Mrs. Purvis threw up her hands, and Laura began to scream in good earnest.

Fortunately two of the keepers entered the room almost immediately, and removed the maniac.

Before the ladies recovered from their fright, the head of the establishment, Doctor Hewett, joined them, apologising for the fear to which they had been subjected, which, he assured them, was the result of an accident.  The poor gentleman whom they had just seen and who, he said, laboured under several delusions, one of which was, that he was the last of the race of men who wore tails like monkeys, had strayed away from his keepers, who had been some time in search of him, and the shrieks of the young lady, brought them to their rescue.

In answer to the inquiries as to the state of Horton, he said that he was—though no longer violent—a confirmed lunatic, and he much feared that he would never be restored to reason.  They could see him if they liked, and perhaps the presence of Miss Purviss might recall some scattered ray of sanity.  Was she equal to the interview ?

She said she was.

Before they quitted the room, Doctor Hewett and Mrs. Purviss, had some conversation apart relative to the gentleman who was found murdered. It had been shown, she said, to the satisfaction of the deceased general's friends, that his death was the result of violence from the robbers who had broken into the house. Their means of entrance and escape had been apparent; they had left some of their housebreaking implements behind them; but the weapon with which the murder was perpetrated was found beside the victim. The villains had evidently mastered Horton, and bouud him in his chair. It was this said the doctor, that had brought on his patient's fearful madness. The amoont of property that had been carried off that night was unknown, but not estimated at any considerable sum, as the bank-notes and valuable papers on the corpse were untouched. The murderers had probably feared to take these, lest, by their means they should be traced.

Having partaken of a little wine, the ladies followed the doctor to Horton's cell.

The doctor entered it first. The madman was subdued,

"My good fellow," said the doctor, " I have brought visitors to see you."

" I will see no one—they shall not look upon me. I am not a show, nor a wild beast."

" But they are friends of yours, they come in kindness."

" They have no right to come to me—I'll not look upon them, they shall not see my face; I will hide it in the earth—deep—deep."

He was lying with his face on the floor, and he turned his face on it, and said—

" Now, let them come, if they will."

The doctor admitted them. They were both very nervous, and there were big tears in the eyes of poor Laura, while consumption's pale ensign was waving in her cheek.

" You will speak to your friends, Horton."

" I have no friends; they all left me when my father died; I have no friends but the spiders, and they and I live together cheerily—ha! ha!—cheerily."

And the hollowness of that laugh entered the breast of Laura like a sword.

" But this is Mrs. Purviss, and her daughter, Miss Laura."

" I don't know them—I don't know them.

"If you look upon them you will remember them, they deserve to be remembered."

He continued only to mutter—"I don't know them," and kept his face close against the floor.

"Speak to him, Miss Laura," said the doctor, "your voice may recal him."

"George," said Daura, in her gentlest tone. At first he took no notice of her, but, as she repeated it, he lifted up his head a little, and turning it, looked full upon the fair girl before him. She started at the fearful appearance he wore. His head had been shaven, his cheeks had fallen, and there was a beard of many days growth upon his chin. His eyes looked like two burning coals of living fire deep set in a broad red rim. He gazed upon the maid without the smallest scintillation of reason in his glance, and then he turned his eyes upon the mother, and the doctor—first from one to the other: at last he seemed to recognise Dr. Hewett, and immediately cowered down, crying out, in a piteous tone—

"Don't send them to me, and I will be quiet—quiet as the grave, if they won't beat me with whips, and lash me again. Do you know," he added, addressing Laura, "do you know, pretty lady, they have lead in the thongs, and if you come here, they will beat you with them on the shoulders—on your white flesh till the blood runs down. Ha! ha! ha! Oh God! how the blood trickles then."

"My dear Miss Purvis," said the doctor, "you will, perhaps, understand that this is one of the peculiarities of the malady under which our poor friend labours." Miss Purvis bowed, and wished to think it might be so.

"Do you think," asked she, "that I might be left alone with him for a little while; then that I might better talk to him—soothe him He would know me, perhaps, after some few minutes. Leave me: indeed, I am not frightened, mamma," she continued, in reply to an anxious look cast upon the lunatic. The doctor seemed at first to think the young lady wished to question his patient as to the treatment he received; but he dismissed the idea almost immediately, and replied—

"I see no great harm, Mrs. Purvis, if we remain within call; he appears to me calm again now: I do not fear any paroxysm. Of course, my dear young lady, you will be very cautious in the topics you choose to speak upon." Taking the arm of the widow, he led her somewhat reluctantly from the cell, while he again assured Laura that she had but to raise her voice to secure his presence and that of the keepers. They were gone.

Horton watched the door close, and then began to laugh. That horrid sound almost frightened Laura from her intention; but she exhibited no sign of her trepidation, when the madman, rising, thrust his face close to her's, and whispered, in that dread peculiar voice, common only to lunatics—

" I know why they have brought you here; it is because that you are mad. I was mad before I came to this place ; but now I am quite well again. Do you know what has become of my old pocket-book?"

" No."

" Nor I; I wish I did—I wish I did. Do you know what I want that pocket-book for? I think *he* has stolen it?"

" Who?"

" He that was here just now: he is bad, very bad. He orders everything, and the men, his men, are devils. Did they ever whip you?"

" George."

" That is not my name."

" No?"

" No ; I have no name: they took it from me when I came in here. They are not allowed."

" But that pocket-book, dear George; why do you want that?"

" What pocket-book?"

" That of which you spoke."

" I didn't. My dear, you are wrong. I haven't got a pocket-book, miss." In a more vexed tone, he added, " What do they bring these mad women to my cell for? Take off your hat!"

" But George, dear, listen to me."

" I listen; but my spiders are calling to me—it is near dinner time. You wouldn't be so cruel as to keep my friends without their food. You'll chain, and whip, and lash them next, and tell them they are mad."

" This pocket-book ; it was an old green leather one."

" Eh?"

" Lined with red, and always had many papers in it?" Horton fixed his eyes upon her, and seemed to try and recollect something ; then he drew his hand across his eyes, and sighed, and said sorrowfully, " I cannot tell—I cannot tell."

" Once you asked me to give you a lock of hair, George, and I remember now you placed it in a pocket-book; that may be the one you speak of. Is it for that you want it?"

The maniac still regarded her; but a little vacant laugh was the only answer.

"I will try once more," she thought. "Look here, dear George; held the book a lock of hair like this?" and she pulled down a soft ringlet, and placed the end of it in his hand.

For a minute he alternately regarded her and the curl; then tears came in his eyes, and his whole frame shook and trembled strangely; then he whispered,

"Where do you come from? Who are you?"

"I am your wife that was to be; that may be yet, if God shall will it so. Laura Purvis—*your* Laura."

"Mine? I have nothing now."

"Yes, dear George, you have kind friends; warm hearts that beat for you yet, and one that will love you ever: 'tis Laura." She repeated her own name a dozen times at least, and each time he said it after her, till at length his rigid features softened, and then suddenly the fire in his eyes went out, and a whole shower of tears came boiling down his cheeks, and having put back her hair, he drew her to him, and clasped her to his heart, and wept hysterically, like a weak woman.

"Laura, sweet Laura, my own lovely girl; I know you now!"

She looked up; she was about to utter a cry of joy. She found herself besmeared with blood! Her cry of joy was changed to one prolonged shriek.

The doctor and her mother entered the cell. They were in time to receive the fainting girl in their arms.

Horton had ruptured a blood-vessel, and never spoke again

Within three months, the grave had closed over the once beautiful Laura Purvis.

Alas! for her mother.

## CHAPTER XXVI.

### THE COTTAGE AT KILBURN—THE VISCOUNT—THE PROPOSAL.

WHEN Jonathan took his daughter home again to Kilburn, he gave his wife strict injunctions not to permit her abroad, without she accompanied her. The stalwart footman had crept back to his master's with his clothes torn and soiled, in dreadful distress as to the fate of his young mistress. Jonathan dismissed him immediately from his service, notwithstanding the intercession of Fanny, who represented with truth and kindness the man's behaviour in a favourable light, though he had been overpowered. It was idle to debate. Wild had made up his mind : it was the fellow's duty to take care of his mistress ; he had failed—he must go.

Late as it was, Mrs. Wild received an outline of the events of the evening, as also did Nancy, after Fanny had retired to her own apartment ; and now Nancy, thinking it best, to a certain extent, to make a clean breast of it, said, when her young mistress told her the history of the self-convicted impostor, that she had all along had her suspicions, that the gentleman who talked to her on the evening of the masquerade, though heaven knows he did not say a great deal, and was rather formal and precise than tender and loving, for the matter of that, yet he did not seem more like a lord than a lord's gentleman. There could not be a doubt of it, and they must have changed the dresses which Mr. Watson had told her they were going to wear. So that her mistress was conversing all the evening with the valet, whom she had taken for the lord, and he had had the impudence afterwards to address her in the streets. Well, she would like to catch him, that's all ; she'd give it to the fellow well, and she meant it too, because after what had passed between them at the discovery in the ante-room, she considered he had made her an equivalent to a declaration, and then to make love to her mistress afterwards, was decidedly against the laws of fair and legitimate courtship all over the world.

The next morning Mrs. Wild sent word to her daughter, that business having taken Jonathan early into the country, she should be glad to see Fanny in her own room to breakfast and chat. Fanny went accordingly, and took the wisest course a daughter can take under any circumstances, and made a *confidante* of her mother.

She told her how she had first met his lordship; how she felt that that interview—nay, it did not deserve the name—that fleeting, swift exchange of glances, had raised in her the first passion she had ever known. She did not cry—she did not sigh out her confession; but she pouted a little, and crossed one twinkling foot over the other, and swung them both, while her heart was tossed a little with a corresponding motion, and she said, in plain terms, that she loved Lord Lisle. It was very hard, so it was, to be so played with, and by a valet. Now would not any lady in the land be as vexed as she was? Would not her mamma?

Madam Wild listened very patiently to all Fanny had to say, and then told her how wrong it was for her to indulge in this dream of greatness. A young nobleman like the viscount would never think of her as wife, at all events; of course she would not allow him to regard her with any but honourable eyes. The young lady did not see the force of this reasoning at all. She could not understand why she should not be a viscountess as well as another lady. Several had been pointed out to her, who, without vanity she said it, were not her equals in appearance. What should she do?

" Forget this folly once and for ever," said her mother. Our heroine made no reply: she saw that it was in vain; but the morning being very fine, she told her mother that she would go for a walk.

" You must not, Fanny; your father has left a special injunction that you are not to go out without me. I am not ready to accompany you now, but I shall be by-and-bye; meanwhile, you can walk in the garden."

" The garden," thought Fanny, as she left the room with a flout, " everybody treats me ill. Oh, the tyranny of fathers; but it was always so. Young ladies never were allowed to love where they liked, from Juliet downward. She loved young Montague, and I young Lisle; her father was a Capulet, and mine's a Wild. Juliet! she was a great deal better off than I am, for she had a balcony, but here, there isn't such a thing in the place."

As she strolled amongst the flowers and shrubs, picking pettishly at the leaves, and mourning her fate, she suddenly heard the sound of carriage-wheels. She looked up, and beheld a handsome equipage at the gate. Who could it be? Somebody who had lost a gold snuff-box, perhaps, and wanted papa to oblige them by asking among his acquaintances if any of them had seen such a thing.   No; it could be hardly that; they would call at the office in West-street : no business was transacted at the country residence.   Soft you now ; the carriage-door is opened by a great footman in gorgeous livery, and a young and elegant gentleman alights.   Can it be?   It is Lord Lisle.

Instantly Fanny is assured that he is there to see her, and she remembers at that moment that she has not got her best " bib and tucker" on.   Her hopes of a coronet may depend upon the figure she cuts that morning.   She rushes round to a door in the rear of the premises, and escapes to her own room, where, in a flutter of excitement, she desires Nancy to pull out all her fine things from the drawers ; she is speedily arrayed, and in very good spirits.   Very sharp indeed with her maid, because she cannot instantly fasten and arrange everything; then she sits down for a moment, and looks in the glass, and is at last quite satisfied with her appearance.   Yes, there is not a doubt about it; she is quite fit to be seen by a lord.

Is it not very odd she is not sent for?   He is considering; they do not wish to hurry her : he is proposing for her to her mother.

Surely they will send for her.   She cannot bear suspense ; anything is better than that.   She'll be bound her mother was not dressed ; that always is the case with mamma, and she really *does* take such an immense time.

" Nancy, *do* go and see."   Nancy goes accordingly, and does not come back immediately.   That girl is getting quite as bad as the rest ; there will be no bearing with her shortly.

To work go the little feet pit-pat, pit-pat, quite savagely against the carpet.   Suddenly she rises, and crosses to the door and opens it—puts her head out and listens : she can hear nothing.   She returns, and again seats herself opposite her glass.   The colour is stronger in her cheeks.

Now she hears a door open—there are steps upon the stairs; they are coming to fetch her to the drawing-room.   Shall she not be ready; shall she keep them waiting—to keep waiting a viscount: perhaps it were better not.   She arranges even her face; her eyes are fixed upon the door.

But the steps descend; the street door is heard to open, and in a minute, the carriage-wheels are heard receding on the road.

Can he be gone—gone without seeing her?   Impossible !

She feels a little faint though, and she is obliged to put her two hands upon the toilet-table.

How silly she is!   He has but sent away the carriage; he will probably stay lunch—lunch with the viscount!   Nancy appears.

" Well."

" Lord Lisle, miss."

" That's right.   Can't you speak?  why, what's the matter with the
girl ?"

" His lordship, after some conversation with your mamma, miss,
has driven back again to town."

Fanny stamped her foot, then turned pale, and finally burst into
tears, and tore with both her hands as much finery from her shoulders
as she could conveniently clutch.

       *     *     *     *     *     *

And where was Jonathan gone?

A day or two before, some people who had been robbed  on  the Oxford-road called upon him to make proposals for the recovery of some
watches and pocket-books which had been taken from them.

Our hero consulted his books accordingly,  for,  as we have before
had occasion to remark, he was very exact in minuting down his orders,
and found that no gentleman under his command had been out on that
road for a fortnight before.  He was very inquisitive to know what
sort of person the robber was who committed the acts, and according
to their description, and other circumstances, he was pretty sure it
must be the cheesemonger, who, as Jack Sheppard told us in an earlier
chapter, was somewhat dissatisfied with his first adventure under Jonathan's banner, and it appeared that the fellow afterwards deserted.
Wild had been searching for him all this time.

Now, therefore, and on the morning when Mrs. Wild and Fanny
took breakfast together, the head of the family had set out towards
Oxford, well mounted and well armed, intending to renew his acquaintance with his cheesemongering friend, who, according to several
reports, had met with good luck on that road.

He jogged on easily, visiting all the villages that lay on the by-roads,
both on the right and on the left, going into every inn, looking into
the stables to see to the horses, drinking with all the landlords, and
inquiring of them what company there was in each house, and what
company they lately had, which was his constant method when he
went in search of a deserter.

He spent a good deal of time in this manner to  no purpose, when,
riding on towards Oxford, he met a coach which had just been robbed,

the coachman warning him, and telling him the place where they had been attacked was not above a quarter of a mile distant. Upon this Jonathan inquired the number of people who had robbed them.

The coachman answered that it was done by a single man, and from the description of him, Wild was assured that it was the cheese-monger.

Jonathan set spurs to his horse, and arrived at the spot which had just before been the scene of action. Like an experienced general taking a view of the ground, considering with himself what a man of discipline would do after such an incident, in order to puzzle and be-guile his pursuers, in case any hue and cry should be raised, he spied a lane upon his right hand, and concluded that if the cheesemonger was a man of conduct, he must have struck down that lane, after he had finished his adventure. The thieftaker doubled his pace, and after a short gallop, came in sight of a man in a great coat, well mounted. Judging now that he was near the end of his inquiry, he slackened his pace, that he might prepare himself for battle. The man before, hearing the tread of a horse, looked back; but seeing no more than one man, thought it had not the appearance of a pursuit. He did not, therefore, move the faster, and at that distance he did not recognise the sweet phiz of Jonathan.

Wild, who was stuck all round with pistols, as thick as an orange with cloves, or like the man in an old almanack, with darts, but took care to be well cocked and primed, and this he managed under his great coat, concealing his war-like appointment, lest it might put the enemy in a posture of defence.

As he further advanced, the man cast another look back, and imme-diately knew that it was Jonathan. The cheesemonger faced about manfully, and drawing his pistol, bade Wild stand off, for he had done with him.

Our hero put on the fox's skin, and employing all his oratory, for he had an excellent talent at wheedling, begged that they might be good friends, and go and drink together, swearing that he loved men of courage, and desired nothing but that they might be as before; but the valiant cheesemonger told him his mind in a few words.

" Jonathan," said he, " you have led me here into a damned trade, which I am weary of, and now I have got money in my pocket, I mean to go over to Holland—"

" And deal in Dutch cheese, I suppose," sneered Jonathan.

" Deal in anything that will get me an honest living, without fear or danger."

Jonathan having a pistol in his hand, under his great coat, which the other could not see, still continued his wheedling, and approaching nearer and nearer still, that he might have a sure mark, suddenly drew forth his desperate hand, and let fly a brace of bullets in the cheesemonger's face. Then drawing forth a sharp hanger at the same instant, he flew upon him like a tiger, and with one blow, felled him at his horse's feet, all weltering in his gore. So, and with as little mercy, may be seen a gallant ox, felled by some fierce butcher, and so like Jonathan will he bestride the mighty beast, and strip him of his skin.

Wild having thus obtained complete victory, as master of the field, now fell to plunder. He found fifty-odd guineas in the fellow's pockets, with some moveables of value, of which having taken *livery* and *seisin*, according to the law of arms, he went to the next town, leading the horse in triumph as a mark of his victory. Inquiring for the next Justice of Peace, he surrendered himself, telling him that he had killed a highwayman, giving at the same time directions where he had left the body. The justice sent, and had it brought into the town, where it was immediately acknowledged by some stage-coachmen and others to be the remains of one, who, as a robber, had frequented that road. At the same time, Jonathan signified to the justice, with considerable dignity, that he was Wild, the great thieftaker: so the justice took bail for him, and Jonathan went on his way again towards his home.

And thus endeth the story of Jonathan and the cheesemonger, which, in addition to the insight it gives us to the character of our hero, and the times in which he lived, has the advantage over and above of being literally true.

## CHAPTER XXVII.

### THE PROPOSAL EXPLAINED.

THOUGH Fanny Wild was not admitted to the interview between Lord Lisle and her mother, there is no reason why we, who know exactly what passed, should not relate it to the reader.

The viscount was as pleasant, and good humoured, and courteous withal as a viscount ought to be, while Madam Wild, with the feelings of an anxious mother excited within her, did not lose for a moment the proud little flutterings of the gratified woman.

" Your lordship does me great honour; if my husband were here, he would be proud to receive, as I am, your lordship's commands."

" My visit, dear madam, is to you, not to your husband, and I am aware of his absence from home this morning, which induced me to call upon you."

" Good gracious," thought Madam Wild, forgetting her daughter in herself, " it is a little suspicions; but it is very complimentary for a young nobleman to visit a lady, who must be, I should think, three or four years older than himself"—(for three or four, read fifteen—*passing remark*)—" in the absence of her husband: he is very good-looking."

" Yes, madam, my visit is to you, and my future happiness much depends upon the reception which, at your hands, I am to meet."

" His future happiness," mentally ejaculated Madam Wild. " Poor young nobleman."

" You do not answer me, madam. You must promise me, at least, that you will grant me your patience."

" Certainly, your lordship. Can I offer you anything else to begin with?"

" Nothing, madam, I thank you, and now you must not express surprise at what I am about to say. Indeed you will not, when you know that I have once seen her, and you must hear me to the end, before you offer observation. Madam, I love your daughter."

" Hem," thought the lady; " I was near forgetting that part of the story. I must be very ignorant of all this." Aloud she exclaimed, " My daughter, my lord?"

" Even so, madam; the fascinating, charming Fanny."

" This is language, my lord, which, however flattering, in one sense, to a mother's feelings, I cannot listen to from one of your lordship's rank. The very fact, that your lordship has taken the opportunity of my husbands absence, to express your love for our child, forbids me hearing more. I have the honor, with your lordship's permission, to retire."

" Stay, my dear madam, stay. I see you mistake me, as I feared, alas! you would. Notwithstanding my application to you, instead of Mr. Wild, my intentions towards your daughter are of the most honourable nature."

No. 13.

" Your lordship proposes to marry her."

" Most certainly."

" Then I shall be mother-in-law to a viscount!"

" Permit me to explain. I am willing to forget all difference of station, and make the beautiful Fanny Lady Lisle, conditionally upon her father giving up his business and retiring, I presume, accompanied by yourself, to some distant part of the kingdom. In that case, to compensate him, in some measure, for the losses he will sustain pecuniarily, I shall be happy to settle upon him or you, and continue to the survivor, an annuity of three hundred pounds a year. I am only speaking now, supposing that I may be fortunate enough to win Fanny's acceptance of my hand."

" Ah! your lordship is not usually an unsuccessful wooer, I'll be bound; but as to the retirement of which you speak, if my husband gave up business, I can understand your lordship not wishing your father-in-law to continue the practice of a thieftaker, even though so distinguished as is Mr. Wild. Yet that he should retire to some distant part of the kingdom—yet more extraordinary still, I should be requested to accompany him, is certainly, to say the least of it, not so flattering as your lordship's *penchant* for our daughter."

" So sensible, and at the same time so agreeable a woman as Madam Wild will not, I am sure, misconstrue that which is only intended to secure the perfect happiness of herself and husband."

" But a distant part of the kingdom, shut out from all society."

" Would be more agreeable and consistent to the great thieftaker and his lady, than an indiscriminate association with peers and peeresses of the precise old school—some of them hardly capable of relishing the humour of my dear Jonathan, or even appreciating the matronly beauty, and many virtues and talents of his amiable lady."

The lady looked hard at the nobleman, to judge, if possible, what amount of satire he intended to convey; but his face wore so placid a smile, together with such a frank expression, that she could hardly believe that he meant other than he said.

" Really, my lord, this is altogether so strange a proposal, that I know not what answer to make you. Why did you not apply to my husband?"

" Because I know the hasty violence of Mr. Wild's temper. I experienced it only on the occasion when I saw the young lady in his office. She had fainted in his arms; I did but utter an involuntary expression of admiration, and lo! he fell into a violent rage, and seemed to be angry with me for only looking at her. Under these circumstances, it occurred to me, whether, if I made this first proposal to you, you might not the better break the matter to him than I could."

"He will be proud of the honor that your lordship confers upon him, I know, and he will think the more of it, since your lordship has not addressed Fanny first."

"Nay, I know not; he seemed so angry at the mere word 'beautiful,' and so jealous of his daughter, I almost doubt if he would give her to a prince."

"He could not refuse, my lord, to make her the wife of a nobleman, who loves her, and whom she loves."

"Ah, my dear madam, think of what you are saying. We have met each other but once; we have exchanged no words together. For a whole evening, I pursued one I thought was her—I was deceived. Powerful as is this love, I feel myself I cannot hope to have awakened at a glance feelings in her sympathetic with my own : if, therefore, in the course of time—"

"You will forgive me, my lord, if I do not say more, than that my daughter has not forgotten you."

"You make me very happy, Mrs. Wild ; but at the same time let me hope that you will yourself give me some promise on your own part."

"I can say nothing, my lord, further in the matter, than that I should be very proud to call myself your mother-in-law, and that I will undertake to sound my husband in your behalf. As your lordship says, I may by degrees be enabled to obtain his opinion and consent, without causing that anger into which any sudden proposal for Fanny, however good, would certainly throw him. And the young lady : I hope your lordship will agree with me, that it will be better not to name the matter to her, until we know something of the feelings of her father."

"Ah, madam, you forget a lover's impatience, and my passion is most impetuous; but I will yield to you, madam, in this, promising you, on my word of honour, not to attempt any communication with Fanny, if I may call her so, till I have heard from Mr. Wild or yourself; but it must be within three days, or I shall hold myself free to woo the young lady as I best can."

"I promise your lordship that within three days you shall hear, meanwhile—"

"Meanwhile, madam, I have the honour to be, your humble servant." And his lordship lifted the tips of Madam Wild's fat, but pretty white fingers, and raised them to his lips.

This formal and precise interview, which appears ridiculous with our present notions, was not at all so in the day of which we write, and Lord Lisle and Mrs. Wild each thought they were playing their parts to perfection.

All that day and evening, Fanny besieged her mother with innumerable questions as to the object of Lord Lisle's visit. Madam, though she refused to satisfy her daughter by a direct reply, further than to tell her it was upon business of her father's, yet she could not help letting fall, by accident, an occasional hint, having reference to that which was mysteriously great, and then recalling her words, as though she had let fall too much. It was very tantalizing to poor Fanny.

What could his lordship think of her? Not a great deal, she imagined, because it would appear that he had talked to her maid for her, and he must, therefore, have a very *waiting*-maidish opinion of her. She might never meet him again; she could have no opportunity for upsetting his belief. What should she do?

Nancy was at hand to assist her, and would, no doubt, very willingly enter into any plot, or practise any scheme they should together devise; but their last intrigue had proved so miserably unsuccessful, she feared to enter on another, and though she knew not exactly why, she had some distrust of her waiting-woman. She could not help thinking there was more than accident in Nancy's adhesiveness to his lordship at the Pantheon. She must have known by the voice that the blue and silver domino was not Mr. Watson, the valet.

It was the next evening, when Jonathan had just returned from his Oxfordshire exploit. Mrs. Wild broke the subject of her interview with Lord Lisle. Half an hour passed, and then Fanny, who had been previously sent up stairs by her mother, was ordered down again.

" Here, my girl," exclaimed Wild, on her entering the apartment, " I have no secrets from you relative to yourself. Not long ago, I told you of an offer that was made to you, and I asked you to give your own answer; I desire you to do the same now."

" What, papa, has any body made me an offer now? Really it's very pleasant to be sought after, and it is such a gratification to refuse them."

" Refuse; aye, that's the word. I know you will; but first, Fanny, you shall hear, and then give the answer yourself. I am insulted most grossly by a man, who takes a base advantage of an accident in his favour, and in the same breath that he so insults me, he asks me for my daughter. What does she say?"

" She says, the man who insults the father is a fool, as well as a villain, to attempt to woo the daughter."

" This man, Fanny, stabs me, where I could least bear a wound; he would thrust me from my home."

" The monster!"

" Deprive me of my means of living and of happiness, at one stroke."

" A wretch indeed!"

" He would drive me into some out-of-the-way corner, that I might rot in obscurity."

" The low villain! O, I could tread upon him!"

" Right, my girl, the low-minded scoundrel; but he shall not rob me of my child."

" He shall not."

" But," said Madam Wild, for the first time joining in since Fanny had re-entered the room, " you have not told her yet the name of this *low* gentleman."

" Ah! that you have forgotten, pa; not that I care to hear it. The last was a carpenter and burglar, and this is—"

" A nobleman and villain."

" A nobleman?" And there was an ashy whiteness in the face of our heroine.

" Yes, Fan, the man who insults your father, and whom you have so nobly refused, is the Viscount Lisle."

" Quick!" cried Madam Wild: " the window there—water, Jonathan. Don't you see the girl is faint?"

# CHAPTER XXVIII.

### ANOTHER YEAR, AND A TRIP INTO WARWICKSHIRE.

TWELVE months went by, and Fanny, who had been very ill, had accompanied her mother into Warwickshire, and now, with Madame Wild, occupied the inside of a stage-coach, that twice a-week (D. V.) made its journey to London.

" How time passes, mamma."

" A very natural observation, my dear, but not a very original one; though, if you had lived as long in the world as I have, and seen the changes I have seen, you might, indeed, have cause to say so."

"'I was only thinking, mamma, of what had happened during the last twelve months."

" And I, within the last twenty years : this part of the country is to me particularly rich in old associations."

" I thought so, mamma, from the fact of our stopping three days at the ' The George,' in Warwick, and you asking so many questions about the people in the neighbourhood. Those Thornton's, now, that you would find an excuse to call upon ; they did not seem to know you, and yet you appeared very much interested in them."

" They would have known me, Fanny, at least, he would, had he heard my name ; but as you must know, my dear, however proud your father is of being called the great Wild, we do not care to be pointed at throughout the kingdom for the great Wild's wife and daughter."

" While I, who really have the right," sighed Fanny, " to be called by another name, am not permitted to assume that which is my own. What is the use of being my lady."

" Hush, Fanny."

" I can't hush, mamma ; I must speak sometimes. What is the use of being a viscountess, if one is only to be called—miss. I really don't think there can be a greater insult, than calling anybody miss after they are married."

" But, Fanny, you look like a miss."

" Do I indeed, mamma? What a pity. I hope his lordship will soon return from those estates of his in Scotland, that require so much looking after. I know I want looking after too."

"Certainly, Fan, your position is not a very pleasant one—a maiden wife, and as you say, my lady, but only known as plain miss. Yet consider; it was very good of me to assist you from secret marriage with Lord Lisle. If Jonathan were to know it, there would be murder."

"What a dreadful thing papa will be so obstinate. After all, 'tis nothing so wonderful he should not like his father-in-law to be a thief-catcher."

"You may be right, Fanny, and indeed, I am beginning myself to think the profession very, very low indeed. I have withdrawn both you and myself as much apart from it as possible ; but I must say his lordship is obstinate too.'

"That was to bring my father to terms, by not marrying me until he consented to retire."

"Whereupon," said Madam Wild, "I must come to your rescue, and before my lord started for Scotland, consent to your secret marriage, conditionally on your separating at the church-door."

And if papa should remain obstinate, after my husband returns to London, he told me that it was his intention to run away with me into Scotland, and never let me see London or my father again."

"I think when your father knows from me of what has happened, and I have represented it in my own way, he will not be so blind to his own interest—to all our interests, however profitable and pleasing may be his profession, as not to abandon it, and see his daughter recognised a lady in the land."

"Ah ! as I said, how time passes, and those Thornton's, mamma, of whom we were speaking, and whose farm you were so anxious to see."

"It was not a bad notion of mine, Fanny, our taking a walk, and my pretending to be ill, seized with a sudden faintness, at their gate ; they were compelled to ask us in."

"True mamma, and really, considering the man was only a farmer he did not do it so badly ; there was rather a manner about him."

"My dear Tom Thornton, as he used to be called, was, eighteen or twenty years ago, a very handsome young man."

"Very likely, mamma; he is not bad-looking now, for a person o the kind. Very respectable, of course, but countryfied and all that. I did not think anything particular of his wife; a good, motherly sort of woman, no doubt."

"Why, my dear, Mrs. Thornton cannot be above five or six and thirty, at most."

" Well, five or six and thirty ! dear me, I think five or six and thirty quite old."

" Miss Wild !"

" I am not Miss Wild, mamma."

" Then my Lady Lisle !  Has your ladyship forgotten that you have a mother?"

" Law, mamma! to be offended with me for that.  I was not thinking of mothers at all ; I was talking of young women, when I said five and thirty was old."

" I can tell you, Fanny, that motherly sort of person, as you call Mrs. Thornton, was once the beauty of Warwickshire."

" Ah, it is easier to obtain a village, or even a county reputation, than a metropolitan one."

" But I remember to have seen her myself, and I believe I am not the worst judge of beauty in the world.  It was on the occasion of a large ball, held at the house in which you and I have lately stayed. I remember Lord Dumbfounder, the late lord that died in a fit of apoplexy, after a grand dinner, was there."

" Were you with either of the old families, mamma?"

" No, my dear, your father and I were staying there together; your father was not very well at the time, and we parsuaded him to go to bed.  I did not care for society myself, and, of course, would not join the dancers.  Not wishing to be alone, I allowed the hostess to sit with me, and during the evening, this Mrs. Thornton, who was then a Miss Hodson, came into the room.  She was quite the *belle* of the evening, and a very beautiful girl, I assure you."

" But was this passing glimpse of a little country girl sufficient to excite an interest in you after so many years?"

" Her story interested me,  and I could not help remembering it ; for that very night, she eloped from Warwick with a captain in the army, one Captain Austen.  He was killed the other day, my dear : you must recollect hearing of the death of General Austen."

" What a dreadful creature—eloped with a captain, mamma !"

" Almost as bad, my dear Fanny, as running away to a masquerade at the Pantheon, and a few months after, secretly marrying a young nobleman."

Fanny coloured, but made no reply, and Mrs. Wild continued.

" Miss Hodson was deceived very cruelly, and this Mr. Thornton, who was an old lover of her's, proved her true friend, and was the means of restoring her to her parents.  I have heard that they both suffered very considerably, but at last, after five years had passed away, Miss Hodson's father died, and before he breathed his last, put his daughter's head into the farmer's, and said—

" She will refuse you no longer, Tom ; she will reward your affection and fidelity, and remember her old father's last wish, that she and you, who now have climbed the hill together, may no longer be parted, but, as man and wife, jog down it, to rest together at the foot.' "

" Quite an affecting story, mamma, though the farmer's wife looks so hearty aed ruddy now, you would never think she had been the heroine of a little domestic drama, and with her round, and apparently motherly-looking honest face, that she ever committed a *faux pas*— how contradictory !"

" Poor Ellen was very unfortunate : but I believe now that she is very happy, and her children are really handsome—the model of their father. I heard a great deal of them from the old landlady at The George, who repeated to me farmer Hodson's dying speech."

Fanny, whose heart was good and kind always, and whose occasional pettishness and seeming affection were the result of being spoiled all her life, and the mistress of everybody around her, as well as almost all her own actions, was much interested in this little episode of her mother's narrating, and inquired who Austen married after all.

" The daughter of a noble house," replied the mother, " who bore him three girls. He died without an heir, and a very considerable estate passed out of the family in consequence."

" If I remember rightly, he met his death during the confinement of his wife ?"

" Yes, it was a strange circumstance altogether, or rather a combination of circumstances : the death of the general—the burglary at the doctor's, and the subsequent madness of the doctor himself; but, my dear child, are you not getting hungry ? I am, and, as it very fortunately happens, agreeably to our appetites, we have arrived just at the end of the stage, where the coach dines. This is Coventry, my dear ; how do you like it ? This is the place where they say Lady Godiva rode through the city, without any clothes, and thought nothing at all of it. I have heard that she had a great deal of hair, that came down almost to her feet, so it did not very much matter ; but I must say, I should not like to do it myself, and in my case, it would be very awkward, as I have not a great deal. Talk of one Peeping Tom, there would be a regiment. I have ridden on horseback, but never in that way."

" Law, mamma, how can you be so ridiculous?"

" Now then, ladies, this is where the coach stops to dinner; there's three hours allowed here, and then we goes on again, ma'am, and the coach stops to sleep at the next stage."

" Pray, Mr. Coachman, when do you think we shall be in London?"

" Why, ma'am, as we always says on the way-bill, D.V., and the weather permitting, we shall be in town to-morrow night, or at the very latest, the morning arterwards, and that ere is what I call the fastest travelling as ever was, or ever will be."

Gas, steam, rail-roads, electricity, and crystal palaces were undreamed of then.

Two days have passed, and a hired vehicle, heavily piled with trunks and many packages, with two ladies in the midst, is making its way to the open country by Marylebone-fields.

" London again, then, mamma?"

" Yes, Fanny; but we are approaching the suburbs now. How pleasant it is to hear all the old cries again."

" I can't say that I think so; to me it has a discordant sound."

" Stop, my dear; there is somebody bawling a death-speech. I must hear it, as I might remember the poor gentleman. I'll be bound your father is doing a fine stroke of business now. Stop, coachman, stop!" cried Mrs. Wild, putting her head out of the window, " I want to hear what that good man has to say."

The coach was stopped, and the vender, who was close at hand, shouted, in a hoarse voice—

" Here ye are; the last dying speech and confession of the notorious Jack She—eppard, who was hung this morning at Tyburn: how he looked—what he said, and what he didn't say, with a full, true and pes-tick-ler account—"

Fanny leant back in the carriage, and complained of faintness. Her mother hastily pulled down the windows, and desired the coachman to drive on.

They had heard enough; Fanny remembered her father's threat to Jack and his mother, on the night they had conveyed her to the cottage; she felt sick at heart.

" A bad omen, mamma; I fear something has happened to papa."

" Pshaw, child! what can have happened? Your father knows how to take care of himself."

They had reached their journey's end. There were many lights in the house, and an unusual commotion.

"Heavens! what does this mean?" exclaimed Mrs. Wild to the man who undid the carriage door. "Where is your master?"

"Oh, ma'am—oh, Mrs. Wild—oh, miss, I am so sorry for you; I pity you, from the bottom of my heart."

"Speak out at once. What has happened?"

"Oh, ma'am, the thief-catcher is caught at last; the constables have been, and taken Mr. Wild, and lodged him in Newgate."

"Ha, ha, ha," laughed a man near at hand, whom Mrs. Wild knew to be Blueskin; "and Jack Sheppard is avenged!"

---

## CHAPTER XXIX.

WE are writing the last chapter of our history.

A new Act of Parliament had been passed, of which the following is one of the clauses:—

"And whereas there are several persons who have secret acquaintance with felons, and who make it their business to help persons to their stolen goods, and by that means, gain money from them, which is divided between them and the felons, whereby they greatly encourage such offenders: be it enacted, by the authority aforesaid, that wherever any person taketh money or reward, directly or indirectly, under pretence or upon account of helping any person or persons to any stolen goods or chattels, every such person so taking money or reward as aforesaid (unless such persons do apprehend, or cause to be apprehended such felon who stole the same, and cause such felon to be brought to his trial for the same, and give evidence against him) shall be guilty of felony, and suffer the pains and penalties of felony, according to the nature of the felony committed in stealing such goods, and in such and the same manner as if such offender had himself stolen such goods and chattels, in the manner and with such circumstances as the same were stolen."

After this act had passed, the Recorder sent to Jonathan to admonish him, and let him know the danger of any longer pursuing his calling; recommending him only to detect rogues and bring them to justice, promising, upon that condition, to give him all encouragement, reminding him of what considerable sums he had made in that way already, by which he might judge that sufficient may be got to do good to the public, and enable him to live honestly.

Whether these admonitions, or the fear of a new law wrought upon his conscience is uncertain; but there had been a damp for a while upon his business; his books were shut up for some weeks, and he even refused several large sums offered him for the recovery of things stolen. Yet during the whole time, he never once lost sight of his friends and dependants, the thieves; but employed them in various small, though safe matters.

In the meantime, all his acquaintance were anxious to know what he would take to next, having a notion that he was too cunning to venture himself within the clutches of the law.

He talked of a new project, which was to open an office for insurance against robbery, pretending to settle a sufficient fund, and give security for the performance of the articles, not doubting, he said, but that all trading people, as well as noblemen and gentlemen, who kept great quantities of plate in their houses, would, for their own sakes, support so useful an undertaking, bragging, at the same time, that it was no South Sea bubble, and he would make a great fortune by it.

Whether he gave out this merely to amuse people, and prevent them from inquiring further into his affairs, is not known; but he took no steps in it: on the contrary, he engaged in another scheme—that of smuggling to a great extent, and he projected a trade with London, and Holland, and Flanders, and went so far as to become part proprietor of a sloop. His chief trading-port was Ostend, where his name is well known, even to this day; then he usually sent his emissaries to Bruges, Ghent, Brussels, and other great towns, where he took to market gold watches, rings, plate, and now and then a Bank or Goldsmith's note, that, in the thieves vocabulary, had been *spoke with.*

One day, however, the vessel was exchequered in the Thames, and he was obliged to stand a trial, in which he was cast £700 damages, which put an end to his trade in that particular way.

With his expenses, however, having the house at Kilburn, and also the house by Saffron-hill to keep up, which latter was only very lately pulled down, and known to the public as the " old house in West-street," while, besides what madam and Miss Fanny cost him in their tour, it was rumoured that he had, at least, half-a-dozen mistresses, we can easily imagine what demands were made upon his purse.

He was now, as of old, frequently importuned by people who had been robbed, to help them to their goods again, and so he ventured to dabble a little once more, every now and then bringing to the gallows some idle rascal who did not mind his business, and who, according to his notions, was fit for nothing but hanging.

But now it was decreed that our hero should reign no longer, and the cause of his fall was this :—

Certain persons having information where a considerable quantity of rich goods lay, supposed to be stolen, obtained a warrant for the seizure of them, which was accordingly done.

Though Jonathan did not go and claim the goods as his own, he had the assurance to commence an action, in the name of Roger Johnston, to whom he pretended the goods belonged, and arrested the persons who seized them.

Thus he pretended to recover goods by law, for possessing which, if they were fonnd upon him, the law would hang him.

So barefaced and impudent a proceeding put persons upon finding out means of bringing so sturdy a rogue to justice.

Jonathan was loudly threatened, which occasioned a report that he had fled from justice, whereupon he published a bullying advertisement in the newspapers, which the author of this has himself read in the British Museum, offering a reward of ten guineas to any person who should discover the originator of the report. At the same time, he ran into public places to show himself and contradict the rumour; yet, in the midst of all this blustering, he was seized and committed to Newgate, and his wife and daughter only returned on the evening of the event.

They sought him out hastily, aad now that there was no longer any cause to keep her marriage a secret, Fanny acquainted her father with everything, and promised how she would use the interest which her husband could command.

Wild now expressed himself in the highest degree gratified with the honour which he esteemed had been conferred upon his daughter, and he embraced her rapturously, and promised, if he got over this difficulty, which he did not doubt he should, he would go and end his days in some retired corner.

Fanny wrote to her husband, conjuring him immediately to come to London, and employ all his influence in her father's behalf. Serious as the matter grew, yet instilled as was the idea into her mind, she could not bring herself to believe that they would hang her father— the great Wild. Madam Wild, from the moment that she had first heard of her husband's arrest, evidently entertained the most serious fears, and though it cannot be said that she loved her husband with all the devotion a wife should feel, yet it must be remembered that Jonathan's own nature was not of a loving kind, and that, except his daughter, he regarded no one thing on earth with any degree of real affection.

Lord Lisle obeyed the summons of his maiden wife, and came to London with all haste.

He did not neglect to exert himself for Wild, and though he did not care publicly to acknowledge his immediate connexion with the felon, yet he behaved in the best spirit towards him, and said to Fanny, in the presence of her parents—

" I am prepared to the fullest to carry out what I have commenced. I am devoted to you, darling, heart and soul, and eager as I am to welcome you to my home, and bid the world call you Lady Lisle, till this life-and-death business of your father's is past, I will not talk to you of love, or a husband's right to the cheering influence of his wife's society."

Fanny, by turns, shed tears upon the breasts of husband and of father."

And now the trial came on, and Jonathan was found guily and condemned to die—he who had hurried so many to the scaffold.

And how bore he his sentence ? All his courage deserted him ; his cheeks were blanched—his knees shook together, and he clutched impotently at the dock rails.

He was taken back to Newgate, and placed in the condemned cell.

No malefactor had ever stood his ground so long, committing every day acts of felony, in sight of the world, and it has been computed, that in eighteen years, he received nearly fourteen thousand pounds for his dividend of stolen goods returned, living the greater portion of the time, though not allowing his family to share, in riot and voluptuousness.

He had no hopes of a reprieve, and the state of his mind was deplorable. A lesson of morality might have been drawn from it, that virtue alone can give true tranquillity, and nothing can support a man against the terrors of death but a good conscience.

His wife and daughter were admitted to him after his condemnation; he drew the latter to him, and for almost the first time in his life, burst into a flood of tears.

He was completely overwhelmed. The time was short betwixt eternity and him. When they were gone, he was visited by one of his old acquaintances—as great, but a less skilful rogue than himself, and it is characteristic of the man to state, that when the other asked him if he was afraid to die, he answered, as he cocked his hat—

"D—me, it is only a dance wiihout music; who's afraid?" Glad should we be, if we could report better of one whom we have chosen for our hero.

The night before his execution, his wife had, according to his desire, and in the firm belief that she had therein done no wrong, brought him some laudanum; but it produced a different effect from that which was intended, and the horrors of that night no pen can trace. When the morning came, and his irons were struck off, he asked for brandy, and it was given him. Then he passed out into the Old Bailey, amid the hootings of the crowd, and ascended the cart.

At that moment, his daughter, in the cottage at Kilburn, was weeping her heart out on her husband's shoulder; her little hand within her mother's, whose tears fell thick and fast upon it.

The cart moved slowly on, preceded by a troop of Horse Guards, bearing javelins in their hands, and all the way along Holborn and the Oxford-road, there were crowds upon crowds, who hooted and yelled.

When he arrived at Tyburn, he was welcomed with a tremendous shout; so hateful had his name become to the populace, that they gladly hailed the catastrophe. They endeavoured, however, to prevent it, by knocking him on the head as he stood under the tree, while the ordinary was performing his last office. They battered the cart with stones and dirt, and all manner of mischievous weapons, some of which, erroneously playing on the robes of the ecclesiastic, made him more expeditious in his repetition than he might otherwise have been, and, perhaps, shortened the career of our hero. This gave rise to the statement of a great satirist, that Wild, in the midst of a shower of stones which played upon him, picked the parson's pocket of a corkscrew, which he carried out of the world in his hand.

The ordinary having descended from the cart, Wild had just opportunity to cast his eyes around the crowd, and to give them a hearty curse; then his mind reverting to his daughter, he cried aloud—

"Fanny, my child, O God protect thee!" And the horses moving on, on that 24th day of May, 1725, Jonathan was swung out of the world.

Lord and Lady Lisle lived a long, retired life in the Highlands of Scotland, and Madam Wild, who dwelt under their roof, lived to the age of ninety, famed to the last in her neighbourhood as a benevolent lady, and a skilful doctress.

www.ingramcontent.com/pod-product-compliance
Lightning Source LLC
Chambersburg PA
CBHW080822250626
47160CB00008B/2834